the other side of
SOMEDAY

New York Times Bestselling Author
Carey Heywood

Lexa,
xoxo,
Carey Heywood

DEDICATION

To Melissa, Jennifer, Lisa and Nasha,
for showing me daily all the laughter and love in friendship.

CHAPTER
I

Courtney

Did I turn off the stove burner? The question was stuck in a loop the whole drive to work. I glance randomly at my cellphone while I sit at a red light. I could sneak a quick text to Mike. I'm trying to be good about not using my phone at all in the car, no calls, no texts, no random checking of Facebook updates. I turn back and look straight out the windshield. I'll be at work in less than five minutes.

Mike doesn't have to leave for another thirty minutes. I can call him and have him check, no big deal. I hate not knowing. The wondering bugs me, the unanswered question of 'if it's still on'. That question gives birth to another. What if Mike decided to go into work early today? Then another. If he went in to work early, is our place burning down as we speak?

When I pull into my usual spot at work, the one that sides up to the second mulch island, I grab my phone. I don't text. I call.

He answers on the second ring. "Hey."

Just hey. "Hi, honey. Can you check the stovetop for me? I can't stop thinking I forgot to turn the burner off."

"Really, Court?"

Shit, he sounds annoyed. "Please, babe."

He doesn't answer but I can hear him move from wherever he was in the background. After a minute, he replies, "It's off. Happy?"

I ignore his shortness. "Did you have to turn it off or was it already off?"

"It was already off. Did you need anything else? I don't want to be late to work."

I roll my eyes; he works in sales, and unless he has an actual appointment, he makes his own hours. "Thank you for checking. I hope you have a good day. I love you."

"Thanks, babe." His tone softens, "I love you, too."

I smile to myself after we hang up. Tomorrow is Friday, and then it's the weekend. Maybe we can go out to dinner or go see a movie. Mike has been so grouchy. I know his job stresses him out. He sells heavy machine equipment. He's always been really good at it. I don't think he's not hit his monthly goals. Considering the last few years have taken a real hit on the construction industry, that's saying a lot.

His problem is he sets his own goals beyond what is expected of him at work. His drive, his ambition is one of the things I love about him. I wish he wasn't so hard on himself.

I'm the first one at work. I'm a secretary. No, it wasn't my lifelong aspiration to be one. I just fell into it. There is something about being the only person in the office before anyone else arrives, a peaceful calm before the storm. I flip on the lights before I make my way to my desk, dumping my purse and umbrella into the bottom drawer before I head to the break room with my frozen lunch to make coffee.

I don't drink coffee every day, and if I do, not in the morning. I'm more of an occasional afternoon pick me up coffee kind of girl. However, I do love the smell of brewing coffee. For this reason, I'm the self-appointed office coffee maker. This way I can sit in the break room and hog all the fresh coffee smell to myself. The sound of movement from the hall surprises me. I peek my head around the corner. No one is ever here this early.

"Hello?" I call out tentatively.

I jump when I see Elliot, another secretary. He looks surprised to see me.

"Hey. You're here early," I say in greeting.

"Uh. Yeah." He looks away. "I wanted to take care of some stuff."

We aren't work besties or anything, but he's acting weird. I suddenly feel bad for not making an effort to get to know him better. I make a mental note to go out of my way to do that. Now is not the time though. I head back to my desk and start my computer. My boss, Mr. Fulson, will be here any minute and he's meeting with a potential client at nine.

Today my long, blonde hair is pulled into a low ponytail; but no matter how frequently I smooth it back, strands around my face always seem to come loose. My hair has curling tendencies, not enough for my hair to be considered curly, enough for it to frizz when it's extra humid out. Which is April to October in North Carolina.

"Good morning, Mr. Fulson," I greet as my boss approaches.

"Morning," he returns, rushing past my desk.

I stand and trail after him to the door of his office. "Can I get you a cup of coffee?"

Most mornings he drinks his brew at home with his wife. Mrs. Fulson is great and I can't help but watch them together, and hope someday that will be Mike and me.

We aren't high school sweethearts as they were. We met in college and we almost didn't meet at all. It was our senior year, a month before graduation. I never went to very many parties because I was on an educational scholarship, which didn't pay room and board. For that reason, when I wasn't studying, I was working.

Jen, my roommate, talked me into going to a party with her. It wasn't a crazy, frat party or anything; I never would have gone if it were. Not many people were there. I didn't intend to stay long; however, once I met Mike that all changed. His gravitation toward sales after we graduated was no surprise. He is a born salesperson. That night he sold himself to me.

I don't know what about me drew him in. I do know, previously, I had never felt so pursued. I wasn't naïve or new to dating; but his level of interest from the start just seemed different. Here we are, eight years later, still together. As intent as he was on us becoming a couple, he seems uninterested in getting married.

We're engaged, have been for three years. Things have happened during that time to explain why we haven't actually gotten married. Understandable things, I guess. Only, I see or hear about couples all the time who have even more going on but still somehow manage to make it happen. I tell him it doesn't bother me, but it does. Most of our friends are married now too; it's hard to go to their weddings and not think about the fact Mike and I have been engaged longer than any of them were.

"Courtney?"

I shake my head and realize I've been standing there lost in my own thoughts. "Sorry, Mr. Fulson. I zoned out. Did you want coffee?"

He looks annoyed. "No, I had my coffee at home this morning. I asked you for the Offenheim file."

I nod, giving him my best professional expression. "Yes, Sir."

I turn and hurry to my desk. The Offenheims are well known in town, and every business locally has tried to add them to their client lists. The company I work for acts as an asset manager. On staff are estate teams, retirement teams, tax advisors, and growth experts. Mr. Fulson is one of the best relationship managers in the business.

I pass Elliot in the hall and give him a small smile. He looks distracted and avoids my eyes. Maybe I could ask him out to lunch; he seems so stressed. I grab the Offenheim file and bring it back to Mr. Fulson. Most of the records we have are duplicates of stuff he could have easily found on our computer network. My boss is old school; he doesn't like reading documents electronically. He likes to spread them out on his desk to review them.

Old-fashioned, yes, but it works in his favor. He has a knack at being able to identify what a client seems to be missing. Most of the time, the clients, themselves, have not been able to figure out how to put into words what they need. He can, and when presented correctly, he has won accounts frequently that way. I look up to my boss. He is a good guy and smart.

I have tried to emulate the way he evaluates situations. It wasn't my dream in life to be a relationship manager. I was a history major. I had hoped to teach; but even though I applied all over, I couldn't find any openings near where we lived. I thought about subbing, but Mike knew someone who was able to get me an interview here.

"Here is the file." I reach out to hand it to him.

"Were you able to add the real estate reports yesterday?" he asks, flipping the folder open.

"Yes, they're right on top." I smile, hoping he would be happy with all of the work I had done yesterday.

"This looks good, Courtney," for some reason he seems almost disappointed as he says it. He pauses before continuing, "They should be here in less than thirty minutes. I'll be meeting with them in the small conference room. Please prepare a beverage tray, and then run to the bakery to pick up a few scones."

I hurriedly start a new pot of coffee before going down to the bakery located on the first floor of our building. Because the food's so good, I avoid the place like the plague. I am past the days where I can eat whatever I want without worrying about gaining weight. Mike still looks the same. He is better than I am about working out.

Sometime over the last eight years, I have managed to put on an extra ten, or so, pounds. It wouldn't be a big deal if I weren't freaking out that maybe the extra weight is the reason Mike is putting off wedding planning. I need to go to the gym; but I don't want people to see me working out until I am smaller. How dumb is that? Avoiding the gym because there are in-shape people there.

There's a small line at the bakery. I glance down at my watch to see how much time I still have before the Offenheims get there. Luckily, when it's my turn to order, I don't need them to prepare anything. I only need five scones and I'm back at my desk in no time. I open the small conference room to air out the stale smell in there, while I set up the refreshment tray.

I transfer fresh coffee, cream, and sugar to a small coffee set we have. I also fill up a water pitcher and add ice. Once everything is set up, I roll my shoulders back a couple of times to release the tension gathering there. I'm only at my desk a couple minutes before I get the call from the front desk that the Offenheims are here.

I notify Mr. Fulson before going out to greet them. He will meet us in the small conference room once I have them seated and offer them refreshment. I glance at my reflection in the glass window of an office before going to greet them. I wore my best suit today to make a good impression.

I hate hose; so today, I only wore pants to work to avoid them. My suit is a simple black with thin white pinstripes that I have paired with a cerulean shell. Mr. and Mrs. Offenheim are joined by their eldest son, Grant. Grant Offenheim is something of a local celebrity around these parts. He is a frequent addition to eligible bachelor lists locally, and I think a national magazine one year.

This is the first time I have met him. He is stutter inducingly beautiful. I plaster my most professional face on and try not to sneak too many glances at him. I don't think it's cheating to ogle attractive men. He seems pleasant. I don't expect him to throw himself at me or be overly cordial; if anything, he seems distracted.

Both Misters Offenheim take coffee, while Mrs. asks for tea. I pass Mr. Fulson on my way to the break room and explain. He looks annoyed I hadn't thought of tea ahead of time. Maybe I'm assuming he's annoyed because I'm annoyed with myself for overlooking it. I return to the conference room with the tea in no time.

I have made one cup by itself and have more tea steeping in a pot on a tray. After I add, per her request, milk to her tea I excuse myself. Our office manager is waiting for me when I get back to my desk.

"Courtney, can you please come to my office?"

I give Beth a confused look. "Sure, everything okay?"

She shakes her head and turns, so all I can do is follow her. Once we're in her office, she closes her door. Why did she close her door?

My palms start sweating and I rub them across the tops of my pant legs to dry them.

"Courtney, after an investigation, we believe you have been misappropriating funds from petty cash. If you are able to replace the amount you have taken, we will not contact the authorities; but in either scenario, your employment is being terminated immediately."

As if it was the starting line of a horse race, my heart begins to gallop. Soon her voice is a dull distant noise against the rumble of the stampede echoing in my ears.

"What?" I stammer, "I haven't stolen anything from petty cash. I took ten dollars today to buy scones from downstairs. I have a receipt. I haven't entered it into the system yet because I was making coffee and tea for Mr. Fulson's appointment."

"I'm sorry, Courtney, but this is more than ten dollars."

"You're joking." I nervously laugh because it doesn't feel like she's joking. "I swear I didn't steal anything. Please give me a chance to somehow prove it to you."

"I will escort you to your desk so you may collect your things. You will need to give me your key at that time. If you are not able to write me a check for the amount missing from petty cash, we will take it from your final check."

When she stands, I mimic her movements blindly dazed by everything she just said. Something isn't right. They have to know I wouldn't ever steal from them. Beth grabs a flattened box on the way out of her office. When we reach my desk, she hands it to me.

They aren't only firing me; they're forcing me to make my own box to carry out my stuff. As she watches me, I decide what to take. Although the stapler is technically mine, will she assume I'm stealing it? I grab the framed picture I have of Mike and me.

I look up at her after grabbing my purse. "Does Mr. Fulson know you're firing me?"

When she nods, I take a deep breath. I had thought to myself, there was no way he would let them do this. Apparently, I was wrong. People are looking and whispering. Eyes of people I have talked to everyday dig into my shoulder blades.

Not one of them says a word to me. I'm not sure I've ever been so embarrassed in my entire life. Beth walks me to the main door. Our lobby is empty, almost as though they timed my exit to avoid any clients seeing it.

I'm half way out the door when she says, "Your key?"

I have to set my box on the floor to get my keys out of my purse. I slip the office key from my ring and hand it to her. "This isn't right."

She offers me no reply, just takes the key and turns, letting the door close without a backward glance. I have been a good employee. What the hell just happened?

Embarrassment propels me toward the exit. I clumsily shift my box to my hip to open the door. My steps are awkward across the parking lot. My ankles seem to have forgotten how to hold me upright. I stumble and find every imperfection in the asphalt. I make it to my car somehow.

My eyes are misty, but I refuse to cry. Shoving my box into the back seat and slamming the door, I climb into the driver's side. With shaky hands, I pull my cell phone out to call Mike. He doesn't answer so I hang up and text him to call me right away.

I'll break my no phone in the car rule when he does. I start my car. I'm hyper-sensitive to each action I take, hands on the steering wheel at ten and two, turn wheel to the left, blinker on, look right, glance at my cell after each movement. I was just fired. I was just fired. There is no way I did what they said I did. I didn't steal money.

I'm halfway home when my car jerks to the right. Thankfully, not the left or I would have hit the Ford in the lane next to me. I brake and ease onto the shoulder. I've had a blowout. I can see from my rearview mirror the remnants of what was my tire all over the road. I try to call Mike again. No answer.

Can this day get any worse? I groan and unbuckle my belt. I smack my steering wheel a couple times before apologizing to it.

My spare is in the trunk. I peel off my suit jacket and toss it into the passenger seat before timing traffic to get out without having my door hit. I get the lift set before it starts raining. There's the answer to my 'can it get worse' question. Great.

I stop to check my phone, hoping Mike has called, texted, or something, and grumble to myself when I see he hasn't. The rain has done nothing to kill the heat of the day. It's as if I'm in an outdoor shower in my clothes.

The wayward hairs, which frame my face, have escaped the rubber band and now are plastered to my cheeks.

I want to cry. I want the rain to disguise my tears. Some stubborn piece of me refuses to allow myself that relief. Every car that passes I both hope and worry that they'll stop. No one does stop though. My wet hands on the crow bar make removing the lug nuts holding the rim of my now destroyed tire a nightmare. My hands slip more often than not.

Squatting there in the rain, a wet mess, I realize it's not so bad. This is the worst of it. My spare tire is now on. I can get a new tire, and I can get a new job. The new job part might be difficult without a reference, but I can do it. I get back in my car and shake some of the rain from my hair like a dog. I search for the closest mechanic on my phone and find one at the next exit. I slowly make my way to it, hazards on.

It's a small garage called Pete's. I clamor back into the rain to the front office.

Seeing no one there, I tentatively call out, "Hello?"

"Be right with you." A voice returns from a back room.

The air conditioning has me shivering in my wet clothes. I cross my arms and rub my hands up and down them attempting to warm up. A moment later, an older man with a backward baseball cap walks out.

"Got caught in the rain," he remarks sympathetically.

I nod. "I blew my tire and had to put the spare on."

"You don't have roadside assistance?" He sounds surprised.

My shoulders sag and I groan. "I didn't even think to call them." I glance back up at him. "It's been a rough morning."

He pats my shoulder. "I can get you all fixed up from here. Want me to check your other tires while I'm at it?"

I shake my head. "Honestly, I want to get home, crawl into bed, and pull my covers over my head."

"That bad?" he asks.

I nod and give him a small smile. I pass him my keys and he directs me to the ladies room telling me to use as much of the paper towels as I want to dry off. The ladies room bulb blinks in refusal before fully illuminating the small bathroom. A roll of paper towels sits on a small table between the sink and toilet.

I wring my shirt and hair before even trying to dry them further. The soles of my wedge dress shoes are soaked. I make a squish sound with every step I take. By the time, I'm back in the front office the rain has stopped. Stupid summer downpours. I try Mike again. At this point, I don't know whether to be angry or worried.

The older man, who I assume is Pete, has my new tire on in no time. I thank him profusely as he rings me up, passing him my debit card. He runs it through the machine twice before cringing and looking up at me.

He rubs his chin, passing my card back to me. "It was declined."

My jaw drops, my lower lip shaking. "That can't be right."

He hesitates. "Do you have another card?"

I shake my head. "I don't."

I don't want to cry. "Let me try to call," my voice trails off as I try Mike again.

To avoid his kind eyes, I turn my face attempting to hold myself together. When it goes to voicemail, I fall into an uncomfortable plastic chair and hold my head in my hands. Fired, flat tire, rainstorm, and now my debit card is being declined. I don't know what to do. I start to call my mom, but stop myself when I see my battery is almost dead.

"Can I use your phone to call my bank?" I quietly ask.

He walks over to me, my bill in his hands. Standing right next to me, he tears it in half.

"I can pay. I just need to…" I say.

"Don't worry about it."

He helps me up, patting me on the back as he walks me to my car. After opening my door for me, he tells me to go home and get some rest. That everything will seem better tomorrow. Once I'm far enough away that he can't see me, I pull over so I can cry. His kindness and his generosity on this being maybe the second worst day of my life gives me hope.

Tomorrow I will call Mr. Fulson and ask them to provide proof. I will call a lawyer and find out if I can get my job back because I have been wrongfully terminated. I dry my tears and get back on the road.

I'll be home early enough to make something nice for dinner. Moreover, I have to call the bank to find out why my card wouldn't work. Even if I have to stop by my branch and pull out cash, I am going to pay that nice man back.

When I pull into our complex, I see a car in my spot and Mike's car still in his spot. I park in a visitor spot further down and slowly walk up to the stairs to our condo. Having a car in my spot has happened before. This car seems familiar somehow. When I'm passing the car, it comes to me. It's Stacy Callahan's car. Her father is Mike's boss.

Stacy is a sweetheart; we've all hung out before. I hurry up the stairs and into the condo. Our front door opens right into the living room and I'm surprised I don't find them in there or in the kitchen that feeds off it. I start to wonder if they're even here when I hear it, a moan, Mike's actually. The sound he always makes right before he comes.

I stand outside the doorway of my bedroom, frozen. I know what they're doing, and I now know why every call and text I have sent my fiancé today has been ignored. I deliberate whether to confront them or not. Do I want to see the man I have spent the last eight years of my life with, the man who asked me to marry him, making love to another woman?

I decide another eight years may need to pass before I want to see his face again or hear his excuses. I grab a sheet of paper and write a quick note. "You sounded busy." I sign it and leave my engagement ring with it on the kitchen counter. I can figure out how or when or if I want anything from this condo another time.

CHAPTER
2

Courtney

That earlier summer shower has nothing on the tears I cry on the drive to my mom's house. The foundations of my ability to trust are cracked and crumbling. Eight years of my life, for what? While I don't have eyewitness proof Mike was with Stacy, the fact her car was there, and in my spot, is too much of a coincidence to ignore. We haven't been close friends or anything; but the fact I'm not a stranger to her and she's been in my house as my guest is painful.

The brunt of my anger is focused on Mike; however, a healthy helping of heartache tones it down. For Stacy, I have no reason to agonize if I'm not enough for her. Mike is who is supposed to be committed to me, not her.

My mother's more heartbroken over what Mike has done than I am. After telling her I will leave and never speak to her again, she stops asking if I think we could work it out. I have spent two days in bed. I have cried, I have punched the pillows on my bed, I even have screamed aloud a couple times.

Mike has called my phone nonstop until my battery has died. I just lie here watching the incoming call notifications. I don't want to talk to him. I'm terrified I'll slip and take him back or tell him I still love him. I haven't eaten much. My stomach feels weirdly nauseated. I drink water though because I need to be hydrated to keep crying.

After three days, I arise. My muscles are screaming at the lack of use. I have thought about double-checking a bible to see what God made the third day. I haven't asked my mother though; she would not appreciate my weird sense of humor.

So not knowing what God did the third day, I still have a plan for mine. I need to call Mr. Fulson. At this point, I don't even want my job back, but I want my reputation cleansed and for them to figure out who was actually stealing from them. I need to figure out what was going on with my checking account, our checking account. I cringe to myself thinking about it.

At least the condo is only in Mike's name. The down payment had been a gift to him from his parents. Nothing there is mine except some clothes and tarnished memories. The checking account is the only thing still linking us, that and our cell phone plan; but it's in his name too. That is something else I need to do, remove my address book from my cell phone and give it back to him.

I don't need a cell phone; and not having one will make the whole not using it in the car goal that much easier. I call the bank first and am informed the happy news that our joint-account had a fraud alert on it. There had been a large debit, originating from overseas; so rather than pay it, they froze our account until they could verify it with one of us.

That explains why my card wouldn't work at the tire place. I have her remove my name from the account and open a new one in only my name. I have a small individual savings account. With the help of the girl on the phone, I link my new account to my savings account.

I have her pull some money from savings so I will have some funds readily available. It isn't much but it's all mine. She seems surprised I don't want to pull anything from the old joint account. Right now, I want nothing that touched anything of his.

My mother has spoken to a friend who is an attorney about the circumstances of my dismissal. He seems to think I have grounds for a wrongful termination suit. While I'm angry I lost my job, I'm also grateful my needing to leave that day has exposed Mike's unfaithfulness to me. My annoyance at my former employer is small potatoes in comparison to how I feel about Mike's infidelity.

Still, my mother has talked me into letting her friend send a letter on my behalf to them, instead of calling Mr. Fulson myself. Her friend is doing it at no charge, and I'm getting the impression he may have a thing for my mom. I tell him to go ahead with it, curious as to how they will respond. Jen, my college roommate lives twenty minutes from my mom's house. I have told her about my phone and she has offered to come over at lunch to show me how to transfer the address book. Now, on the third day post my worst day ever, I already have completed my to-do list; and it's not even lunch yet.

I'm about to shower when I realize I have nothing clean to change into. When I got to my mom's house Thursday afternoon, she loaned me some sweats to sleep in. I wore those all day yesterday. I could borrow some more clothes from her; but that would also mean borrowing a bra and underwear. For some reason, this grosses me out. I look like shit, like actual shit, but decide to head to Wal-Mart because, for some reason, even on my worst day at Wal-Mart, someone always looks even worse.

I don't have a ton of time or money to shop. I grab two five packs of cotton bikini briefs, four inexpensive bras, and a multi pack of socks. My mom and I are about the same size; so until I decide for sure if I even want my clothes back, I can borrow stuff from her. Everything that I own has been touched by him in some way. We lived together. He has tainted everything.

I'm showered and changed before Jen comes over. She is smart enough to bring her charger since we have the same kind of phone.

"You look awful," she blurts the moment I open the door.

I nod. "I feel awful."

"I'm sorry," she amends, "I shouldn't have said that."

I wave my hand; maybe I look extra awful because she looks so amazing in comparison. She's a knockout in general, all tall with flowing long black hair and pale blue eyes. "Whether you said it or not, it doesn't change the fact it's true, so get your butt in here and help me figure out my phone."

"This will be the blind leading the blind. I should have brought my niece. She knows how to work my phone better than I do."

I snort. "It's because you're old."

Her eyes widen. "Who are you calling old?"

I point at her, covering my mouth to muffle my laughs with my other hand.

"I'm only four months older than you," she grumbles, moving past me.

I follow her to my mother's office. Jen has known me long enough to know the layout of my parents' house. Before my dad passed away, she even lived here with me one summer. She also doesn't have to stand on ceremony waiting for me to offer her food.

"I'm starved. What's for lunch?"

"I thought you were picking something up for both of us on the way over?" I ask.

She pouts. "Please tell me you're toying with my emotions right now."

"I am," I console. "I'll be right back with food."

I don't make anything special, some BLT's with chips on the side, but I know they are her favorite. Her eyes light up when she sees them. She already has my phone plugged into the computer.

"Don't get overly excited, but I think the computer and the phone do it automatically," she confesses, picking up her sandwich.

"You're joking." I peer over her shoulder at the screen.

She attempts to speak around the bite in her mouth but gives up and finishes chewing. "I was as surprised as you are. When I plugged it in, a screen popped up asking if I wanted to back up data. I hit okay and it's been doing its thing ever since."

"That's so cool," I smile.

"You didn't even need me," she adds.

I shake my head. "I will always need you. Besides, I don't have my charger cord so I wouldn't have been able to plug it into the computer without you."

Her face relaxes as she goes back to being content at being needed.

Once she's done eating, she asks how I'm doing. I knew it would come up. To a certain extent, it already had when I called her to let her know I would be staying with my mom for a while. On the phone, I could tell her I was fine; and as long as my voice didn't shake while I said it, she would have no other choice but to believe me.

In person, I couldn't lie to her. "I need to go to the doctor. I'm on the pill, so I know I'm not pregnant, but we haven't used condoms in years, Jen, years. What if that girl isn't the first girl? What if I have a disease?"

She reaches over to rub my arm. "Have you talked to him?"

I shake my head. "I've ignored his calls and texts; and thankfully, he hasn't come here."

"You can always come stay with me, if you want."

I rub my forehead. "Nah, besides I'd be crashing on your couch if I did. I'm okay here. My mom has been really cool about it. I think she's more upset about me leaving Mike than I am."

She looks into my eyes, seeing right past my attempt at a joke. "We both know you don't mean that."

My eyes well and I rub my lips between my teeth to keep the sob that threatens from escaping. The quiet sympathy in her eyes is what leads me to fail miserably at not crying in front of her. Nodding, I ignore the torrent of tears streaming down my face. She pulls me to her shoulder and I bury my face in it. I loved him; I loved him so much. Cheating on him didn't even seem fathomable; and the idea he didn't feel the same way about me has shaken my belief system to the core.

If I couldn't even trust the person that I loved, the person that wanted to marry me, how can I ever trust again? Jen rubs my back, promising me that everything is going to be all right, that I'll be okay. Problem is I don't believe her. Sure, I know I will get another job. I won't live with my mother forever. I don't see falling in love as an option of something I ever want to do again.

I pull back from her to grab a tissue from the desk before my nose runs all over her pretty shirt.

"Your shirt is really pretty," I mumble around my Kleenex.

She laughs at me. "It's old, babe. I think I've had it since college."

"Don't they say stuff always comes back in style?"

She lets my question and subject change stand and I'm grateful for it. "You might be waiting a while for that to come back in style." She motions toward my mother's kitten t-shirt.

I snort. "Cats are cool. Besides, maybe I'm being ironic, which is trendy, right?"

"Nice try," she giggles. "There is no way you're talking that shirt into being cool. Speaking of, if you are hell bent on not getting any of your clothes back, we need to go shopping."

"I went to Wal-Mart today and got some stuff. In addition, I need to save money."

"It'll be my treat." She holds her hand up when she sees me start to argue. "Consider it my birthday and Christmas presents for the next couple years if you need to."

"I don't feel comfortable letting you do that," I admit.

Her eyebrows furrow. "You aren't letting me do it. I offered. Besides I need some new stuff and I hate shopping by myself."

"Nowhere expensive," I plead.

"We can go to Marshalls or Ross," she agrees, and then adds, "as long as you change your shirt before we leave."

I smirk at her and grab our plates. She starts to take them from me and tells me she'll take care of them while I go change. I set them down and hug her before giving them to her. No matter how shitty everything else is right now, I'm lucky to have a place to stay and a friend to cheer me up.

I raid my mom's closet for another shirt, settling on a blue one. Since there is no writing or animals on it, I figure it's safe. Jen nods in approval when she sees me.

Walking out to her car, I feel deja vu. She's had the same Honda since college. "God, it's been forever since I've ridden in your car."

She smoothes her hand over the steering wheel with a smile. "It crossed over one hundred thousand miles last month."

Jen isn't much of a spender. She is an editor for a regional magazine and takes pride in repurposing old things. Her place somehow avoids looking cluttered even though she has a hard time throwing things away. Jen has the ability to see the value in things in a way no one else I've ever known does.

A strip mall not far from my mom's house is where we go. I gravitate toward the kind of clothes I usually wear. Jen stops me, reminds me I'm single now, and should think about flaunting my goodies.

"I have no desire for anyone to see my goodies," I whisper over the rack.

She ignores me. "We should go out dancing tonight."

"Dancing?" I ask. "I'm single, not a different person. I've never liked dancing."

"But you're cool with going out?" She sneaks in, "As long as it isn't dancing."

"You're trying to trick me into something." I shake my finger at her. "Not interested."

Her shoulders sag. "But you're finally single again, and I'm single, and OHMYGOD, I need to get laid."

"Jen, shut up. I think you just traumatized someone's grandma on the next row. I promise I will be single for a very long time, and there is no way I'm going out with you tonight."

"I can't believe I'm going out with you tonight," I groan.

"Oh, hush, you look amazing. Anyway, I've heard this place is super low key."

"Where are we going again?" I tug at the hem of my dress.

"It's a jazz place. How cool is that? Jazz?" Her enthusiasm is infectious.

"I didn't know you liked jazz." I peer at my reflection in the mirror, my eyes lock with hers. "Are you sure about this?"

"Change is good; besides, you always let me cut your hair in college." She twirls the scissors around her finger and aims them at the mirror like a pistol.

"Trim," I correct her. "I let you trim my hair. I have way more hair than you've ever cut before."

"Gotta have faith. Worst thing that can happen is you won't like it and you'll have to grow it back out. It's hair, not a limb. You need to banish your ponytails."

I close my eyes and take a deep breath. "Okay, do it."

"That's my girl."

I keep my eyes closed the whole time. It's relaxing and nerve wracking at the same time. I can't remember the last time someone played with my hair. I only hope she doesn't mess it up. I have agreed to a simple bob, long enough for me to tuck my hair behind my ears and short enough not to sit on the back of my neck. It's the most hair I've ever had cut at one time, maybe six inches.

When the scissors stop clipping and she starts styling my hair, my heart starts racing. What if I've made a terrible mistake? What if I don't have the face for shorter hair?

"Courtney, you look beautiful." My eyes flutter open at the sound of my mother's voice.

I turn my head to meet her eyes. She's standing in the doorway to the bathroom. I turn back to the mirror and my jaw drops. I lift my hands to my hair to feel the bounce and how light it feels after having shed those extra inches.

"It looks amazing, Jen," I gush.

She unwraps the towel from around my shoulders. "I am pretty fabulous," she agrees, humble as ever.

While my mom and Jen talk, I stand to inspect myself in the mirror. It has been a long time since I got dressed up or wore this much make up. Was that the reason Mike had to look elsewhere? Because I stopped taking care of myself? I don't want to cry, ruining the makeup Jen has so carefully applied; but I couldn't help but wonder about that. Was I partly to blame for Mike cheating on me?

"Stop looking so serious." Jen's attention was back on me. "Tonight is about going out with your oldest friend and having a couple drinks."

"You will always be my oldest friend," I tease with emphasis on old. Couldn't help it, she walked right into it.

"You think you're funny," she deadpans.

We do a final appearance check before we leave. Jen looks fabulous. She's always had a gypsy vibe with her long black hair and almond shaped eyes. Her maxi dress shows off her curves and covers her, well, most of her. The top part of the salmon shaded dress is sleeveless leaving her sun-kissed shoulders bare.

I'm a little top heavy, so strapless dresses are not part of my wardrobe options. I loved this light green sundress in the store; but now it seems more low cut and shorter than it did in the dressing room. The green makes my hazel eyes seem brighter and my new haircut makes my blonde hair look young and fun.

I glance at Jen. "Are you sure I don't look stupid?"

"Only when you open your mouth to ask questions like that."

God, I love her.

When I ask my mom if she wants me home by a certain time, both she and Jen groan. "What?"

Jen and my mom share a look while they decide who will talk. "You are thirty years old, Courtney. I'm not giving you a curfew."

"That's not what I meant. I didn't know if you had to be up early. I was trying to be considerate."

She winks. "You might meet someone and not come home at all tonight."

I tilt my head at her. "Are you suggesting I go home with some random guy tonight?"

She shrugs as if it's no big deal.

"Mom—"

Jen cuts me off walking over to high five my mom. "You are so much cooler than my mom." She turns back to me. "Come on, hooker. I got your mom's permission to get you laid tonight."

I turn around and head back toward my room.

Jen runs to catch me before I reach the stairs. "We're teasing you. Now, let's get a move on so we can get a table near the stage."

The bar is past her place but not by much. Still, it's the direction and the same road I would take back to my old condo with Mike. Three days. I've only been apart from him for three days and people expect me to move on. Each morning that I've woken up in my mother's house, I've forgotten where I was, and then had to remember all over again what he did.

It almost feels like the last eight years of my life have never happened. It's not as if I have anything to show for it. The worst part is, while Jen is thrilled to be going out, I'm terrified. I don't want to assume I'll be approached; but on the off chance that I am, I don't know how to flirt anymore.

I haven't had a conversation as a single woman in almost a decade. There were so many rules to dating back then. Are they the same now or different? What if

I'm not approached? Will that be worse than if I am? Will it mean I'm no longer attractive to the male gender? Clearly, Mike felt that way if he had to look elsewhere.

"You're quiet. Whatcha thinking about?" Jen asks, turning down the stereo.

"I'm nervous," I admit. "It's been a long time."

"What? Since you've gone out? Come on." She pushes my leg. "You and I went to dinner and a movie last month."

"This is different and you know it," I argue.

"Why does it have to be different? Relax and focus on having a nice night out. Nothing else matters. There is no expectation for you to meet or talk to a guy tonight. Ignore every single one of them for all I care. I only want to see you happy again."

"Oh, my God, what if Mike is here?" I panic.

Jen gives me a weird look. "Courtney, think about it. Mike at a jazz place? Seriously?"

We lock eyes for a couple moments before we both crack up. "What was I thinking?" I struggle with my next breath. "What was I thinking?"

Same words, only so different. Jen reaches out to clasp my hand. "Honey, we don't have to go out if you're not ready."

"But you got me this dress and you made me look pretty; and you look pretty and you deserve a night out. I won't be a mess, I promise. I'm fine."

Only I'm not. I'm not fine. Life moves on and I have to accept the fact I need to make a new one for myself.

Jen turns into a busy strip mall. A grocery store is at the far end and the bar hugs the opposite corner. Parking is already hard to find. Jen manages to find a spot in front of a sandwich place a few businesses down from the jazz place. We both flip down the visor mirrors to do a quick face check.

"So you're good?" Jen double checks with me one more time.

"I am," I lie, opening my door.

After we make our way to the front entrance, we are carded. I find this funny and flattering at the same time. There is no way this bouncer can think either one of us is under twenty-one. The place is on the dark side. There are round two, and four-seat-er tables in the main area between the stage and the bar.

The tables are a dark wood, which matches the heavy fabric lining the walls. There is low lighting throughout the bar and larger lights are directed to the stage. A band plays music more bluesy, in my opinion.

We are able to find a table for two midway between the bar and the stage.

"What do you want to drink?"

I think about it. "Do they have any sangria?"

"I can check. Do you want a merlot if they don't?"

I grin, which she takes as a yes, and I turn back toward the stage. I do my best to relax, not to look at the people around me. I feel even more alone sitting by myself. I know Jen is only at the bar; however, I can't help but wonder if people are judging me. My engagement ring was my shield. It told the world I wasn't alone. Now, all I have is the faint tan line where it was. I cover my hand, feeling bare without it.

"What do you think of the band?" Jen asks, passing me my drink.

"I like them. Will there be a singer or just the band?" I ask before taking a sip of my drink.

"I'm not sure." She leans over to tap the shoulder of a guy at the table next to ours, and asks.

I envy her uncanny ability to start a conversation with anyone. That is something I've always struggled with.

She turns back to me and introduces her new friend. "This is Tony." He stands to reach across the small table to shake my hand. "He says there are singers, a guy, and a girl, who switch off throughout the night. One of them should be going on any minute."

I smile my thanks and he offers to buy us a drink. I decline. I've barely had any of the one I just got but Jen accepts. He asks her to keep an eye on his table and not let anyone steal their spot because his friend stepped outside to take a call. She laughs and slides into his chair to protect his table while he goes to the bar.

There must be a lull at the bar because he is back with her drink and one for himself in no time. He sits in the seat vacated by his friend while Jen stays in his seat, leaving me alone at our table. I'm going to kill her. I'm meditating the method of how when Tony's friend returns. Jen in her infinite wisdom tells his friend to sit in her spot at our table. She absolutely has a death wish.

When he sits, I'm stunned to see he is none other than Grant Offenheim.

He squints at me, reaching out his hand. "Have we met before?"

I nod. "I worked for Don Fulson, but I don't work there anymore."

"So you know my name, but I don't know yours." He smiles and his trademark dimples appear.

I try not to let them affect me. "Courtney." He gives my hand a squeeze. "Courtney Grayson."

Any further conversation is impeded by the first singer. She is amazing, and beautiful. She has an Adele feel and big voice to match. I find it impossible that I sense Grant's eyes on me and not her. When I finish my drink, he offers to get me another. I nod, still surprised by his attention. He could be talking to any woman in the room. It seems like a shame he's wasting his time on me.

Jen slides into his chair when he gets up. "So, he seems nice. Tony is a doll."

"Do you know who that is?" I whisper.

She shrugs. "No clue. Why? Should I know who he is?"

"That's Grant Offenheim, North Carolina's most eligible bachelor," I answer.

"That's great. That way you know for sure he's single."

I glare at her. "That's not the point. I'm not interested in anyone right now."

"Then consider this practice for when you are. You are under no obligation to like him or even talk to him ever again."

I nod. I can do this. I can have an adult conversation with an attractive, scratch that, insanely hot single man. In fact, having a trial run with a never going to happen option might be what's best for me. Getting my feet wet by cannonballing into the ocean will make dipping them into a puddle when I'm ready all the easier.

She moves back to the table with Tony as Grant approaches with my drink.

"Thank you." I take a sip, time for courage. "Have you ever been here before?"

Lame conversation starter, I know, but this is practice. He moves his chair closer to mine and I can smell his aftershave. It's woodsy but not overpowering. I try to picture him camping and giggle to myself.

His dimples make another appearance. "Did I say something funny?"

I shake my head and cover my mouth. "No, I just thought of something funny. It's nothing."

He tilts his head and I feel strangely evaluated. "You can tell me."

He is going to think I'm crazy. Okay, here goes. "It's silly really; when you moved closer, I could smell your cologne or aftershave and it reminded me of a forest."

"What's so funny about that?"

I blush; I hope he doesn't think I'm insulting him. "I don't know why, but I pictured you in a plaid shirt chopping down a tree. And that's so different from all the suits I've ever seen you in."

He looks hurt. "I don't make a good lumberjack?"

I try, but fail, not to laugh as I shake my head.

He smiles. "I bet I could surprise you."

Grant Offenheim is flirting with me, I think.

CHAPTER 3

Courtney

"So, are you going to call him?" Jen asks as she pulls into my driveway.

"I don't know. He seemed nice, but I need to get my feet back on the ground before I even think about dating."

I still couldn't believe he asked for my number. I didn't want to give him my mother's, so I gave him my email address instead, and he gave me his number. I had been so surprised, I blurted out 'why' when he asked for it. I smile thinking about his reply, "I have to show you what a good lumberjack I can be."

"What about Tony? He seemed nice," I ask, effectively changing the subject.

"Your guy was cuter but beggars can't be choosers. We're going out next Friday. Want me to ask him to invite Grant, and we can double up?" She knocks her elbow into mine.

"You're lucky I love you," I tease, getting out. I lean down to look at her before shutting my door. "Seriously, don't do that."

When a mischievous look crosses over her face, I add, "Promise."

She crosses her heart and blows me a kiss. I shut the door and wave at her while she backs out of my driveway, and then I turn around to head inside. It's late, but not that late. My mom is in bed; but when I hear the TV is still on, I knock and pop my head in.

"Hey, Mom. I wanted to let you know I'm home."

"Did you have a good time?" Her expression is hopeful.

"I did but..." I don't want her to get her hopes up. "I think tonight might be it for a while though."

She nods. I'm single, not a different person.

I change and get ready for bed. Tonight was fun but it didn't feel real. I can't allow my thoughts to be distracted by Grant Offenheim and his stupid, sexy dimples. I needed a job and to get my own place. I am lucky I have no major bills to speak of. I paid my car off last year. So barring any mechanical issues, I only have to worry about insurance.

Mechanical issues? Shit, the tire guy! I hop out of bed and walk across my room to my dresser to grab a notepad and a pen.

-Go pay tire guy.

I tear the sheet off and set it on my bedside table so I'll see it first thing tomorrow.

When I wake and head down to the kitchen, I realize the house is empty. I find a note from my mom on the door to the fridge telling me she is checking out some yard sales. Some things never change. My mother has been obsessed with other people's treasures for as long as I can remember.

After I pour myself some orange juice and make some toast, I turn on a TV morning show to watch while I eat. When the doorbell rings, I'm not one hundred percent sure, whether I really heard it or just imagined it, so I wait to see if it rings again. When it does, I cringe at my current attire but head to the door anyway. When I open it, I am face to face with Mike 'we almost shared a last name' Hudson.

I start to shut the door but he puts his hand up to stop it. "Please talk to me, Court."

I turn and walk to my mother's office letting him follow me. He's a born salesman. "Nothing happened; she forced herself on me; I want you back; I've only ever loved you; please don't leave me." And other versions of not apologizing trail my steps. When I reach my mom's office, I pluck my old phone off her desk and hand it to him.

"That's for saving me the trip to the post office."

His jaw drops. "That's it? That's all you have to say?"

I nod, squeezing past him to lead him back to the door. He reaches out from behind me, a hand on each of my biceps.

"I can't lose you."

He doesn't understand I probably could have forgiven him for anything else. It would have been hard; but whether it was money or an addiction, I would have stayed with him and made it work. Cheating is something else altogether. Short of him providing a doctor's note proving he had been drugged and forcibly raped, I would never trust him again.

the other side of
SOME DAY

I glance back at him, into the eyes I thought I would spend the rest of my life waking up to, and say, "You need to leave."

His arms fall. He's known me long enough to believe me.

His reticence is replaced with a sneer. "You haven't even asked about your things. You don't even want them back. Make one mistake and I'm as good as dead to you, aren't I?"

I turn, facing him fully. "Make me the bad guy, Mike. Twist it around so you aren't to blame. Do whatever it is you have to do to live with what you did."

I hold his gaze until he looks away. I know few things right now; but I do know that I deserve fidelity. I was good to him; I never led him on or lied to him. When I loved him, I left myself vulnerable. I'm not sure that's something I will ever forgive him for. Now I know, no matter how perfect things seem you cannot ever trust another person.

"I miss you. I don't know how to live without you." His voice breaks, and for the first time, I see the differences in him. He doesn't look like he's slept or eaten; his hands are shaking, and he looks close to tears.

"I'm not coming back." As hurt as I am by what he did, there is no point in being cruel now.

I don't have the energy to hurt him like he hurt me. Some piece of what makes me who I am, a part of me that I never had to see before now, allows me to accept all I can do now is move forward. The tears that threatened him before now spill. All I can do is stand here and watch the man I once loved crumble. I'm strangely detached watching him break down.

My mind recognizes the lie in his behavior, the falseness in his pain. If he loved me as much as he claims, he never would have betrayed me the way he did. All I want is for him to leave, to wipe his presence from my memories. At this point, he's a ghost; he was never real.

"If you could box up my things and drop them by, it would mean a lot to me," I say it more for his sake than mine.

It gives him the unfortunate opportunity to see me again. With any luck, I can work it out so I'm not here when he comes by. I could go my whole life without seeing him again and that will be fine with me.

"What are you doing for money? I know you took your name off the joint account."

My mouth drops. "What I do now is none of your business. You should be happy I didn't clean it out and leave you with nothing."

He looks up at the ceiling, his shoulders sagging. "I can't keep your money Courtney. At least let me write you a check for half of what's in it." As much as I want to refuse it, some of that money is mine and would come in handy right now. "Not half, you put more into it than I did."

When he reaches out as though to grab my hand I step back, watching his hand fall back to his side. "What can I do Courtney? I'll do anything."

Shaking my head, I open the door. "I don't want any guilt money."

Reaching into his pocket, he pulls out a check. "This isn't guilt money. It's yours and I won't keep it. I'm..." he hesitates, his eyes searching mine for something that died the day I learned he betrayed me. "I'm so sorry."

Lifting my hand, he presses the check into it then leaves. I sag against the door once it's closed behind him.

My hopes of accomplishing anything today are dashed. I only want to sleep now. Maybe Mike isn't a ghost, but a vampire because I feel drained from being near him.

I stagger back up to my room. I'm still in bed when my mom returns, her face flushed with the excitement of her finds. Her expression falls when she sees me.

"Mike stopped by," I whisper.

"Oh, honey." She's by my side, perched on the edge of my bed, her hand on my back to comfort me.

"I'm not sad. I feel as though, maybe, I finally have figured out we never were supposed to be together."

"Don't say that. You had something special."

I know she's only trying to make me feel better; but how can that comment help me now? If what we had was special, clearly, it wasn't special enough to keep him from fucking someone else.

"Mom, I need some time to myself, if that's okay."

She squeezes my shoulder and hesitates before leaving, gently closing my door behind her. I glance around my room, the room I grew up in. I've never felt more of a failure. I'm thirty, never married, cheated on, no job, and never even held a job that had anything to do with my degree. I'm at square one.

My self-disgust, more than anything else, propels me into the shower. There is one thing I can do today, reimburse that nice man for the tire he gave me. I am starting over. I don't want to tarnish my clean slate by owing someone.

When I go to shampoo my hair, I remember it's now half gone. Well, I won't have to waste any of my time drying it is my only thought. I change into a new cream-colored dress courtesy of Jen. This one hits my knee and isn't as dressy as the green one I wore the night before.

"Where are you going?" My mom seems surprised to see me rushing down the stairs.

"I'm driving out to pay that man for the tire he gave me."

She nods. "Are you okay for money?"

"I'll be okay." I need to do this.

I don't have much in the way of funds; the check from Mike will help though. My mom already has refused my offer to pay her rent. Once I figure out a job, I'll be able to build up a cushion of my own. The drive to Pete's is quiet. I don't turn on any music. I have no cell phone to distract me. I have only the buzz from air conditioning and the other cars to pull me from my thoughts.

I recognize the exit from my hellish day. I can only think about the things I didn't know, the last time I took it. Business seems slow, like the last time I was here. I feel better at my decision to pay back the owner. I have no idea how solid his business is and I would hate to think helping me in any way hurt him.

I park and, after getting out of my car, smooth my dress before walking to the office. A bell I don't remember from my last visit chimes to announce me.

"Be right out." A voice calls out from the back.

My eyes move over the sales posters on the wall. Shocks, brakes, and one type of oil or another. It's somewhat daunting how little I know about how my car runs.

"How can I help you?"

I turn at the sound of the voice and I am greeted with startling blue eyes. I blink suddenly, certain mine are deceiving me. In addition, I seem to have lost the ability to talk. I stare and gulp as my eyes process the man in front of me. He's tall, not as tall as Grant Offenheim my mind argues, which is odd.

My open perusal of him seems to amuse him. He gives me a crooked smile while my eyes take him in; no dimples, my brain screams. I direct my gaze to his biceps clearly straining his white t-shirt. My brain offers no argument to them.

Once I find my voice I speak, "I was…" My tongue feels heavy and fatter than normal. "Looking for an older man who works here."

His eyes narrow. "My dad isn't here. Is there something I can help you with?"

I wonder at his chilly response. "I had a flat tire last week and my card was declined when I went to pay. Your dad told me not to worry about it, but I wanted to come pay for it."

"Shit," he mutters under his breath.

"Excuse me?" I stammer.

He takes a deep breath. "I'm sorry. It's just-" he stops to drag his hand through his wavy hair. "My dad has a heart of gold, you know?"

I slowly nod and he goes on. "You're here to pay, which is great. I don't want to dump all over you for doing the right thing. It's that my dad has to stop letting people not pay or he's going to lose the shop."

"That's awful. I'm so sorry. Here." I take out my wallet. "Please let me pay you."

He gives me a half smile. "Do you remember what the total was?"

I groan, to which he raises his eyebrows. "It was embarrassing when my card was declined," I explain. "Trust me; I remember what the total was."

As he rings me up for the figure I give him, I feel the need to tell him why my card was declined. "Someone tried to pull money out of my account from overseas. My bank wouldn't authorize any new transactions until they could confirm whether or not I knew about it. I didn't know about it but that's all straightened out now." I gulp. "I don't want you to think I couldn't afford the work."

His eyes widen, but I can tell he gets it. He quietly hands me my receipt. "Is your dad taking the day off? I'd like to thank him, personally, at some point for what he did," I babble on. "You have no idea what an awful day that was. Your father not charging me was the one nice thing that happened." His expression hardens, so I start backpedaling. "I'm being silly, I know. Maybe, if you tell him thank you for me. I don't want to waste your time."

I turn to go, but he reaches over the counter to grab my wrist. I shake my head and stare at his hand, not fully understanding why he stopped me.

He releases me, putting his hands up. "I'm sorry. I wanted to tell you something before you left." He pauses, his eyes lifting from my arm to my face. "I'm Clay, by the way."

"I'm Courtney," I stammer, weirded out by the random introduction.

"I don't usually work here. I'm only helping out because my dad fell and broke his hip."

"Oh, my God! That's awful," I blurt.

Clay walks around the counter and sits in one of the plastic waiting room chairs. "He's so stubborn. He needs to sell this place and retire, but he won't."

My mouth drops.

"You don't need me dumping all of this on you. Absolutely, I'll tell my dad you stopped by to thank him. It will mean a lot to him."

"But what about the garage?" I blurt.

He squints at me. "What do you mean?"

"I can work here." I think I've lost my mind.

He cocks his head at me, an amused grin spreading over his face. "Do you even know anything about cars?"

I scratch the back of my neck before shrugging. "Not really."

He stands, moving closer to me. "You're adorable."

"Pardon?" I take a step back.

"You seriously want to become a mechanic?" He's teasing me.

"No," I admit. "I don't even know where that idea came from."

"Too bad. I wouldn't mind working here from time to time if he hired someone as cute as you."

"Ugh." Cute? Adorable? I head for the door.

He follows me through it. "I didn't mean to offend you. Aw, don't get mad."

I turn to face him. "This has been great fun; but since I'm all paid up, I'm going to head home."

"Would you like to go out sometime?"

"Not even a little bit," I snap.

He grins. "Not even this much?" He holds his hand up with a sliver of space between his thumb and his index finger.

I can't help it, I laugh. "I don't like you."

He looks at me. "I think you might."

"I just got out of a really serious relationship," I begin.

He jumps in. "All the better to go out with someone you don't even like. It'll be like practice for when you meet someone you do."

"That's a terrible idea," I argue.

"What if I take you to see my dad?" He pauses to gauge my reaction. When I don't immediately argue he goes on. "You said yourself you'd like to thank him in person. And think how much it would cheer him up to see you."

"That's unfair," I grumble.

CHAPTER 4

CLAY

Worst weekend ever, check. Spending the day at the hospital helping my mom get my dad checked out and over to their house sucked. I missed lunch with my niece, Mags, because of it, so now I can add a self-imposed guilt trip to my already full mental dance card. I worked until o'dark thirty getting as much shit done for my actual job as I could.

Since I've been here, the phones have been ringing off the hook all morning. I think I have a cramp from running back and forth from the bays to the office to answer all the calls. For a smart guy it took me longer than I care to admit to unplug the phone and move it to the bay, so I wouldn't have to run to grab it.

Half of the calls aren't even to schedule work, but to check on my dad. I had to swallow the urge to shout 'call their fucking house' to them. My mom's retired, and loves to talk. This is her type of stuff, not mine. Still, as annoyed as I've been, I have to remind myself not to be an asshole. I'm not usually one. I blame stress.

It's gotta be the mindfuck I'm dealing with, considering I'm even here. I never expected today to go this way when I woke up this morning. My dad's been on my ass to take over the shop since forever. Now I'm here; all he had to do was break a hip to make it happen. I have nothing against the place; I don't want to work on cars for a living.

My dad isn't thrilled that I'm in IT; but I like what I do and it pays the bills. My business is thriving. There isn't a company on the planet that doesn't already have or want a website. Since I can build and maintain them, I'm so busy I've turned jobs down.

Last thing I needed was to deal with the garage. I'm already crazy busy with my shit. So, one minute I'm stressing over how I'm going to balance my own projects with temporarily taking over my dad's shop, to trying to think of a way to keep this girl from leaving. I'll figure out those other things somehow.

Those other things don't seem to matter as much anymore, which is crazy. Speaking of crazy, I'm trying to talk a girl I've never met before into coming to meet my parents. It was the best I could come up with at the time. She's too cute to let her walk away. I haven't felt this…attracted, interested, I'm not even sure what… in I don't even know how long.

How could I not? Her concern over my dad did something to me. I'm used to people only being interested in one thing, themselves. A cute little blonde thing, her offering to work at my dad's garage because he hurt himself blew my mind. This Courtney chick is nothing like the girls I'm normally into, not that I've been into anyone recently. I've barely had time for anything. I've had my head down working my ass off this past year.

"What is?" I ask.

"You're using me wanting to thank your dad to get me to go out with you."

Nodding, I reply. "Sure am. Did it work?"

When she smiles, I make a fist and pull my elbow down to my side, biting my lower lip.

All for spontaneity, I jog back to the office to flip the sign to closed and lock the door.

When I start closing the openings to the bays, she gasps. "Right now?"

"Why not?" I grin. "I need to take a lunch anyway." I reach my hand out to her. She gapes at it for a moment, before gently placing her hand in mine. My fingers close around hers, and I give her a squeeze before leading her toward my truck.

Her mouth drops as we near it. If only I can make her panties as wet as my truck does. "Hungry?"

She glances back at me, a blush coloring her cheeks. I walk her over to the passenger side, opening her door for her. She's not short, but still needs to use the running board to get in. I walk around the front of the truck, grinning at her the whole way. Once I'm in and buckled, I turn the truck on with an added rev of the engine just for her. She blushes again and I grin.

I turn to look at her after popping it into reverse. "You really shouldn't get into trucks with strange men."

She gulps and reaches to put her hand on the door handle.

When I see her reaction, I hit the brake, feeling like an ass and shift the truck back to park. "I'm not going to hurt you, Courtney. I promise."

When she continues to hesitate, I go on. "Why don't you take a picture of me and text it to someone?"

I hope that she'll relax since I'm sure a serial killer wouldn't want his picture texted to someone.

"I don't have a cell phone."

I still haven't put the truck back into gear because I wasn't expecting her to say that.

"Everyone has a cellphone. My niece is ten and she has a cellphone," I argue.

She seems at war with herself deciding what to say.

Finally, she replies, "I just don't. It's a long story. If you want, I can use your phone to do it, if it will make you happy. I'm not some crazy anti-technology person who doesn't own a TV or something. I know how to work a cellphone. I had one up until recently. For reasons I don't feel like getting into, I don't have one anymore. Okay?"

It's time to change the subject. "Are you still nervous about driving away with me?" I ask.

She shakes her head. It's not until I've pulled onto the main road, that I notice her shiver. I had the air on full blast.

"Sorry." I move to turn it down. "I run hot."

She hugs herself, and still manages to blush at my words.

She blinks at me in surprise when I pull into my 'parents' driveway. The house I grew up in is a simple rancher. It's funny how the place seemed huge when I was a kid. The house is the same for the most part; the same white siding and maroon shutters, I'm what's changed.

Trying not to startle her further, I quietly tell her, "Here we are."

With that, I get out of my truck and start making my way to the front door. I purposefully walk ahead of her, away from her. The pull I feel toward her is messing with my head, stupidly, I wonder if distance will dull it. Half-jogging, she quickly catches up to me, sliding in front of me as I hold open the door for her.

"Mom, Dad. I've got a visitor for you," I call out from the foyer.

Standing beside me, she straightens her dress and looks around. I glance at her, wondering what she thinks of me, my parents' house, and being here. Their foyer has a warm wood toned chair rail with thin wooden panels beneath it. Above the chair rail, the walls are painted a pale green with a border of painted ivy leaves near the ceiling.

"Visitor?" My mom calls out from further down a hall.

"They must be in the den." I tilt my head for her to follow me.

We pass a sitting room on the right and a dining room on the left before entering a large white kitchen. From there the den is off to the right. An oversized flat screen is on Sports Center.

"Who do we have here?" my mom asks, arching a brow in Courtney's direction.

"Courtney, this is my mom, Judy. Mom, this is Courtney."

She reaches out to shake my mom's hand, who looks happily confused I brought a girl home. I can't help but wonder what she thinks.

"Your husband gave me a tire last week. I stopped by the shop today to pay him back and thank him," she explains.

Where I was annoyed at hearing what my dad had done, my mother gets a sweet faraway look in her eyes and smiles. "That's my Pete."

She walks further into the room to lift a remote off the coffee table and mute the TV. "Honey, you have a visitor." She beckons Courtney to her side.

My dad's in an oversized recliner. "He's on some serious painkillers." My mom explains his sleepy expression.

"I'm so sorry to intrude. I only wanted to thank you for the tire."

Mom links her arm through Courtney's, giving it a squeeze. "You aren't intruding. You stopping by has made my day."

"You're prettier today." Pete grins up at her.

Mom laughs. "Always such a flirt, this one."

"Clay should find a pretty girl like you and marry her," he continues.

"Dad." I stand behind the recliner frowning down at him.

"It's the pain medicine," my mom explains.

"No. It's not. I've been married to your mother thirty-three years. She's made me the happiest man alive."

My annoyance evaporates. "I know, Dad."

"She can't cook worth shit though," my dad continues to no one in particular.

Courtney bites back a laugh and glances at my mom, who doesn't look surprised by his statement.

"Good thing you didn't marry me for my cooking skills." she teases, releasing Courtney's arm and bending down to kiss Dad's forehead.

He smiles up at her before his eyes flutter closed.

She turns to look at me. "I could have held off on giving him his dose if I knew you were coming."

"It's okay, Mom. We'll get out of your hair." I put my hand on the small of Courtney's back and turn her toward the door.

My mom's eyes widen before she reaches her hand out to Courtney. "It was real nice to meet you Courtney. You are welcome to stop by anytime."

"Thank you, and please thank your husband again for me when he wakes up."

The heat of her skin through the thin material of her dress warms my hand. We walk quietly back through my parents' house, her eyes drifting over framed pictures of me throughout the years.

"Do you have any brothers or sisters?" she asks when we reach the front door.

"I have a younger sister."

I don't elaborate and drop my hand from her back once we are back at my truck. I open her door, and wait for her to settle before closing it.

The sun has banished any trances of air-conditioned air from the truck. The heat is now solid against my limbs, beads of sweat erupting in my hairline.

"Shit, it's hot in here," I exclaim. Once I'm in, I quickly start the truck and crank the AC to max.

"I should have cracked the windows before we went in." I turn toward her. "Sorry about that."

"It's okay," she smiles.

"Do you have to get right back or do you have time for lunch?" I ask, shifting into reverse.

Her mouth drops. "Are you asking me to have lunch with you?"

I shrug. "I need to eat whether you come along or not."

She laughs, covering her mouth. "Way to sell it."

I pause, deliberating before responding. "I know a place that makes a great burger."

"I am hungry," she admits.

That's response enough for me.

Work is the last thing I want to think about with Courtney sitting next to me. I glance over at her; I have to admit she looks pretty good in my truck. I can't stop looking at her legs, if her dress was a little bit shorter I could—. I force my eyes back on the road before I end up driving off it.

I have to concentrate on not coming off like a jerk. Part of me wants to though, caveman style. Throw her over my shoulder and have my way with her in the nearest cave, or up against a tree, maybe in a field bending her—.

I jump when the car behind me honks letting me know I've been sitting at a green light. I look over at Courtney and shrug. She smiles sweetly at me; thank God, she isn't a mind reader. If she were, she'd be running in the other direction right about now.

Or would she?

She did agree to come with me pretty fast. Was it because of my dad or me? Even if she came mainly because of my dad, she would have driven separately if I had given her a bad vibe.

I grin, yep, still got it.

We're not far from my favorite diner. I wonder if she's one of those girls who only eat salad or if she eats real food.

CHAPTER
5

Courtney

As we drive, I try to place where we are. I grew up an hour from here but never explored this area. There are plenty of shops and neighborhoods; but overall, it's more rural than where my mom lives.

"Do you do this a lot?" I ask, breaking the silence.

"Eat?" He jokes.

"No. Take women you just met out to lunch," I clarify.

He turns into a small diner with a red and white striped awning. "It's been a while since I've taken a woman anywhere."

He turns off the truck and slips out his door, walking around to open mine.

I beat him to it. "You don't have to open my door."

"I don't mind." He pushes it shut behind me.

I follow him to the entrance, not surprised when he opens the door for me. Despite my argument, I like it. I can't remember the last time Mike opened a door for me. I guess that's how it goes. The romance dies over time. It didn't seem that way with Clay's parents, or even my parents before my dad passed away.

Clay motions me toward an empty booth. There are menus standing in a holder against the wall with the condiments. He passes one to me before leaning back in his booth and watching me.

The burgers on the menu are straightforward. I know I'll have one but I check out the other dishes to satisfy my curiosity.

"Do you have a boyfriend?"

My eyes snap from an old-fashioned meatloaf to Clay. "What?"

He pushes forward, leaning over the table, his chin on his hand. "Do you have a boyfriend?"

I take a breath, closing my menu. "I do not."

His eyes hover on my lips before easing up to mine. "How come?"

I drop my hands to my lap and rub the spot where my engagement ring was for so long. "Like I told you before, back at the garage, I just got out of a long relationship. I'd rather not talk about it."

"What? Did you catch him cheating on you?" He says it like a joke, his expression falling when I gasp.

I look down, my hands darting up to cover my face. I don't want him to look at me.

He hops around to my side of the booth, draping his arm across my shoulders, and pulling me into him. I will not cry. I will not cry. I stiffen in his grasp; instead of letting me go, he pulls me closer, dropping his lips to the side of my head.

"I didn't know." His breath gently fans my ear.

I pull away, scooting closer to the wall. "Please don't make a big deal about it."

He slowly returns to his side of the booth. "I didn't mean to upset you."

I look over his shoulder to the scrolling curve of the wood topping the booth. "Let's just eat."

He lifts his hand to let a server behind the counter know we're ready. She brings out our drinks first. I fold the paper wrapper of my straw repeatedly until it makes a small triangle. Neither of us speaks, an awkward silence is putting it mildly. I unfold my wrapper and start folding it again.

"I was a cheater."

I suck in a breath and look up at him. "Why?"

"Vanity, immaturity, it was a game to me. Trying to see how many toys I could accumulate." He doesn't look proud.

"What made you stop?" I ask, not even knowing if he has stopped.

"It cost me my best friend."

"How? What happened?"

Our server brings our food and he waits, thanking her before he answers. "Owen was a lot like me, until he met Chloe. It pissed me off. I was losing my wingman and he was so whipped over this girl. I set out to break them up."

"But if they really loved each other," I start.

He shakes his head. "I seduced her."

"You didn't drug her did you?" I stammer.

He jerks his head up. "I was an asshole, not a criminal. I wormed my way into her affections; and then, set it up so that Owen would catch us together."

"That's horrible."

"It was. I have no excuse for what I did. I didn't see it at the time, but I know it now. I thought it would only break them up, but it also ruined the friendship I had with him."

I nod. "Have you spoken to him since?"

He shakes his head. "That was five years ago. The last I heard, he moved out west. Some things, sorry won't fix."

"I saw my ex today. He wants me to come back. I could barely look at him."

We both eat for a while before he asks, "How long were you together?"

I set my burger down and wipe my hands on a napkin. "Eight years."

"Damn." He shakes his head.

For whatever reason it doesn't seem weird to confess since he went first. "The day I got the flat tire."

"You weren't lying about just getting out of a relationship. Shit, that was last week."

"It's strange. It feels like it's been longer, like so much has happened since then." I push my plate to the side and refold the paper from the straw, my hands on the table now. "Part of me is scared that I haven't fully dealt with it; that I'm in the eye of the hurricane, and the impact of what happened hasn't hit me yet."

"Do you still love him?"

I shrug. "I hate what he did. I don't wish ill on him, or her. I mainly feel stupid. I wonder how long it was going on. I still love what I thought we had."

He reaches his hand across the table to rest it on both of mine. "You'll get past this better off than you think."

My hands melt under the warmth of his. "How do you know?"

He squeezes my hands before pulling his back into his lap. "I have a feeling about you."

When the check comes, he refuses my offer to pay. Once we're out the door, I turn to read the name on the sign, Holliswood Diner, cementing it to memory.

"That was a great burger. Thanks for treating."

He opens my door. "Growing up, we came here once a week."

"Old habits die hard," I reply, before he shuts my door.

"Yep," he replies, getting in on his side, "I have lunch here every Sunday."

"Why Sundays?"

"Like you said, 'old habits' and all. If I lived closer, I'd probably eat here more often. I live an hour away. I'm running my dad's shop till he gets better or sells it."

"How'd you manage to get the time off?"

He shifts the truck into reverse. "I took a leave of absence."

Curious, I ask. "What do you do?"

His eyes stay on the road. "Nothing exciting, a boring old office job. What do you do?"

I sink further into my seat. "I'm between jobs at the moment."

He glances over at me. "Were you serious about working at the shop?"

I pick at the hem of my dress, encouraging it closer to my knees. "I don't know anything about cars. I'm not even sure why I offered."

"Can you answer phones, schedule appointments?"

I stare at him. "You can't be serious."

He laughs. "Why not? I'm the only one at the shop now. Every time the phone rings, I have to stop what I'm doing to answer it."

"Can I think about it?" I stutter.

"Nope." He shakes his head, grinning. "You need a job and it'd help me out. Don't think about it, just do it."

"You're crazy," I giggle.

"Like a fox. You know you want to. Besides, this way you can treat me to lunch next."

"Now, I'm buying you lunch?" I joke.

"It's the least you can do, seeing as how I'm solving your employment dilemma."

"Well, when you put it that way..." I trail off.

He stops at a red light, turning his body toward me. "Will you do it?"

Ahhhh. Think, shit. I need a job, but a garage? I meet his eyes and think about having an excuse to see him again. As quickly I argue that thought, it's too soon even to think about a guy. In fact, the very last thing you should do is take this job.

"I'll do it." Holy shit! Did I really say that?

His face breaks into a dangerous smile, the kind of smile that makes my body ignore my brain.

There isn't time for a long goodbye when we get back to the shop. There's a red Toyota waiting.

Clay doesn't open my door. "I'll see you Monday morning, eight AM."

"What should I wear?" I question his back.

He glances back at me. "Anything you want," he says, before greeting the owner of the red car and opening the shop door.

What have you gotten yourself into? Is all I can think walking back to my car and for most of the drive back to my mom's house.

She meets me at the door. "You've been gone so long. I started to worry."

I grimace. "I'm sorry. I didn't think I would be gone this long, but the good news is I got a job."

She follows me to her office and I fill her in on Pete, his hip, Clay, lunch, and my job offer.

She clucks her tongue at me. "I think that boy is trying to get in your pants."

"Mom." I push her knee, trying to ignore the blush spreading across my cheeks at the thought of Clay in my pants.

She hangs out with me while I check my email. I stop listening to her the second I see two exciting, for very different reasons, emails in my inbox. One is from my mother's lawyer friend, the other from Grant Offenheim. I struggle with which one to read first before clicking on the one from Grant.

I am unable on my first read to grasp the entire message, only certain words pop out at me; Friday night and dinner. On my second attempt, would you and with me. My third run through, I speed-read it, my jaw dropping. Grant friggin Offenheim is asking me out on an official date for next Friday night, a whole week notice.

You're not interested in dating anyone my brain tries to argue; but it has its own comeback of, *this is Grant friggin Offenheim we're talking about.* I reread it, taking an absurd amount of time to try to read between the lines of each sentence.

Why am I even reading anything into this? What type of guy sends a polite email to ask a girl out? I start to wonder what Clay would do instead. Something tells me it wouldn't be polite. There is something almost primal about him. I should be disgusted by him given his lunchtime confession. Instead, for whatever reason, it almost endeared him to me.

In knowing his flaws, I want to fix him. I find something desirable in how wrong he is compared to the rightness that someone like Grant Offenheim represents. I know I'm not dating him, and there isn't anything overtly romantic in his email. Maybe he only wants to be friends.

I reply, accepting, and asking for a bit of detail as to what I should wear. Good thing I have a job because I see more shopping in my future. I open the email from my lawyer next. He sent a strongly worded email to my former employer asking for evidence of my thefts and threatening a wrongful termination suit otherwise. The email is nothing other than a copy of the letter.

I open it, and then skim it and all the legal speak. "Geez, your lawyer friend kinda kicks ass, Mom."

She leans over my shoulder to read the letter he sent. "He's been asking me to go out with him for months."

My mouth drops. It's awful but I see her as only being capable of loving my dad.

I keep my eyes forward. "Do you like him?"

With her hand resting on my shoulder, she gives me a squeeze. "There'll never be another one like your dad, but I guess Jim is all right."

I spent two hours last night obsessing over what I was going to wear to work today. I even laid an outfit out, and then panicked and changed into something else this morning. I want to make a good impression. Glancing down at my clothes, I suddenly feel overdressed. I'm wearing black slacks and a new blue sweater. I made a Target run yesterday to pick up a few things.

Is it awful the only reason I got this short-sleeved sweater is that it reminds me of Clay's eyes? I sit up straighter in my seat as if having proper posture will disguise my thoughts. I'm nervous, not just about the job, but about seeing him again.

Other than Jen and my mother, who both think I have lost my mind in taking this job, I was somehow able to talk to Clay about Mike. He feels safe, which shows how dangerous he could be. I sympathize with his former friend's girlfriend. If Clay is intent on getting something, I can't see him not succeeding.

Hell, he got me to agree to work with him without even telling me what he would pay me. My heart starts thudding in my chest; he is planning to pay me isn't he? A mixture of excitement and what the hell have I gotten myself into propel me the entire drive to the garage. I'm early but it turns out Clay was even earlier.

I park next to his truck and check my face in the mirror of my visor before heading in. Clay is behind the counter, leaning against it. The windows are tinted, so I couldn't see him as I walked up. If he has been there the whole time, he must have watched me walk across the parking lot.

The thought of him watching me gives me a secret thrill. "Good morning."

"You're early." His eyes start at my feet and slowly make their way up my body.

I hold my breath waiting for his eyes to meet mine. When they do, I release it as if I'm blowing out a candle.

"Trying to impress the boss?" He face is more serious than his teasing words.

I shiver. "I do what I can."

"We'll see about that." He lifts the opening in the counter for me to come behind it.

I feel his breath on my neck as I ease past him. Luckily, he speaks first because his nearness is leaving me tongue-tied. He gives me a quick tour; other than the waiting room, bathrooms, and counter area, there is only a small back office. He offers me his hand for the step down from the office through the doorway into the actual shop.

I feel his touch, simple, innocent, throughout my entire body. My lungs seem incapable of holding a full breath. I swallow poofs of air, doing everything in my power not to pant. When he releases my hand, I rub him off my skin and onto the tops of my pants. There are three bays. Only one of the doors is open even though there are cars on the lifts in the other two bays.

"Why don't you open those bays?" I ask, looking for something to say.

"I'll open them around mid-day; but for now, I'm trying to keep some of the cool air in."

I follow him back toward the office. The door is still propped open; but he pauses next to it, letting me go ahead of him. I feel his eyes on my back. I hear his steps approach me and gulp before turning to face him. It's hard to concentrate while he gives me a quick rundown of their phones and scheduling system.

I'm pleased to see it's on the lower tech side. I dealt with more complicated systems at my last job; but I also didn't spend half of my training wondering how soft my instructor's hair was. Because it looks so soft, I have had to fight the urge to touch it. It drives me nuts when it falls into Clay's eyes as he leans forward.

He slips into the back office and the fog of his presence lifts for a moment. I stand, straighten my shoulders, and vow not to make an ass out of myself the next time he stands near me. That lasts all of two minutes when he is back with employment paperwork for me to fill out.

As I work on it, he pulls out his phone. "What's your number?"

I glance up from my tax withholding worksheet. "I can give you the number to my mom's house."

He rubs his jaw. "That's right, no cell phone."

I nervously tap my pen on the counter. "My old cell was in a plan with my ex and I didn't want to get a new one before I got a new job."

"What happened with your last job?"

Such a simple question, such an awful answer. No good will come of lying.

"I was fired for stealing." I watch as his face hardens right before my eyes. I lift my hands up. "But, I never stole anything from them, I swear. My mom's friend who is a lawyer sent them a letter demanding proof or he said I might sue them for wrongful termination."

My explanation does nothing to soften his expression. "I can show you the letter that was sent to them on the computer if you want."

His jaw ticks back and forth, as I watch him decide whether to take my word.

"Am I going to regret giving you this job?" he quietly asks.

I shake my head. "You won't. I promise."

He rubs his hand over his face before directing his gaze back at me. "You really need a cell phone. What would you do if you broke down?"

I shrug, I hadn't really thought about it. "I was waiting to get a job."

He nods. "We can go at lunch."

My mouth drops. "Why would you go with me?"

He turns, shuffling some papers on the lower edge of the counter. "In case you broke down between here and there."

I fold my arms across my chest. "How far away is the closest cell phone place?"

He moves a step closer to me, straightening a stack of business cards. "A shop for the company I use is only fifteen minutes away."

I can't help it; I reach out and touch his arm. "Why are you so hell-bent on taking care of me?"

His eyes don't leave my hand; he eases out of my grasp and through the door to the bays, grumbling. "I don't know."

There is a window in the wall between the bays and the office part of the shop. When the phone isn't ringing or the waiting room is empty, I watch Clay while he works. His attention is mostly on whatever car he is working on so I can watch him without fear of him knowing.

He wears a pair of navy Dickies and a grey t-shirt that fits snugly across his chest and arms. Sometime between leaving the office and now, he pulled on a baseball hat, wearing it backward to keep his hair out of his face just like his dad did. I'm so lost in the show, I jump when the door dings.

"Courtney?"

I'm too surprised to disguise it. "What are you doing here, Grant?"

He clears his throat. "I didn't expect to see you here." He walks closer to the counter and leans toward me. "I got your email. I'm looking forward to Friday night."

The door closing behind me ensures Clay heard that.

"Something I can help you with?" he asks from behind me.

I can feel the heat radiating from him and mentally have to stop myself from closing my eyes and inhaling him. I must be losing my mind but I've never been more turned on by sweat in my life.

Grant frowns at how close Clay is standing to me before answering. "I was looking for the owner, Peter Bradshaw."

Clay drops his arm on to the counter, leaning forward slightly, erasing more of the already minuscule space between us. "My dad isn't here. Who are you?"

Grant offers his hand. Clay has to move away from me to shake it.

"I'm Grant Offenheim."

If Clay recognizes the name, he doesn't say. "What's your business with my dad?"

Grant reaches into his breast pocket to hand Clay his card. "Have your dad call me." He glances at me and winks. "I'll see you Friday."

I lift my hand in a motionless wave letting it fall back to my side once the door closes behind him.

"I thought you said you didn't have a boyfriend?" Clay snaps from behind me.

I spin around, leaning back against the counter. "I don't have a boyfriend."

"But you're going out with him," he argues.

"Why do you even care?" I demand.

He advances, caging me in with his hands on either side of the counter behind me, his blue eyes frowning right into mine. "I don't care."

I lift my brows, and were I not breathing the same air as he, I'm sure I could have come up with an intelligent response or at the very least a 'liar, liar, pants on fire' response. Instead, I'm locked in his gaze and trapped in his arms.

Finally, I manage, "I think you care."

He gulps, slowly straightening, my chin following his movement until I'm looking up at him. He turns and walks back through the door and into the bays. There's a water cooler right outside the door. He fills a paper cup with water and gulps it down three times in rapid succession before glancing up at me through the window, crumpling the cup, and throwing it away.

I snap my eyes forward, away from him and stare at Grant's business card. Clay must have dropped it on the counter. What in the world, could he want with Clay's dad?

CHAPTER
6

CLAY

Fuck. Fuck. Fuck.

Fuckity fuck.

Whatever plans I thought I had for Courtney need to change. My plans for slowly getting to know her before asking her out are shot. I'm an idiot for not assuming someone else would be interested in her as well. She's not going to be single for long the way Offenheim was looking at her.

Something about her draws me in. Any game I've got is pure luck at this point. I'm still surprised I told her about all that shit with Owen. I've heard about pheromones; but Courtney seems to breathe out truth serum. I want to be nothing but upfront with her. She's the type of girl you want to have around no matter what.

After I brought her back to the shop yesterday, I haven't been able to stop thinking about her. Luke even called me out on being distracted when I went to the gym last night. I brushed it off, told him it was the mess with my dad.

Sure, she's pretty. That's an understatement. She's fucking beautiful. First thing I thought of this morning was I'd get to see her today. Christ, it's as if she's infiltrated my subconscious.

Already, I haven't been able to get jack shit done today. I came so close to putting new brake pads on the wrong car earlier this morning. My mind keeps drifting to the girl sitting up in the front office with no fucking clue how sexy she is.

I almost got hard this morning watching her walk across the parking lot. What the fuck is that about? That hasn't happened to me since Mrs. Callahan wore a red bra under a white shirt and watered her flowers while I mowed her front yard. My only excuse for my reaction that time is I was in middle school for Christ's sake.

Two things are driving me nuts right now.

One, she abso-fucking-lutely called me out on wanting to take care of her. Am I turning into my dad? Charity cases seem to gravitate to him on some sort of cosmic pull. What is it about her that makes me want to take care of her? And, why does it piss me off so much?

Two, she's fucking going out with that asshole. You don't live in this part of North Carolina without knowing who Grant Offenheim is. That pretty boy is in the paper almost every other week. He's the closest thing to a local celebrity we have. Knowing they're going out is pissing me off. I don't even want to think about him touching her, kissing her.

Fuck.

I drop the hood of the Impala I'm working on with a satisfying bang. There is one thing in my favor. Grant might get to go out with Courtney on Friday, but I'm here with her now. I pull my phone out and check the time. Just holding it reminds me she needs a new one. Turning toward the front office, I stop trying to hold back my grin.

Her eyes widen when I push open the door, my attention fully on her. If I were a betting man, I'd be going all in, certain I affect her, too. There's no way she could do the same to me if she wasn't also feeling something. I'm a man who gets what he wants, and I can't remember wanting anything more than I want her.

"Let's go."

"Um, where?" she asks as I flip the Open sign to Closed.

"To get your new phone." I push open the door, waiting for her to follow me.

Her jaw drops. "Right this second?"

"No time like the present," I reply with a grin.

She leans over to grab her purse with a huff. "I don't see why you're making this such a big deal."

I shrug as she passes by me and walks into the parking lot. I'm enjoying the view as she makes her way over to her car.

Locking up quickly, I call out to her, "We're taking my truck."

I'll never know for sure, but something about the dip of her right shoulder as she readjusts her purse strap makes me certain she just rolled her eyes at me. Could be worse though; she might be annoyed, but she is still walking over to my truck. I'll consider it a victory.

Once we're in and on the way, I try to sell my cell company to her.

"Why should I use the provider you use?" she asks, probably wondering why it even matters.

My fingers tighten on the steering wheel. "Let's see, they're reputable, they have good service ratings, they have good local coverage, and I guess that's it."

"Don't lots of cell phone companies have those things, too?" She pushes.

"I guess so; but because I'm also with them, if you were ever low on minutes or something, it would be free to call me."

She gulps. "I don't even know your number."

"Are you asking for my number?"

She folds her arms over her chest and looks out the side window. "You are something else."

Our arrival excuses me from replying. I hold the door for her, smirking as she passes in front of me. Luckily, there isn't a wait and she picks out an older model smart phone with a basic plan.

Once her phone is activated, I hold out my hand for it. She rolls her eyes but still passes it to me. She tilts her head and watches as I take what seems like a long time to enter my phone number. My phone beeps as I pass it back to her. When she looks to see what I've entered, her brows pull together.

It's not everyday I plug my number, the number to the shop, my email address, and home address into a girl's phone.

She almost drops it when it buzzes in her hand. She has a text notification. She laughs reading it. I had sent, "Can I take you out to lunch?" from her new phone to mine, and then replied, "Sure, but I'm buying."

She holds her phone up, still laughing. "Really?"

I open the door for her, and reply, "Pretty girl asks me out to lunch, answer is always yes."

"You do realize you asked yourself out? You get that, right?" She jokes.

"It's all semantics. I don't see you fighting it."

She hops into my truck and waits for me to get it cranked. "Cute guy offers to buy me lunch..." She trails off.

"So you think I'm cute?" I ask, suddenly seriously.

"Shut up! You know you're good looking. I'm not stroking your ego."

"Is there anything you are willing to stroke?" I tease.

She folds her arms across her chest. "You're awful. Rein it in or you're losing your lunch date."

I lift my hands up in mock surrender. "Fair enough. No more talk of stroking unless you start it."

She shakes her head as we pull away. I can't believe I've only known her for three days, it feels like much longer. I take us back to the Holliswood Diner. She orders the chicken strips today and pairs them with a vanilla milkshake.

"Vanilla," I scoff. "You strike me as something less tame."

"Nothing wrong with vanilla," she argues, before taking a long pull from her straw.

It must be an insanely good milkshake; she closes her eyes and sighs. When she opens her eyes, I'm staring at her intently. She's playing with fire. I glance away before she manages to burn me. She behaves herself for the rest of our meal. I miss her subtle flirting.

"You're awfully quiet." I tap on the table to get her attention.

"Second thinking your choice in lunch dates?" she replies.

I swirl a fry in ketchup before popping it in my mouth. "Not at all. Just wondering what's going on in that pretty little head of yours."

She shakes her head. "Trust me, you don't, it's a giant mess right now."

She watches me, almost mesmerized as I continue to dip my fries into the small lake of ketchup on my plate and eat them one by one.

"Why do you say that?" I ask.

Swirl, bite, she follows my movements with her eyes almost hypnotically.

"So much has changed for me. It feels like every aspect of my life is up in the air. Seems like every other thought I have is about what I'm going to do with myself."

She looks down at her lap, not even noticing she has folded up the paper from the straw. I reach across the table, leaning forward, using my fingers to lift her chin until her eyes meet mine.

"Life isn't a race. Where you are right now is okay."

She turns her head and I drop my hand. "That's nice of you to say."

She turns back to look at me, her eyes softening. "It really is, but it doesn't make being thirty and moving back in with my mom any easier."

I squint and cock my head to the side. "You're thirty?"

Her mouth drops. "Don't say that like it's a bad thing."

"I'm not, seriously. You don't look thirty."

"How old are you?

I push my plate to the side and rest my chin in my hands. "How old do you think I am?"

"Ugh," she groans. "I suck at this game."

I just smile and bat my eyelashes at her.

She taps her lip and looks at me; I mean really looks at me. I've never felt the weight of someone's stare or appraisal like this.

She drums her fingers on the table. "Thirty-one?"

My smile widens. "Good guess, but I'm thirty-three."

"So old." She giggles and sips her milkshake.

I smirk and signal the server we're done eating. We talk the whole way back to the shop. No uncomfortable silences; just an easy conversation the whole way. When I go back to work in the bays, I miss talking to her. She seems to miss me too.

She pops her head in the door fifteen minutes later. "Still want to teach me stuff about cars?"

"Sure." I motion her to come to me.

"What about the phones?"

I head over to her, stepping up into the office and unplug it before tucking it under my arm. "There's a jack we can use in the bay. Grab a notepad to write down any messages."

"Wouldn't it be easier to have two phones?" she asks, following me.

I hold the door open for her. "The last phone broke and I haven't gotten around to replacing it."

Ignoring her, I plug it into the back wall of the second bay, pulling a small table over to rest it on. She follows me and sets the notepad and pen next to it.

"I'm changing the oil on the Mazda next." I stand behind her, my hands on her biceps as I shift her over a couple steps.

She shivers despite the heat. I can't help but notice that, and the way the back of her neck reddens, and the smell of her hair, so faint I want to lean in so it's all I can smell.

Instead, I take time to tell her about the different components of the engine. The car is on a lift so I walk under it as I point different parts out.

Next, I slide a big plastic barrel with a giant funnel under the engine. After removing a cap, a stream of oil flows into the barrel.

"Once it's done draining, I'll switch out the oil filter and fill her back up with new oil." I step around the barrel and toward the car lifted on the third bay.

"This car is having two new tires put on. The two tires with the best tread will be moved up front. The new ones will go on the back. "

"Why the back?" she asks.

"Don't want any cars fishtailing on slick spots," I explain.

"I never even thought of that." She glances toward her car in the parking lot.

"Do you want me to check your other tires for you?" I ask, following her eyes.

She shakes her head. "No, you're busy."

I ignore her and head toward her car. I check all four, pressing on them and inspecting the tread. I can sense her eyes, hot against my back, almost like a caress.

An unmistakable giggle comes from behind me.

"Am I amusing you?" I ask, looking over my shoulder at her.

She nods then changes the subject. "How do they look?"

"They look good. I'd have to grab a gauge to confirm the tire pressure but none of them seem low."

She exhales, clearly relieved.

I notice. "Were you worried about it?"

She shrugs, turning back toward the shop. "I didn't want to have to add new tires to the to-do list."

I stop her, my hand closing around her wrist. "I could've covered it."

She covers my hand with her other hand, gently easing it off her wrist.

She gives my hand a squeeze before letting it go. "The one thing I've learned through all of this is I need to be more self-sufficient."

She heads back toward the bays.

I call out after her, "Don't let one asshole change your ability to trust."

CHAPTER 7

Courtney

I head straight for the water cooler, using a drink as an excuse not to snap at Clay. I know he's being sweet. However, after his confession the other day and the fact I barely know him, these things would make me an idiot to trust him. Was he even talking about himself? I refill my paper cup and remind myself trust is earned.

With the exception of a couple calls, our afternoon is free of anything personal. I sit in a chair and watch as he changes the tires, first slipping them onto a rod, which spins them onto the rim. He hums to himself when he isn't explaining something. I recognize the tune but can't place it.

Three customers arrive at the same time to pay and pick up their cars. Clay comes with me to the office to walk me through checking them out. He leans against the counter and watches me handle the third one all by myself.

"You're a fast learner." It would seem like more of a compliment if he hadn't sounded so surprised.

"Thanks," I mumble.

"Why do you sound annoyed?" he snaps.

I shrug, turning away. He pushes himself from the counter and circles around me to face me. "I'm serious."

My shoulders sag and I glance upward to the dated drop ceiling. "What you said was nice. You sounded so surprised when you said it."

"Now you know me well enough to define the tones of what I say?" he growls.

My eyes widen, and I stutter, "I guess I don't."

He advances on me, his lips hovering right above mine. "Do you want to know what I was really thinking?"

My eyes flick from his lips to his eyes. I can't speak; my lips part and I nod. His hands coast up my sides without actually touching me, fisting when he reaches my shoulders, and dropping back down to his sides.

"I'm surprised by how badly I want you," he breathes before turning and walking back into the bays.

My heart thunders in my chest as I stare after him. I silently pray for the phone not to ring so I have no reason to go into the bays. I don't know how to handle his confession. Part of me wants to fly into his arms and lose myself in him, but the part of me that's struggling so hard to find my feet is stopping me. I also don't want things to get awkward between us.

After flipping the office sign to Closed, I slip into the bays. Clay is lowering the doors. I wonder if he knows I'm watching him when he pauses with his back to me after lowering the last one.

Breaking the silence, I speak, "Clay."

He doesn't turn. "You should head home, Courtney."

I almost ignore him. I turn, heading back to the office. When I'm almost through the door, I look back at him and see him watching me. Our eyes lock as the door slowly closes. The click of the latch catching breaks my trance. I grab my purse and hurry out the door.

If I knew Jen's number by heart, I would have broken my no talking on the cellphone in the car rule. Instead, I have to wait until I get home and look up her number on the file I saved on my mom's computer. I text her first telling her it's me, this is my new number, and to answer the phone when I call her in the next minute.

"Everything okay?" she asks instead of hello.

I give her a Cliff Notes rundown of Clay and everything that has happened today.

"So a crazy, hot, nice guy told you he wanted you?" she asks once I was done.

"Yes, what should I do?"

"I'm trying to figure out why the fuck you're talking to me and not hitting that right now?"

"Jen, I'm trying to have a serious conversation right now," I moan.

"I am being serious. You have been in a relationship for the last eight years. You have no idea what it's even like to be single these days. This guy is hot, employed, and hot."

I interrupt her. "You already said hot."

"Shut up, this is my list. Okay, where was I? Right, hot. Courtney, you have a hot, employed, single guy who wants you."

"It can't be that bad being single," I argue.

"Do we have to discuss the WarHammer guy again?"

I snort. "No, point made. Oh shit, I didn't even tell you Grant Offenheim asked me out."

"I hate you a little bit right now."

"What? Stop it."

"No, seriously. You have been single what? Like a week? And you already have two hot guys hitting on you. I give up. Want to meet me after work and help me pick out a cat?"

I'm holding my stomach I'm laughing so hard. "You are killing me."

"What's sad is even though it's funny, it's kind of true." She pauses. "What's wrong with me?"

"Nothing is wrong with you."

"Look, I don't want you to think for one second I'm not thrilled your love life is on an upswing. It illustrates how dismal mine currently is."

"What happened to the guy from the blues place?"

"He has my number; he hasn't called."

"Maybe he's been busy," I suggest.

"No guy is too busy to get laid, Court."

"So what kind of cat do you want?"

"Very funny," she huffs.

I bite back a laugh, "Hey. It was your idea. I'm just trying to be supportive."

"I'd rather go see a movie. Wanna go with me to the dinner movie place? We can drink there."

We make plans for next week, and then hang up. As much as I love her, I'm not ready to take her advice and throw myself at Clay. Being hot and single isn't enough for me. I need to figure out a way to tell him that without offending him or ruining our friendship before it even has a chance to begin.

I'm not sure I have ever been so physically attracted to someone. That part scares me. Am I being stubborn and ignoring something real, because of timing? I don't want to jump into something for the sake of having a rebound. Or maybe, that right there is my problem. Mike wasn't the first serious boyfriend I've ever had.

If anything, I'm a serial monogamous woman, jumping from one long-term relationship to another. Maybe because I haven't put myself out there, I'm missing something. I don't have any interest in sleeping around; but maybe, I should try dating around.

I already have a date planned with Grant. Perhaps, I should go out on one with Clay. Maybe I need to date a bunch of guys, not at the same time or anything, one at a time for three dates. I might be able to find another couple of guys to go out with; and then after going out on these dates, I would have a better idea of what kind of guy I actually wanted.

I want balance in my life though; I have zero interest in my soul mission being a guy. I lost pieces of me during my relationship with Mike. I enjoyed reading for fun when we first started dating. I can't even remember the last time I picked up a book. That needs to change. I've always wanted to learn how to cook, nothing crazy, a couple of things, and a cake. I want to bake a cake from scratch.

I walk upstairs to my room to write my list of ways I'm going to rediscover myself. As much as I love my mother, I need my own place. I smack my forehead and groan. The one thing Clay and I didn't discuss today was how much he's paying me. That's kind of weird, to consider dating someone who pays you.

Thinking about it makes me uncomfortable and leads to one question after another. Is that why he hired me, to be some type of on the payroll girl for him?

Anger propels me to call him. As it rings, I question my sanity.

"Courtney? Are you okay?"

The concern in his voice subdues my rage. "Why did you hire me?"

"What?"

"Why did you hire me?" I repeat.

"I heard you the first time. I wasn't sure I heard you right." He pauses. "I hired you because you needed a job and I wanted to help you out."

"But you don't even know me. Why would you want to help me?"

"I don't know why. I've never done anything like that before."

"Do you have some sort of expectation from me because I work for you?"

"Whoa. Where the hell is that coming from?"

"I have to know, please."

"Christ, Courtney. I like you; in no way do I have any expectation anything will ever happen between us. I want to be your friend, if that's what you want."

I gulp. "Would you like to go on a date with me?"

"Are you asking me out?" He teases.

CHAPTER 8

CLAY

Funny, how I could go from pissed off to turned on so quickly during one phone call. I was livid when she asked if I assumed something was going to happen with her because she was currently working for me. What the hell? Sure, I've flirted with her. I'm so attracted to her I hardly know what to do with myself.

Knowing she could wonder if I would use my supposed power to expect something from her really got to me. Part of me wanted to forget all about her the second she asked me that. Thankfully, she stunned me by asking me out right after it. I respect her for it. Besides, her cute little come-on was hot. I like a girl who knows what she wants; especially if what she wants, is me.

I shake my head and try to focus on the website I was working on when she called. Unfortunately, WordPress is not as appealing as she is. Good thing I can do this in my sleep. I force Courtney from my thoughts.

The site I'm working on is more of a favor for a friend. A trainer at my gym is expanding his online presence. Luke's a good guy, as long as he doesn't try to get me to drink another one of those nasty-ass green smoothies. He isn't pressuring me, or anything, but I feel like an ass for taking longer than I told him I would with setting it up.

Mainly, I build websites for larger companies. I've only done a couple of these simpler sites on a one-off basis for friends. I should have been finished with Luke's site three days ago.

I've been distracted by a cute blonde with a killer ass. Fuck, distracted again. I forgot to ask if her going out with me, means she's canceling her date with that Grant guy. She's going to learn pretty quickly I don't share.

I pop my knuckles and get back to work. If I can go sixty minutes without thinking about her, I might finish this site tonight. I laugh at myself knowing there is no way I'll be able to go that long.

I give up after ten minutes, deciding a walk might clear my head. Trying to balance everything that has cropped up recently is destroying my ability to focus. The list of shit I need to get done seems to only get longer, and I haven't been able to get anything marked off it.

Somehow, I need to convince my dad I'm not taking over the shop. The fact I'm covering for him isn't helping. If Mom wasn't so distracted with Nicole, she could easily convince him to let it go. My mom is stretched as thin as I am though. Last thing I need to do is add any more stress to her plate.

I skip the elevator and take the stairs, two at a time, so fast I'm dizzy when I hit the ground floor. I'm not dressed for a jog so I settle for a brisk walk. I head toward a twenty-four hour minimart. I can kill two birds with one stone and pick up some shit I'm low on.

If only life was as easy as a grocery store list; Dad off back - check; sister straightened out - check; work caught up – check; Courtney Grayson in my bed - I'd have to check off that one more than once.

As big a pain in the ass my family and work have been recently, why does she consume most of my thoughts? I haven't been this worked up over a girl in, shit, forever. What stresses me out the most is part of me knows I can't compete with that Grant guy when it comes to money and privilege.

Courtney hasn't come across as the kinda girl those things matter to; but it's not as if I know her well enough to be certain of this. Could she be interested in both of us at the same time? Maybe since she saw me working in a garage, she only plans to use me for a good time, to slum until she's really with that Grant guy.

The whole thing is fucking with my head. When did I become the guy who cares about what people think of me?

The store is a short walk. I distractedly amble up and down the small aisles. I pluck necessities as I go. What they stock is limited but still covers the basics. Once I've picked up everything, I stand behind a couple of guys picking up a case of beer.

Their conversation is a distraction to the mess in my head. They're going to a house party and a girl one of them wants to be with will be there. She recently broke up with her boyfriend. His genius plan is to get her drunk and make his move.

I can't keep my mouth shut. "Why does she need to be drunk?"

He looks back at me and shrugs. "Girls think too much when they're sober."

"Yeah, but if you actually like her, don't you want her to know what she's doing?"

He cringes. "I don't want to get her wasted, man, just relaxed."

"Trust me, it won't feel right if it's forced."

He nods. "What would you do?"

This kid doesn't know me from anyone; but for whatever reason, he's looking for my help right now.

"If she drinks too much tonight, be there for her. Take care of her but don't make a move. Pay attention to her; subtly let her know you're interested. Tell her the other guy didn't know how lucky he was to have been with her. Then let her come to you, but only sober, man, trust me. You want her to know what she's doing."

He pays for his beer and turns back, nodding. "Thanks, man."

Now, if only I can follow my own advice.

CHAPTER 9

Courtney

Clay has been the biggest flirt imaginable at work this week. His sails lost a bit of wind when I informed him I was still going on my date with Grant; and I also intended to try to date a couple of other guys as well. Jen is creating an online dating profile for me right now.

After I told him, he got that look in his eyes; you know the one where a guy realizes something is a competition. I thought that would mean he would ratchet his flirting up a notch. Honestly, I was looking forward to it. Instead, he got quiet and stayed in the bays the rest of the day.

I managed to learn what my new salary was on Wednesday. Clay told me he would match whatever I was making at my last job, which was ridiculous considering how much easier this job is. Since he has no idea what I made there I lowballed it, and then got a lecture about staying at a job that paid me so little.

I don't have to pay rent, so the pay cut isn't a huge deal. I'm still applying to other places whose jobs are a better match to my skill set. As far as I am concerned, this job is a temporary excuse to get out of bed and shower everyday.

I went out with Jen last night to buy a dress for my date with Grant. The dress Jen talked me into getting is a simple black sheath. It's a classic; the skirt may be a couple inches shorter than anything I normally wear.

She has loaned me a cute Kate Spade clutch to go with the dress and I already have black wedges. I have spent a bit more time than I normally would on my hair and makeup. I want to make a good impression. I don't think I'm the kind of girl Grant normally takes out.

The look of surprise on his face when he saw me at Pete's was crystal clear. All I can do is shatter any preconceived notions he might have about me. I speed walk to my room to double-check the time on the alarm clock. He should be here soon. I head back to the bathroom to give myself a last once over and brush my teeth.

"Honey, a car just pulled into the driveway."

"Mom, get away from the window or he'll see you. Better yet, go wait in the kitchen until I leave."

"I don't get to meet him?" My mom pouts.

"Um, no. Awkward. I love you but go, go, go." I kiss her cheek and nudge her in the direction of the kitchen.

"Have fun. Remember you have no curfew," she calls out over her shoulder as the doorbell rings.

I tug at the skirt of my dress before opening the door. Grant is standing there all dimply holding a bouquet of roses. I push the screen door open and usher him into the foyer.

"You look beautiful." He smiles, passing me the flowers.

I give them an obligatory whiff. "Thank you so much, Grant. You didn't have to get me flowers."

He shrugs. "I wanted to."

"Wait here." I hold my hand up to stop him from following me. "I'm going to put these in water."

I walk quickly toward the kitchen. My mom is ready, her hand up to take them. I blow her a kiss and whisper, "Thank you." Then, I head back to Grant.

He takes my hand as he walks me to his car. I'm not a car person at all; but even I can tell it's fancy, having an old school Batman feel. I don't recognize the brand. It's even nicer on the inside, all leathery with lots of buttons. It looks high-tech. I purposefully don't touch anything for fear of breaking something or firing off a rocket.

When he starts the car, it rumbles, vibrating through my seat. I glance at him and have to stop myself from giggling. I can't wait to tell Jen about his vibrating car. After pushing a few buttons a bluesy songstress, not unlike the one we heard at the bar, sings from the cars speakers.

He gives me grin before backing out and onto my street. "You have a lovely home."

"Thank you. I'll let my mom know you said so. It was a nice place to grow up."

We talk along the drive, nothing overtly personal; all casual, polite conversation stuff.

"How do you like Pete's garage?"

"It's fun. I'm learning a lot about cars, or at least more than what I already knew, which isn't much."

"Are you working on the cars yourself?"

I burst out laughing. "No. I've watched Clay do some work, but I do office stuff." I pause. "Maybe if it's really slow one day, I might see if I can do an oil change. Or help on one. I think that would be fun."

"I've never taken a girl out who could change my oil," he teases.

"Your car is way too fancy looking. You're probably safer sticking with the dealership."

He pulls into the valet parking of a new French Cajun restaurant. "Have you eaten here before?"

I shake my head.

"There is another one in New Orleans. I've been there before but wanted a good reason to check out this place."

"Hopefully, I'm your good reason," I joke.

"You most certainly are," he confirms before opening his door for the valet.

"Hello, Mr. Offenheim," the valet greets.

Another valet opens my door and Grant meets me, taking my hand. "I thought you said you haven't been here."

"I haven't eaten here, but I have been to this building." He turns to the valet. "Take good care of her, Sam."

He turns back to me and leads me toward the double glass doors of the entrance. Someone is waiting there with the door open for us. "Good evening, Mr. Offenheim."

"Is that how they all know you?" I ask as we walk in.

"My family deals in commercial real estate. This property is one of the ones we own. I've been here for a couple of meetings; but it was before the kitchens were put in, so I haven't had a chance to eat here."

The hostess doesn't even ask for his name before we are led to a table off to the side, overlooking an outdoor garden. "If it wasn't so humid, we could eat outside."

I try to picture Grant sweating, seems impossible considering how well put together he is. "I have big plans for the pool this weekend. It's the only way to beat the heat if you have to be outside."

"Do you swim often?" Grant asks, unfolding his napkin and draping it across his lap.

"It's been a while. I was always too busy to make time for it before. This weekend will be the first time in forever. I plan to hangout poolside with a book."

When our server comes, Grant asks me what I'd like to drink, and then orders for me. Mike would order for me occasionally; but without asking first, and most of the time, I'd end up with something I hadn't wanted. The way Grant did it felt both chivalrous and attentive.

When the server returned with our wine, he proposed a toast. "To the first of many meals shared."

I tapped my glass to his. "That's a bit presumptuous."

I try to be offended, but he smiles and his dimples make me feel less so. "A guy can hope, right? You've already brightened my otherwise dull week."

"I can't believe you say your life is dull. From the outside looking in, it seems pretty exciting."

"You'd be surprised."

"Try me," I encourage, curious.

He tilts his head to the side, looking upward as he thinks before his eyes coast back down to mine. "I've never had a home cooked meal."

"You're joking," I gape.

"I'm not. I've eaten at home; but we always had a chef, so it never felt like a regular dinner."

"My mom is a great cook," I offer.

He laughs. "Not you?"

I cringe and shake my head. "I can scramble eggs."

"See, that right there." He ignores my confused look. "Before you, if I told a woman I've never had a home-cooked meal, her response would be the exact opposite of yours."

I arch a brow. "How so?"

"Bare minimum, she would offer to cook for me."

I snicker. "I'm doing you a favor by not offering that."

"That is how you're different right there."

"But that's a bad thing if you want a woman who could cook, anyway."

His eyes lock on mine. "I'd rather date a woman who is real."

I don't even know how to begin to respond; and thankfully, I'm saved by the waiter arriving with our food. Long manicured fingers grasp his utensils. I straighten in my seat suddenly nervous I have bad posture. Everything about him is meditated and confident. His confidence makes mine nosedive. I am not on the same playing field as this man.

I know I'm just dating for the sake of experience, but I'm in the deep end without water wings. I've never excelled at small talk. Silence blooms as we eat. I take minuscule bites of my coq au vin, trying to mimic Grant's form. Concentrating on not embarrassing myself is exhausting.

Is it always like this for him? The easy smile, the observing eyes from each table around us?

"You've tensed up. Is everything all right?"

I twist my napkin in my lap. This is all in my head, my own insecurities. I'm not serious about him. Why do I even care what he thinks of me? Well, I want him to like me; but that's it. I want him to like me. Me, not a careful caricature of me.

I grin. "I have to be honest. I feel intimidated by this place and you."

"You didn't seem that way before now. What happened?"

My cheeks redden. "Promise not to laugh." He nods so I continue, "You are really good at cutting your food." His eyes widen and his lips tense up. "You have noodles. I haven't seen you slurp even one of them."

He gulps before his dimples appear on full display. "Slurp?"

"Yes, slurp," I groan. "You are the neatest eater I've ever seen."

He immediately sets down his fork and knife, as though he doesn't want to be defined by them. "How about you pick the next place we eat."

I try to picture him at a barbeque place I love. "Deal."

He picks his fork back up. "You agreed fast. Should I be scared?"

"Very."

Grant was a perfect gentleman throughout dinner and after. When he brought me back to my house, he walked me to the door. When I remembered to tell him I bought a cell phone, he pulled out his to program my number. Our next date is for the following Wednesday. I giggle to myself thinking about it. A sweet kiss on my cheek and he was gone.

I putter around the house avoiding my bed. I should sleep, but it's the last thing I want to do. I contemplate reactivating my Facebook account. I could not bear the thought of changing my relationship status so I deactivated my account instead. With the exception of Jen, who was solely my friend, most of our friends were communal.

The time escape of peeking into my friends' lives was the draw. I've lost hours of time scrolling my timeline. There is something safely voyeuristic about it. I want to look up Clay and Grant. I assume Grant doesn't maintain an account, but it would be interesting to compare them side by side if he did.

It has been driving me crazy not knowing what Clay has planned for our date. When I asked him what I should wear he said, "Clothes, but only if you really want to." I should have been offended. I wasn't. Those words sparked a fire in my belly with the realization no man, save Mike and my OB-GYN, have seen me naked in the last eight years.

Not that he is going to see me naked, or that he would even want to see me naked. I no longer have the figure I once had. I'm not out of shape, but I have no plans of entering any swimsuits competitions either.

I wander up to my room hoping the nearness of my bed will inspire me to get in it. I pace back and forth, from my nightstand to the door. Does nervous energy burn calories? Maybe I should do a couple crunches.

When I was in high school and thought I was fat, I would religiously do 100 crunches every night. I would kill for the body I had back then.

I freaked out over what I was going to wear for my date with Grant. Why am I worrying about what I'd look like naked for my date with Clay? No getting naked, no getting naked.

I slump into bed but sleep doesn't come. Somehow, my mantra evolved into wondering what Clay looked like naked or at least shirtless.

The shirts he wears at work don't disguise his chest. He clearly takes care of himself but isn't overly bulky. He's just right.

Sometime while thinking about him, I drift into dreaming about him. He is standing, shirtless, gorgeous in front of me. Each time I reach out to touch him though, he takes a step back. I move closer, over and over again.

Each time I raise my hand, my fingertip a breath away from his skin, he retreats just out of reach. I plead, begging him to stay still. He nods and I try again only to meet the same result.

The sounds of my mom puttering around downstairs wake me up. My dream lingers as I wake, my arms tired from reaching out all night. My brain argues with my limbs that it was only a dream, but they remain unconvinced. I plod down the stairs, blinking at the sunlight streaming through the kitchen windows.

"God, it's bright." I reach to drop the blinds.

My mom passes me a mug for my tea. "I read somewhere living at home reverts adults into displaying teenage like tendencies."

I lean over the island to kiss her cheek. "Sorry, Mom, I didn't sleep well last night."

Her switch flips from teasing to worry in an instant. A cool hand presses against my forehead. "Do you feel okay?"

"I don't have a fever, Mom. I couldn't get my brain to turn off last night; and then when I finally fell asleep, I had the weirdest dream."

She gives my shoulder a squeeze before turning on the burner under the kettle. "Want to talk about it?"

Knowing it would make her happy to talk, I tell her about my dream, getting up to make my tea when the kettle sings.

She's pensive before saying anything. "And Clay is the boy you're going out on a date with tonight?"

I don't correct the boy reference and nod.

"Do you like him?"

Both of our heads turn at the chime of the doorbell. Her eyes meet mine with a quizzical glint. The microwave confirms it's barely past 10.

"I wonder who it could be?" my mom asks as she heads toward the living room.

I stay in the kitchen but move to peer around the corner when I don't hear the front door open. My mom is rushing toward me.

"It's Mike. What do you want me to do?"

My mouth drops and I walk backward, further into the kitchen; unconsciously, trying to put more distance between the front door and me.

"Tell him I'm not here," I whisper.

"But your car is parked out front," she argues.

"I don't want to see him."

She nods, jumping when the doorbell rings again. Composing herself, she squares her shoulders and heads back into the living room. I inch to the corner of the kitchen. He's brought my things. The screen door creaks with each box he brings in. Once, twice, three times, four times, and on and on until I count a ninth creak.

My life with him totaled nine boxes. Pressing my back flat against the wall, I strain to hear their conversation. The dips and crests of their tones are audible but incoherent.

If he was only dropping off boxes, why are they still talking? Minutes stretch like hours as I wait for him to leave. *Just leave,* I will him mentally. The tension holding me upright evaporates when the sound of the door reaches me. I sag and slide downward on the wall until I'm sitting. Rushed footsteps approach.

My mom glances around the kitchen briefly before she sees me sitting on the floor. She moves the recycling bin out of the way so she can sit down next to me. Putting her hand on my knee, she gives it a squeeze as I drop my head to her shoulder.

Tingles precede the numbness as my tailbone protests the tiled floor.

"He wanted to talk with you."

I shake my head and start to stand. "He no longer gets what he wants when it comes to me."

"You were together a long time, sweetie."

I refrain from snapping, silently counting to ten, and offering my hand to help her up, before I reply, "This isn't something we'll ever be able to work out, Mom."

Her lack of anger when it comes to what Mike did makes me wonder if she ever went through a similar situation herself. That whole "stand by your man" concept has never set right with me. What about standing by your woman and keeping it in your fucking pants? What about that?

My tea is cold and I don't feel like zapping it. In silence, I pour it out, watching it flow down the drain. My mother's concerned eyes are a weight against my shoulder blades. I leave the kitchen and use checking email as an excuse to ignore the same wall of boxes now in the living room.

I think about asking my mom if she'll unload them. The idea of Mike's hands being the last to touch my things doesn't feel right. Maybe she can wash my clothes for me, erasing his fingerprints from them before I have to see them again.

An email from my mother's lawyer friend pulls my attention away from the boxes. I read it twice before calling my mom in to make sure I'm not reading it wrong.

"They want to settle?"

She shrugs. "I guess it means they don't want to go to court."

"But does it mean they're admitting firing me was wrong?"

She frowns. "I don't know. Are there any other emails?"

I double check my inbox and check my junk folder as well to be safe. "Should I call him or just email him?"

She fluffs her hair. "How about I call him and try to sweet talk it out of him?"

Mothers never stop being embarrassing. I love her so much, but the idea of her sweet-talking anyone is cringe worthy.

"I'm not really sure this needs that, Mom. I'm pretty sure if I ask him, he'll tell me. Unless, do you want to call him?"

She blushes. "What? No, I mean, only if it would help you. I'm not thinking about me at all."

Right, but I figure it can't hurt to give her an excuse to call him. "Maybe it would be best if you called him."

Her eyes widen. "You think?"

"Sure. Why not?"

Not wanting to watch my mother attempt to flirt, I decide to brave my way past the boxes and up to my room. I take a shower giving myself an internal pep talk about tackling the boxes on my own. I'm thirty; I shouldn't need my mother to manage my breakup.

I change into some yoga pants and borrow an old t-shirt from my mom. The positive outcome of being a big girl and going through the boxes, is my wardrobe is about to triple. I go into unpacking mode with a clear plan of attack. My clothes will all be washed, whether they appear to be clean or not.

There is some closure in that. Any type of photo album or keepsake from our life together will be avoided at all costs. No lingering, no reminiscing; any of those items will immediately be moved to another box to deal with at a later date, if ever.

Books will be split into read and not read. The read can stay boxed until I have a more permanent living situation. I love my mom and that she has provided me a comfortable place to crash. I can't get too comfortable here; I want independence.

I'm on the second box of clothes when my mom comes out of her office. "So, you were on the phone a long time."

She gives me a small smile.

I groan. "Are you going to tell me what he said?"

She moves to sit next to me and pulls a third box toward her. "You can probably have your job back, if you want it."

"I don't ever want to go back there. That was one of the most embarrassing things I have ever gone through." I shiver. "People just watching as I packed up my desk, and then they walked me out."

My mom holds up a white t-shirt. I point to the piles of clothes behind me. "Lights, darks, and what was I thinking."

She tosses the shirt onto the pile of lights. "Jim said whether you go back to work for them or not, they are willing to discuss a cash settlement to avoid court."

Money could be helpful in getting my own place. "Did he have any idea of how much?"

She puts her hand on my knee. "Now I don't want you to get overly excited if it doesn't end up being this much; but he said, given their size, it could be up to two hundred fifty thousand dollars."

I blink at her, my heart pounding. "Excuse me?"

CHAPTER 10

CLAY

I look at my watch again, only checking it for the hundredth time tonight. She's out with another guy right now. For all I know, she goes out all the time. Though knowing she's out with another guy right now fucking sucks.

"You're someplace else again, man. Are you still stressing out about your pops?"

I set the hand weights I was using down. "Sorry, Luke. My dad's doing good, already started physical therapy. It's not him; I've got stuff on my mind."

His eyes meet mine in the mirror. "Want to talk about it?"

I shrug. "Don't worry about it. I'm good."

He smirks at me. "Listen, a new restaurant opened up down the street. I've been meaning to check it out; I heard some people talking about their healthy options menu. Want to come?"

I almost say no, but all I'm going to do if I go home is think about Courtney with Grant. "No green smoothies?"

He rolls his eyes. "Deal."

I didn't work up a sweat, so I skip the shower and am checking emails outside the gym, when Luke walks outside.

"It's this way," he says, jerking his head to the left.

One thing I like about my gym is I can walk to it. That's a perk of living downtown. Finding parking in general is a bitch, so I tend to walk everywhere.

"So, why were you so distracted in there?" Luke asks as we walk.

I cringe, knowing I'm going to sound like a bitch. "There's this girl."

I watch his eyebrows lift from the corner of my eye.

He's smooth though. "And?"

"She's on a date with another guy right now," I confess.

"That blows man. Does she know you're interested in her?"

I nod. "This date was set up before we met. I haven't known her that long."

"But, you're hoping this might be her last date with another guy?"

Luke's sharp, he took the words right out of my mouth.

I roll my shoulders. "Exactly."

"Have you asked her out?"

"Yep, got something set up for tomorrow night."

We reach the restaurant and he pauses before opening the door. "Are you nervous?"

"I'm something," I admit.

He grins, opening the door. "You must really like her."

"Don't make me punch you."

He flexes, making the mouth of the hostess drop. "You can't take me."

I shrug. "I fight dirty. Now put those things away before that chick drools on our menus."

He winks at her and it's impossible not to laugh as she stumbles over to us. I predict her phone number will somehow make its way into Luke's hand tonight.

"So what's new with you, man?" I need him to distract me.

He sets his menu down and rubs his hands together. "I haven't told anyone yet, but I might have swung a guest spot on a weight loss TV show."

His smile is infectious. "That's great news, man. It couldn't have happened to a nicer guy." I pause. "You aren't thinking about going all Hollywood on us are you?"

He shakes his head. "No way, man. My whole family is here. I'm all for some traveling here and there, but this is home."

"As long as I don't need to find a new workout partner."

When I reach for a piece of bread, he smacks my hand.

"What the hell?"

"No carbs."

I hold one hand up defensively and grab the breadbasket with the other. "More bread for me."

"At least, go easy on it," he pleads.

"Luke, I take care of myself so I can eat what I want. Don't be a diet Nazi; and I swear, I'll stop giving you shit about those smoothies."

He smirks. "They're not that ba-"

I cut him off with a shake of my head and a belly laugh. "Right."

He ignores me and goes back to looking at the menu. When it's time to order, he tries one of their healthy options and I go with a burger. Thankfully, he doesn't give me shit for it.

"So, tell me about this girl."

Where do I start? "Her name's Courtney. I met her at the shop and…" I pause, picturing her walking across the parking lot. "She's beautiful; and it's not only that, she's cool too, you know, sweet."

"When are you taking her out?"

I grin, "Tomorrow night."

"Does she have any friends?" Luke jokes.

"Did you see the way our waitress was checking you out? Trust me man, you do not need a set-up."

"She was?" Luke glances around for her.

"Stop playing around. You had to have noticed. She practically fell down walking over here when you looked at her."

He laughs. "I didn't. I suck at reading girls. The second I think one's into me, I get shot down."

My eyebrows lift, "You're joking, man."

He frowns. "I wish."

Our waitress comes back to drop off our drinks. This time I pay close attention to their body language. Now

Luke knows she might be interested, he makes a point to talk to her, look at her. The way she inches closer to his side of the booth, leaning over to give him a nice view down her shirt is proof my instincts were spot on.

Once she leaves, I wait for him to admit I was right. It takes a moment for his eyes to meet mine, considering they were glued to her ass as she walked away.

"Fine." he grumbles, before taking a drink.

CHAPTER II

Courtney

My mom offers to drop the clothes I don't want off to Goodwill. I start laundry while she's gone. I haven't been able to get that figure out of my head. At this point, I almost wish I didn't know it is even an option. Now there is a number, I am mentally spending it.

Nothing crazy, I have visions of a little house or condo and a padded savings account. Maybe I'd get a dog; Mike had been allergic. Laundry started, and the clock confirming it's safely past noon, I call Jen to give her the news. She's in favor of a trip for the two of us to the Caribbean.

After the excitement is over, she asks how I feel about my date with Clay tonight. I tell her about my dream. Her theory is it's a manifestation of how badly I want to touch him. I can't argue even though I think dream interpretation is normally less straightforward. I can't ignore the fact he does have a habit of consuming my thoughts.

When she reminds me I gave her permission to set up an online dating profile for me, I cringe. I forgot. She went on to explain two guys have winked at me, which is weird but I guess that's how it works. She wants to know if I want to wink back or not. I get her to agree to hold off for now; but only after promising I wouldn't jump into a relationship with either Grant or Clay.

My head's spinning by the time I hang up with her. I go downstairs to clear my head and eat. My mom's back from Goodwill and making grilled cheese sandwiches. I instantly think about Grant, and how I told him, I can't cook, wondering if grilled cheese counts. I can rock out an awesome grilled cheese sandwich, Mike used to...

I force myself to think of something else and go start another load of laundry. My sandwich is ready when I come back into the kitchen. I pour each of us a glass of iced tea and come sit next to my mom.

"Did Jim say anything about them finding out who was stealing money?"

"I asked." She grabs a napkin to cover her mouth as she finishes chewing. "He only said their investigation was ongoing, and they were able to confirm it had not been you."

"I still can't believe they thought it was me at all. I thought they knew me better than that."

She puts her hand on top of mine. "It's their loss. I'm happy you don't want to go back there. They are clearly idiots."

I giggle at the idea of Mr. Fulson ever meeting my mom; he wouldn't stand a chance. After lunch, we move the boxes I'm not going to unpack from the living room to a closet in her office. The box of books I haven't read goes up to my room. After putting away some laundry, I pick up a mystery novel and read until it's time to get ready for my date with Clay.

I spend a ridiculous amount of time agonizing over what underwear to wear. He isn't even going to see it, but I want to feel confident and sexy. Finally, I decide on a pretty, mint-shaded set, which doesn't give me panty lines. It's also pale enough not to show through the white sundress I'm wearing.

I try a smoky eye look, a magazine Jen gave me falsely claims is easy, before washing my face and opting for my usual sweep of eye shadow. I'm leaving my hair down but slip a hair clip into my purse in case it starts annoying me. Simple sandals and a baby blue cardigan finish my look. I bring my book downstairs with me to read in the living room while I wait for him.

My mom steps out from her office. "Do I need to go hide in the kitchen again?"

I feel stupid now for even asking her to do that. "Nope, I have met Clay's parents; I guess he can meet you."

She must not have been expecting that answer because she runs upstairs to change her shirt and put on some lipstick. When she comes back downstairs, she flutters around the living room looking for something to do.

"Mom, sit down. You're making me nervous."

"I'm not sure what I should be doing."

I set my book down. "Jen gave me a magazine. Want to flip through it?"

I start to get up, but she motions for me to sit back down. "It's in the bathroom," I call out after her.

I shake my head as I pick my book back up. My mother is more nervous about meeting my date than I am. I can only imagine what she'll do once she sees Clay. Nervous energy blooms in my gut. I will myself not to cave into it, not wanting to give my mom a reason to be even more nervous.

She hurries back down the stairs and rushes to look composed and comfortable. I bite back a laugh, happy she has distracted me from my own nerves.

By the fourth time she's uncrossed and re-crossed her legs, I give up. "Why are you acting so nervous, Mom?"

She lays the magazine across her lap. "Courtney, you dreamed about this man."

I stop myself from telling her I've also had multiple dreams about Alexander Skarsgard. Whatever else she is about to say is interrupted by the sound of a truck pulling into the driveway. All the composure I had gained is lost. My hands shake as I set my book on the coffee table in front of me.

"Should I answer the door, or do you want to do it?" my mom asks as I stand.

"I'll answer the door."

I move away from the door, to a mirror in the dining room. I don't want him to think I'm standing by the door. I check my hair and my lip-gloss, and give myself a 'you can do this' grin. When the doorbell rings, I grimace and glance over at my mom.

I'd laugh if I weren't so nervous; her expression is a mirror image of mine. I take a deep breath and head over to the door. I sneak a peek out the small window next to it, immediately regretting it. He is too good–looking, and my boss, my good-looking boss.

If he were standing there in a pair of grease-covered Dickies and an old t-shirt, I might stand a chance. No, he had to add a pair of dark wash jeans and a crisp, buttoned dress shirt that destroys any hope I have of not wanting him. I pull the door open and remind myself not to drool.

I push the screen door and he opens it the rest of the way. "Hey, Courtney." He leans in to kiss my cheek, his lips lingering by my ear. "You look amazing."

Heat spreads across my cheeks. "Thanks, Clay. Come on in. I want you to meet my mom."

If he's thrown by this, it doesn't show. "Mom?"

She nonchalantly looks up from her magazine before setting it next to her and coming over to us.

"This is Clay Bradshaw." I turn to Clay. "This is my mom, Melissa Grayson."

He offers her his hand. "Nice to meet you."

She blushes; apparently, his blue eyes affect all women. "It is so nice to meet you too. You kids have fun tonight."

I give her a quick kiss before I grab my purse. Clay reaches for my hand and holds it as he walks me over to the passenger side of his truck. His eyes flick quickly to the now closed front door of my house before his lips are on mine.

My purse drops before I brace myself against his shoulders. His lips are surprisingly soft as they claim mine, his hands gripping my hips. My knees start to buckle as my mind races to catch up. The car door is behind me, holding me up as his body molds to mine, and then he's gone. Stunned, I watch as he reaches down to pick up my purse.

After he brushes it off and hands it to me, I ask. "What was that for?"

His finger brushes gently across my bottom lip. "I've been thinking about doing that since the day you walked into the garage."

He tugs me toward him and reaches behind me to open my door. Even though my door is open, I don't move away from him. I breathe him in. I memorize him with each of my senses until he all but picks me up and sets me in my seat.

He grabs my seatbelt, reaching it across me through my open door and clicking it into place.

He fingers dance up my arm, over my shoulder and trace the neckline of my dress. "Safety first."

I gulp. He closes my door and my eyes track him as he moves confidently around the front of his truck.

He's in and belted before he turns toward me. "Any guesses where we're going?"

I ignore his question. "You've wanted to kiss me all week?"

His engine rumbles as he gives it gas, backing out onto my street. "That and more. Based on that kiss, I think you did too."

Any argument would be a lie. "So where are you taking me?"

"No guesses?"

I shrug; my brain only wants to replay our kiss. "I'm hoping somewhere with food. I haven't had dinner."

His eyes are on the road, so I watch one side of his mouth pull up. "I'll take good care of you."

Somehow, I'm not sure he's talking about food. He reaches out for my hand and gives it a squeeze when I slip it into his.

114

"Hey, guess what?" I don't wait for him to reply. "I heard from my mom's lawyer, and my old employer is willing to hire me back and pay me a settlement to avoid me taking them to court."

His body tenses. "Are you quitting?"

I laugh. "Don't be silly. I'm never going back there. I'm happy they know it wasn't me who stole from them."

He relaxes instantly. "Do they know who was doing it? Have they fired anyone else?"

I twist my lips. "I'm not sure. My mom is the one who talked to him. I think they like each other. She hasn't dated anyone since my dad passed away."

He squeezes my hand again. "Sorry to hear about your dad."

It usually annoys me when people apologize for things they didn't do. It's not as if they caused his heart attack; however, there is comfort in the way Clay says it. It seems almost as though if it were in his power to have fixed my dad, he would have. I don't talk about my dad much. I never know how hard the emotions of missing him will hit me.

As we drive, I try to guess where we might be heading. All I know is we are seriously in the sticks. Twenty minutes later, when Clay turns down a dirt road, I'm even more lost.

"Where are we going?" I ask.

"It's a surprise, and we're almost there."

I glance out the back window toward the main road. Clouds of dust churn gray in contrast to the darkening sky. Smooth as the ride of his truck is, we still bounce and rock down the dirt road. The road itself has a thick forest of trees to the left and wide expanses of farmed fields to the right. Up ahead it curves to the right, hugging the edge of the fields.

From where we are, it's hard to see past the curve. Curiosity has me trying though. I'm certain it isn't a restaurant given the remoteness and lack of signage. Clay glances over at me a couple times. He seems amused by keeping me in the dark. As intense as our kiss was, it's fun to see this mischievous side of him.

When we're finally past the curve, I see a charming southern farmhouse with a postcard–ready matching red barn.

"Do you know the people who live here?"

"It'd be pretty awkward if I didn't," he teases but doesn't let on anything else.

He parks near the house and rushes over to my side to help me out. He plucks me right out of my seat, his hands on my waist, as inch by inch he eases me down his body. I'm out of breath by the time my feet touch the ground.

"God, I love this truck," he jokes, shutting the door behind me.

I smack his arm and smile when he acts like it hurt. He takes my hand and leads me toward the front of the house. A young couple is making their way down the stairs, as a Labrador races toward us. Clay steps in front of me and bears the brunt of his excitement.

"Down, Colt," commands the man.

Colt ignores him, still jumping up on Clay. "Courtney, these are my friends, Brad and his wife, Jenna."

I give a half wave from behind Clay's back. Brad wrangles Colt back as Jenna comes over to hug me in greeting. She is beautiful, as in could stop traffic beautiful, in a grown up Little Mermaid way. With Colt trapped between his legs, Brad stretches his hand out to me.

"It is so nice to meet you." Jenna smiles as she leans against Brad.

"Everything is set up," Brad says to Clay, before he looks back at me. "It really is nice meeting you, Courtney."

"Have fun, you two." Jenna waves and she, Brad, and a disappointed Colt head back into the farmhouse.

I am beyond confused. "We aren't eating with them?"

Clay's hand finds mine and he leads us toward the red barn. "Maybe another time, but not tonight."

As we walk around the barn, I see the side not facing the road is painted white, not red. There is a cushy loveseat with a table facing it.

My eyes widen. "What is this?"

He releases my hand and walks over to the table. Picking up a remote I had not seen, he turns toward the wall of the barn and presses a button. The whole side of the barn lights up with the logo for Paramount Pictures. I now see a projector on a small stand in the grass a few feet in front of the loveseat.

When I see what movie it is, I turn to him. "Titanic!"

From a basket next to the table, he pulls two plates before looking up at me. "Does dinner and a movie sound good?"

I nod shyly and move to sit down. As the opening plays, he loads our plates with wrap sandwiches, pita chips, sliced cucumbers, watermelon, and cantaloupe.

He passes my plate to me before leaning over the loveseat to light two citronella torches behind us.

"White wine okay?"

After I nod, he passes me a glass, holding my hand around the stem as he fills it. When he lets go to fill his own, I take a drink.

"Good?" he asks.

I smile. "Delicious. Thank you."

The loveseat is clearly not outdoor furniture, and not large. I sink into its soft cushions, and when Clay sits, his thigh is pressed to mine. He tucks me into his side, draping his arm across my shoulders. I hold my plate in my lap and lean into him.

"This is incredible," I whisper.

"Shh. I'm trying to watch a movie here," he jokes.

I mock glare at him. He removes his arm from behind me, leaning forward to set his plate on the table. Then he places a hand on either side of my face and drops his lips to mine.

Pulling back, with his hands still on my face, he grins. "I don't really mind. I've seen it before."

I place my plate on the table as well, before coiling my arms around his neck and pulling his lips back down to mine. When I sigh, his tongue slips into my mouth. Everything about his touch, his kiss feels so right. His hands have moved to wrap around me, my chest firmly pressed to his. I am on the verge of crawling into his lap, when he pulls back.

I press one of my hands to his chest to stop from falling into him. I'm confused, unsure why he stopped, but happy we stopped before either of us got carried away. We ignore the movie, our eyes locked on each other.

His hand comes up to trace the side of my face. "I don't know if I've ever wanted someone as much as I want you, Courtney."

"I want you, too," I confess.

His eyes soften. He leans forward, picking up my plate, and gently setting it back in my lap.

He reaches for his own plate. "Now, let's watch the movie before I do something that will make Brad and Jenna never talk to me again."

I pop a piece of cantaloupe into my mouth.

He dips his head toward mine, motioning with his thumb to the screen. "I think she likes him."

I cover my mouth and talk around my bite, "I think she does."

We eat and talk throughout the rest of the movie. Seemingly prepared for everything, Clay produces a box of tissues at my first sniffle.

"There is totally enough room for him on that board," I argue, dabbing the corners of my eyes.

He pulls me closer. "I know."

I still argue. "It just isn't fair."

"You're right. It isn't."

It's silly I'm so upset. I've seen this movie before, but never in a theater. Somehow, projected larger than life on the side of this barn, it feels more real than ever before. My heart breaks because they don't get their happy ending. I relax further into Clay, stop thinking about the movie, and start focusing on him. I let his cologne imprint its scent into my mental favorite things file.

I rest my hand on his thigh, the warmth of his skin unmistakable through the fabric of his jeans. His hand crosses over to cover mine. Something about Clay makes me forget my fears. That even if I fell so deep into everything that is him I would be all right, I wouldn't want to climb out. Every promise I made to Jen about playing the field and dating before I became too serious about someone is broken.

"Have room for dessert?" Clay asks, sitting up and pulling the basket closer to him.

I lean over his knee trying to get a glimpse. "Depends, what's on the menu?"

He lifts a rectangular Tupperware container out. "Like éclairs?"

"Silly question." I hold my hand out for one.

He moves the container out of reach, shaking his head. "Open up."

CHAPTER 12

CLAY

I hold her eyes as she wets her lips before opening her mouth. My hand shakes as I bring the éclair an inch away from her lips. She leans forward; putting both of her hands on my thigh and closes her lips around the tip. My eyes never leave hers, my mouth dropping when she bites down. This may be the most erotic thing I have ever witnessed.

She pulls back only slightly to chew before leaning forward again to take another bite. I watch in riveted silence as she continues to eat.

On the last bite, the tip of my thumb slips between her lips and she kisses it softly before pulling all the way back. My hand remains suspended in air for only a moment before both are buried in her hair and my lips crash into hers. She hasn't swallowed and our tongues find each other within the chocolate and cream. I'm struggling to breathe when I break our kiss.

Rubbing a hand over my face, I stare at her. "You are so hot."

Her blushes somehow turn me on even more, like what she just did had been a first. If I don't put some distance between the two of us right now, I'm going to embarrass myself.

I stand. "I have to unplug the projector and put it and the basket in the barn."

I use the excuse to step into the darkness and adjust myself. Courtney offers to help, but I motion for her to stay where she is.

I look back at her once the projector is off, now the yard is fully blanketed in darkness. She's beautiful, an angel sitting in an island of light from the citronella torches.

I'm carrying the projector to the barn when I hear a timid "Clay?"

I turn in time to see her scream and jump as Colt goes flying at her. I drop the projector and take off in a sprint to her.

She's laughing and petting him by the time Brad and I reach her.

I ask if she's okay while Brad simultaneously apologizes. Colt looks up at her and tries to lick her face, settling for her hand. Brad continues to apologize again as he grabs Colt by the collar and tugs him off her.

"I'm okay, really," she calls out after Brad as he pulls Colt back toward their house.

She glances up at me but my eyes are on her legs. When Colt jumped into her lap, the skirt of her dress slid up. She blushes and tugs the material back toward her knees. My eyes burn when her eyes lift back up to mine again.

I hold my hand out to her. "I need to get you home."

She slides her purse strap up her arm and shivers when my fingers wrap around hers. I top each torch with its lid blanketing us in night. Using my cellphone as a flashlight to guide our steps as we walk quietly back to my truck, I open her door, waiting as she climbs in. I linger briefly before closing her door.

"I'll be right back."

I hurry back over to where I dropped to projector and finish putting it away. I have to remember to tell Brad I dropped it, so he can make sure it isn't broken.

When I get back to the truck, and climb in, she reaches for my hand.

I use the high beams to navigate back down the dirt road. Halfway, I slow to point out the glowing eyes of two deer standing in the tree line. Once we're past them, I pick up speed, turning off the high beams when we reach the main road.

"Thank you so much for tonight," she murmurs, breaking the silence.

"Did you like it?" I ask quietly.

She makes me nervous in a way I haven't felt in a long time.

"Best date ever," she replies.

Nervous Clay is gone. "Good to know."

When I pull up to her house, I wish for a way to turn back time, so this night will never end. Neither of us moves when I park. I want to kiss her again, but I don't want her to think I'm being forward.

We both stare through the front windshield at the front door of her mother's house. She peeks at me, and I tighten my hand around hers. If there wasn't a console between us, there is a good chance I'd have pulled her into my lap by now.

"Clay?"

Turning to her, I gulp.

"Please kiss me."

I drop her hand as my fingers find their way into her hair, my palms flat against the sides of her neck as I pull her lips to mine. My touch is gentle, reverent. It's a black hole I've fallen into, spinning and swirling uncontrollably, with no wish or hope of ever escaping. We've kissed for lifetimes and only seconds. I could taste her lips forever but it would still be over too soon.

When we break, my plea is desperate, "Can I see you tomorrow?"

She doesn't even pause. "Yes, when?"

My fingers stroke her jaw line. "I'll pick you up for lunch. There's someone I want you to meet."

"Who?"

I shake my head. "It's a surprise."

I lean forward missing the feel of her lips. We fall again.

I don't want to let her go, but it's late. I get out, and walk her to her front door. Sure, it's an excuse to feel her entire body molded against mine as I kiss her one more time.

Once she's safely inside, I walk back to my truck thinking this was the best first date in the history of first dates. It's so hard driving away from her house. All I want to do is pull her back into my truck, take her back to my place, and do very bad things to her all night long.

God, watching her eat that éclair. Fuck, I'm going to be dreaming about the way her lips looked wrapped around it. The way her eyes stayed locked on mine. Sexiest, fucking thing I ever saw. I can't stop thinking about her big eyes staring up at me as her lips are wrapped around my cock.

I need to adjust myself thinking about it. What is it about this girl that makes me want her around? A date tonight and lunch tomorrow; she's gotten under my skin big time. What's crazy is I don't mind it at all. Besides, if this works out and I'm going to be spending more time with her, I need to see how she'll react tomorrow.

I don't want to come on too strong, or scare her away. I know she's attracted to me. I know it. She felt perfect in my arms, and her lips, shit; all I want to do is taste them again. She's all I think about while I park and ride the elevator up to my condo. A girl tries to talk to me before she gets off on the third floor. Not interested, sweetheart.

I sag onto my sofa, not ready to go to bed, but not able to do anything but replay our night either. I owe Brad and Jenna big time. I've never brought a date out to their place. As far as I could tell, Courtney loved it. I wish Colt hadn't scared her; but the sight of her dress pushed up to uncover those beautiful thighs will be etched into my memory.

I stand, aimlessly walking into the kitchen to get some water. Maybe it will cool my rising body temperature. I try to catch up on some lingering projects in an attempt to push her out of my mind. There is always something to do.

The website I'm updating right now is for the private school my niece goes to. They hired a local photographer to come take pictures of the campus and classes. I'm less of a designer, but in this case, the principal had clear ideas for how she wanted everything to look. Stuff like this is easy.

I struggle with the design stuff. Tell me you want a shopping cart on your site, boom, done. Ask me to make it "pretty" and we'll have a problem. I focus on building the desired functions and let a graphic designer handle the appearances.

I refer out business all the time to some designers who I know, and they send folks my way for technical stuff. I manage to finish some stuff and head to bed.

Before Courtney walked into my life, all I could think of was figuring a way to talk my dad into retiring. The shop has gone from being the biggest pain in my ass to the place I can't wait to go to everyday. As I drift off to sleep, it's clear to me Courtney is the reason for that.

CHAPTER 13

Courtney

I had possibly the best sleep of my life last night. I was in the dream I had the night before, only this time Clay didn't pull away. This morning, my neck and jaw line are slightly tender from the rub of his scruff but it gives me a deliciously naughty feeling. I'm humming to myself as I make breakfast when my mom walks in.

"Good morning," I grin. "Want some scrambled eggs?"

"Sure." She pauses. "That must have been some date. What time did you get in?"

"You were already in bed, but it wasn't crazy late."

"Did you have a nice time?"

I turn to face her, clutching the spatula to my chest. "It was the best date in the history of best dates."

She laughs, plucking the spatula from my hands to take over egg duty while I tell her all about it. We've both finished our plates by the time I've finished sharing. I leave out the parts about our hot make out sessions and that I kinda performed oral on a dessert.

"That sounds like some night," she concedes. "Are you still going to see Grant again?"

"Shit. Sorry," I cringe. "I forgot I have a date already planned with him for this week."

She shrugs. "You could always cancel it."

I kiss her cheek and collect her plate. "You are a genius."

She looks skyward. "She finally notices."

"Ha ha." I load our plates into the dishwasher.

"So what do you have planned for today?"

I pull a dishtowel off the oven handle and dry my hands. "Clay is taking me out to lunch."

Surprise colors her expression. "So soon?"

I don't know how to explain the connection I feel with him without sounding like a pop song. It's been only a few hours since I've seen him, and I feel like I'm going through withdrawals.

"I like him, Mom, a lot."

"It makes me nervous to see you move so quickly."

"It's not like I've slept with him or am moving in with him," I argue.

"I know, sweetie. I just don't want you to get hurt."

I know she means well; but I walk upstairs to get ready feeling like she pissed in my Cheerios. It's too early to text Jen 'operation cancel online dating profile' or call Grant to cancel our date.

I agonize the whole time I'm getting ready that maybe I like Clay more than he likes me. I purposefully wear gray slacks so I won't look too eager. I pair them with a short-sleeved black sweater and some wedges. I twist my hair up and clip it back in a low bun. I look more like I'm going to my old job than on a lunch date.

I head downstairs to finish some more laundry from the day before and catch my mom as she's walking out the door. "I'm heading to the outlets. Did you want me to pick up anything for you?"

"No thanks. Have fun shopping."

She pauses, taking in my look. "Is that what you're wearing for your date?"

I grimace. "Is it bad?"

"Why don't you wear a brighter colored shirt?" she suggests, not saying I don't look bad.

"I love you, Mom. Bye." I close the door behind her and dash upstairs to change.

Second time around I'm wearing a knee length black pencil skirt topped by a beige short-sleeved sweater with a black peter pan collar. I wear the same black wedges I had on before. I hope he'll be turned on by the little bit of leg with an innocent looking sweater. I leave my hair up and makeup simple. I hear his truck and a couple moments later the doorbell.

My peek through the side window leaves me certain my attraction for him has not dulled overnight. He's wearing gray slacks and a black buttoned up dress shirt rolled to his elbows. We would have matched like crazy had I not changed. As I pull open the door, he opens the screen.

"Is your mom out? I didn't see her car."

"Yeah, she went-" Was all I managed to get out before his lips crushed mine.

He steps backward, pulling me with him, until his back is flush with the wall on the other side of the door. I stand between his legs, his hands gripping my hips, molding my body to his. When I'm breathless from his kiss, he lifts his lips, wrapping both arms around my waist.

He peers down at me; an impish smile lifts the corners of his mouth. "Had to make sure your mom wasn't home for a hello like that."

I lift up onto my toes to brush my lips across his again. "Hi."

He arms tighten around me, holding me up. "Hi."

His grip loosens as he controls my descent.

His hand lifts to tuck some escaped strands of my hair back behind my ear. I shiver as the pad of his finger caresses the edge of my lobe. He could ignite a flame with the fire in his eyes.

His voice is strained. "We need to leave now or lunch isn't happening."

Our hands link, bare forearms pressed together. I pluck my purse from its perch and we go. I'd be embarrassed about my compulsion to feel his skin, but he's equally affected. His fingers seek my skin, sometimes the cap of my knee, other times the inside of my arm. When he pulls away to put both hands on the steering wheel, I mourn the absence.

I recognize the diner from our previous lunch. "You sure love this place."

He parks, coming around to help me out. My pencil skirt does not make getting into or out of his truck any easier.

Instead of taking my hand, he tucks me into his side, resting his arm across my shoulders. "I have a standing lunch date here every Sunday."

"Oh, am I one of many?"

He turns to face me, dropping a chaste kiss to my lips. "You are the first date I've ever brought here."

Warmth blooms in my belly, crawling outward through my limbs and across my cheeks. We enter, and he leads us toward the same booth we ate at before. This time one side is already taken by a small brown-haired girl.

"Uncle Clay!" He drops his arm around me to catch the human projectile coming toward him.

"Hey ya, Maggie." He gives her a squeeze before setting her back onto her feet.

He tugs me back to his side. "Maggie, I'd like you to meet Courtney."

Her mouth drops. "Is she your girlfriend?"

I stifle a laugh and hold out my hand to her, waiting to see what his response will be.

"Let's just say I really like her."

Good answer. I shake her little hand and we all slide into the booth, Maggie on one side, Clay and I on the other.

"Maggie is my favorite niece."

She rolls her eyes. "I'm your only niece."

He drops his cheek to his palm. "Doesn't mean you still aren't my favorite, and don't roll your eyes. It's rude."

She scrunches her nose at him but takes his reprimand without argument.

"Want a menu?" Clay asks me.

I look at Maggie. "Do you know what you're going to order?"

She nods. "I always get the short stack with bacon and a vanilla milkshake."

"That sounds delicious." I tilt my head toward Clay remembering our lunches here. "Does he ever give you a hard time about getting vanilla?"

Her mouth drops. "How did you know that?"

My breath hitches as Clay drops a hand to my knee, his thumb circling the side of it. "He did the same thing to me."

"You get vanilla milkshakes, too?"

I grin. "They're the best."

She solemnly nods her head. "They're my favorite."

"So what grade are you going into?" I ask, not remembering if school started in August or September here.

Start dates seemed to vary by as much as a couple of weeks depending on what county you lived in.

She slumps a bit. "I go to year–round school."

"Wow. How does that work?"

She perks up slightly. "We get longer marking period breaks but not a whole summer break." She pouts slightly, sad eyes directed at Clay. "It'd be so nice to have a real summer break."

"You go to one of the best schools in the state." He glances at me. "It's a private school."

"I know," she huffs.

"And," he continues, "You have your best friends there."

At that, she sits straight and presses both hands to the tabletop. "Oh, my gosh, I have the most exciting news ever. Amber's mom got her tickets to see The City Boys and she invited me. Can I go? Please? Please? Pleeeeeeeeeease?"

I wonder at her asking his permission.

"What did your mom say?" he asks.

She nervously rubs her hands together. "See, that's the thing. Mom is going to be out of town that weekend and she wanted me to see if I could stay with you."

"Do you know what weekend it is?"

She whips out a smartphone. "I know it's in September. I can text Amber to find out for sure."

He nods, and her thumbs fly as she texts her friend. Clay uses her distraction to rub the tip of his nose along the edge of my ear. I shift closer to him, leaning into his touch as his hand tightens on my knee.

We are oblivious to the waitress standing next to our booth until she clears her throat. Clay's eyes flick from mine to hers before quickly giving her our order. Maggie's phone chimes a reply from her friend.

She holds her phone up as proof. "It's the third Saturday." Her eyebrows lift. "Please?"

He grimaces slightly. "Do I have to go?"

She rapidly shakes her head. "No, Amber's mom will take us. She booked a hotel room in the city, and we'll spend the night there after the concert."

He drums his fingers on the tabletop. "Now, it's a sleepover, too?"

She nods, innocently.

He twists his lips to one side as he deliberates. "Have I met Amber's mom?"

She nods again, lifting her clasped hands to her mouth. "She's a teacher at my school. She was the mom who did the lock-in in the library last year."

He rubs his hand over his face. "I need to talk to Amber's mom first. As long as everything you told me checks out, yes, you can go."

She bounces in her seat. "Thank you, thank you, thank you, thank you, ohmygosh, thank you. Can I tell Amber?"

He nods and her thumbs take flight again.

I turn my lips to his ear. "You're a good uncle."

He wets his lips. "I'm good at a lot of things."

I blink, the restaurant dissolving around us. All I see is him, and I'm certain I've never wanted someone more. In a haze, I eat when the food comes; I speak when the conversation calls for it. I do none of these things with my full consciousness; a part of me is focused fully on him.

A part of me is behaving in a purely scientific manner, observing and storing data. When he leans forward to steal a slice of bacon from Maggie's plate, some hair falls forward. It doesn't fall as it has before. Did he get a haircut? I glance at the hair partially hidden by the collar of his shirt. I want to bury my fingertips in it, measuring, and memorizing him.

I'm amazed I maintain some semblance of disaffected casualness. After lunch, we take Maggie to his parents' house. I'm less nervous this time entering their home.

Judy seems pleasantly surprised, pulling me into a hug. Maggie introduces me as the girl Uncle Clay likes. Judy drapes an arm around her as they both look at me. Maggie seems jealous when Judy tells her she met me first. Clay rescues me and I follow him toward the den.

Pete, his dad, is in his same recliner, only less drugged.

"Hey, Dad. Remember Courtney?"

His dad squints at me. "How could I forget? How are you, dear?"

His lifts his hand and I reach out and give it a squeeze. "Much better, thank you. How are you feeling?"

He sighs. "Sick of this chair; but I'm starting physical therapy next week. So I hope I'll be up and around soon."

"Don't rush it, Dad." Clay cautions.

Pete's eyebrows rise. "You want to keep running the shop now that there's a pretty girl there to keep you company."

Clay slides behind me, wrapping his arms around my waist. "Can you blame me?"

On our way back to my mom's, Clay hesitates at one turn. "Before I take you home, would you like to see my place?"

His place, alone with him, at his place. "Yes," is all I can manage.

Where he would turn left to my mom's, instead he goes right. I memorize the route. I mentally repeat each street as we turn. He lives closer to the city, almost passing my mom's house on his way to the garage. He pulls into an underground parking deck, sliding into a spot numbered 74.

The tension between us builds as we enter the elevator. He presses a button and we stand shoulder to shoulder watching the doors slide shut. Dull metal doors reflect our images. I see his reflection move before he's in front of me, hands on my face, lips on mine.

He breaks our kiss, waiting until my eyes open to speak. "We don't have to do anything. I didn't want to take you home yet."

I nod, his hands moving with me as my head tips up, and then back down again. His lips drop back to mine and I wrap my arms around his waist. Our kiss is interrupted by our arrival at his floor. There is a console table facing the open elevator doors. A beige carpet with navy checks and a solid navy border lines the floor; a pale grass weave wallpaper adorns the walls.

There are only four navy doors visible. His is to the right of the elevator doors. Once the door is open, he ushers me in, his hand on the small of my back. My eyes are drawn to a wide expanse of windows on the opposite wall.

"Wow."

"You like it?"

The living space is open concept, white walls, and high ceilings. I venture further into the space. A flat screen TV is mounted to the wall in front of a charcoal colored sectional sofa. A black leather ottoman rests on a rug striped in various shades of blue. An office is set up in what normally would be the dining area. Beyond that, is a stylishly modern kitchen with tall white cabinets, granite countertops, and a matching island.

I walk toward the windows. "They're tinted."

I look back to see Clay watching me. Just thinking about what we could do without anyone seeing, makes me quickly look away. I concentrate on the view. The building next to his is an above ground parking deck. I can barely see my reflection. I gaze past it to watch a small red car circle each level in search of a spot.

CHAPTER 14

CLAY

I walk up behind her, my reflection mirrored in the window. Lifting her right hand, I slowly release the fist she's made and press her open palm to the glass in front of her. I repeat this with her left hand before pressing my body against her. Her hands keep us from falling into the glass.

My hands grip her hips, my lips at her ear. "It was a bad idea bringing you here."

"Why?" She exhales.

I suck her earlobe between my teeth. "I might not let you leave."

She presses back against me, her mouth dropping open. "Clay."

"I need to touch you."

"Please. Please, touch me," she pleads, her head falling back onto my shoulder.

My hands slide up her sides and under her sweater cupping her over her bra. She moans, grinding her ass against my cock. I've never been so aroused, hard, pressing back against her. I grind into her, squeezing her breasts. I pull the cups down, freeing them from her bra. Then I roll her nipples into tight buds before pinching them.

She cries out, bucking against me. I press my face between her shoulder blades, my breathing ragged. My hands slide back down her sides to grip her waist. This is too fast. I'm one-step away from hiking her skirt up and fucking her hard against this window. I release her, taking a step back. She cranes her neck to watch me.

"I've got to take you home."

She sags, pressing her cheek against the window. As she breathes, the space by her mouth fogs. "Why did you stop?"

I move back to her, her face in front of mine as I pull her into my arms. Out of the corner of my eye, I watch her fingerprints dissolve against the glass.

I lift her chin, bringing her eyes to mine. "I won't stop if I start."

Silencing any response she might have, I place my lips on hers.

My hands slip back inside her sweater, only to fix her bra with a gentle touch.

"I haven't seen your bedroom."

I nip her lower lip. "Oh, you will, but not today."

My hand gripping hers is the only part of my body that touches her as we leave my condo and ride the elevator back down to my truck. That and a brief graze of her hip as I help her in. My place is only twenty-five short minutes from her mom's house. Her mom's car is there when I pull into the driveway. After I park, we sit there silently for a moment.

She reaches out to open her door. "Wait."

Dropping her hand, she turns to me. "Yes."

"We've only known each other a week."

She looks down. "And your engagement just ended."

Her eyes close. I don't want to embarrass her. I hardly know her and I don't want to pressure her.

"Courtney, please look at me."

She shakes her head and opens her door, slipping out. I jump out as well and cut her off at the front of my truck.

"I wasn't trying to upset you." I wrap my arms around her. "I don't want to rush you."

Shyly, she tucks her face into my neck. Gently, I tell her, "I don't think I've ever liked someone as much as I like you, and I've never had a healthy relationship."

My grip around her tightens. "I can't even believe I said relationship."

"I like you, too," she whispers against my neck.

I loosen my grip so I can kiss her. "Let's take it slow then."

She nods. "You make it hard."

Dropping my head to her shoulder, I laugh. "No Courtney, you make it hard, in more ways than one."

She blushes.

"I don't know how I'm going to get any work done tomorrow."

Pressing her cheek to my chest, she sighs. "Me either."

I don't want to let her go but somehow I do.

She's all I can think about on my drive home. I can't believe I took it that far with Courtney tonight. Seeing her in my home turned me on in ways I can't explain. Thank fuck, I didn't show her my bedroom or she'd be in my bed right now. That's exactly where I want her, but I'm trying so hard to do this the right way.

I like her enough to think long term. She has a ton of shit going on in her life right now, and I don't want to

overwhelm her. I still can't get over how much I like her.
I've been attracted to girls before, but this is something
completely different.

Maybe the way we met is the reason. If I had met her
in a bar, would my brain have reacted differently to her?
Nope, she had to walk into my dad's shop, intent on
paying him back. Not everyone would do that, especially,
if that person had recently lost their job. She's honest;
there's something so sexy about that.

I know she isn't playing games. If she's nervous, she
tells me. I have no undercover bullshit to wade through.
If she was any other girl, I might not have stopped
tonight. She's special; if we go there, end up having sex, I
don't want it to be because we both happen to be turned
on.

I want to be sure I'm the only one in her life. It's too
soon for that. She needs to be the one who makes that
decision. One thing I will do though is make sure she
knows she's the only woman I'm seeing. No pressure, I
want her to trust me.

After that asshole cheated on her, I figure it will take
time for her trust to grow. By stopping tonight, I hope
she knows I did it because I want her for more than her
hot–ass body. Thinking of her trembling under me
makes me hard. I change and head to the gym.

I'm pretty sure Luke's there. I'm not technically a
client of his anymore. At this point, we're friends. He was
my trainer when I first joined the gym where he works.
I wasn't in a good place after all that shit went down with
Owen and Chloe. God, I had been an asshole.

A good friend would have been happy his friend
found a girl he could see a future with. Instead, I had
pursued his girl with the intention of proving she wasn't

right for him. Why did I think that was up to me? Sure, I proved my point, but I lost my best friend in the end. It had always been Owen, Brad, and me.

Brad didn't talk to me for the longest time after Owen moved away. He and Jenna already were a couple when we all met in college. She's the reason Brad and I are friends today. If it hadn't been her pushing Brad to forgive me, I might have lost two friends that year.

I stopped hitting the bars and started hitting the gym instead. The chain gym I belonged to was a fucking meat market. I quit and found the gym Luke works at instead. Not many women go there, and it being close to my place made it what I needed at the time.

I spot Luke the second I walk in. He gives me a chin nod.

Not planning to change afterward, I walked over in old basketball shorts and a tank top. I have a sweat towel around my neck and drop it on the ground next to the free weights.

"Hey, man," I offer, dropping to the floor to stretch out my calves.

"Legs today?" Luke offers in greeting.

Fuck. I hate leg day. "Sure," I mumble.

He looks like he wants to laugh but thankfully keeps it to himself.

The seated leg press is going to make me its bitch tonight. Luke winks at me as he adds an extra twenty pounds to the amount I usually do. This is going to hurt tomorrow. The positive is if I can't walk, maybe I won't be tempted to bend Courtney over the front counter.

CHAPTER 15

Courtney

After my dates with Clay I knew it wasn't in me to go out with Grant again. He was a nice guy and perfect on paper but he didn't make my blood race like Clay does. Jen will think I'm crazy but I want to see where this thing with Clay goes.

When I came into the shop the next day, I was surprised to see not only Clay, but Pete as well. Our unexpected chaperone makes keeping our hands to ourselves much easier. Part of Pete's rehab homework is to keep moving. Judy drops him off every day after his appointment. He uses a walker to keep weight off his hip. During his surgery, he had a partial replacement. He can't navigate the steep step up from the bays into the office.

Clay and his dad spend much of the week bickering. Nothing overly tense, they just talk that way to each other. Clay thinks his dad should sell the place and retire. Pete wants Clay to take the place over and keep it in the family.

On a day Pete stays home, Clay and I go grab some takeout for lunch. He drives us to the back parking lot of a local park. He jumps out and lowers the tailgate. Grabbing a blanket from the floor behind our seats, he lays it across the bed of his truck. After boosting me up, we sit side-by-side, backs to the cab and eat.

"Tell me something I don't know about you," he says.

"I've never been outside of the country. I've never even been on an airplane."

"Where would you go first, if you could go anywhere?"

I lean closer to him. "That's hard." I pause. "Maybe someplace that gets a lot of snow. Okay, your turn."

"Where would I go or something about me?"

I shrug. "Either, both, whatever you want."

He leans down and kisses the side of my mouth. "Whatever I want?"

"You know what I meant." I pull back, smiling.

He pouts. "If I could go anywhere, I would go to Hawaii. I've always wanted to see a volcano."

"So you want heat and I want cold."

"You know what they say about opposites."

I imagine him shirtless on a beach. "Hawaii sounds nice, too."

"And something you don't know about me." He taps his fingers along my thigh. "I have a couple tattoos."

I sit up. "Really? Can I see them?"

He gets a mischievous glint in his eyes and leans in to me. "I hope so." He kisses me before pulling back. "But not today."

Frowning, I pull back and he laughs at me. I can't stay annoyed at him. I change the subject and ask him about the shop.

"My dad needs to give that dream up. I don't want to be a mechanic."

I crumple up my wrapper and drop it in the bag. "What do you normally do?"

He attempts a basketball type shot with his wrapper, missing the bag entirely. He crawls forward to retrieve it and tries again.

"I work with computers."

I laugh when he misses again. "Do you like it?"

When he gets his wrapper, he throws it at me. I block it and we both scramble for it. Somehow, I end up pinned under him.

He grins down at me. "This is an interesting turn of events."

My hands reach up to his neck. I tug his face down to mine, sinking my fingers into his hair.

I'm in his lap by the time a friendly park employee tells "us kids" to "hit the road." There is a decent probability he's younger than both of us are.

Once we're on our way back to the garage, I ask him again about his job.

"I love what I do," he admits.

He is an independent contractor so he has the flexibility of taking time off to help with the shop. I am lost as he explains his job involves writing code to upgrade and establish websites. Companies also hire him to design proprietary programs for back office functions.

"That is all over my head."

"If you ever want to learn it, I know a guy."

"Private lessons?" I tease.

His breath hitches. "That sounds way hotter than what I was picturing."

My mom comes with me to Jim's office. He has received the settlement offer from my previous employer, and he wants to review it with us in person. I wonder if it's a ploy to see Mom in person. Clay has told me to take the day off, but call him after to let him know how it went. Jim's office is in an older building downtown, complete with gothic adornments.

A wide marble staircase in the main lobby has us skipping the elevator since his office is only on the second floor. My mom fidgets nervously, picking at her clothes before Jim comes out to greet us. For someone my mom's age, he is nice looking, has that whole silver fox thing going for him.

He ushers us back to his office, complimenting my mom along the way. He goes over the settlement, paragraph by paragraph, explaining the legalese. They are offering me three hundred seventy-five thousand dollars.

"If you want, I can go back and attempt to improve their offer."

I blink. "That's– " I count in my head. "Ten years salary and more than you thought it would be."

"You need to understand there is the potential the award you could receive, should we go to trial, could be substantially higher."

I gulp. "It's already much more than I ever thought it would be."

My mom leans forward. "Should she turn down the offer?"

I shake my head. "This isn't about the money for me. Sure, it's an incredible bonus to the whole thing; but I really only wanted them to admit they were wrong, and I didn't steal anything."

"That is all covered in the settlement document," Jim replies.

"Did they ever find out who did it?"

He glances toward his door. "I'm not supposed to know this; but they believe it was a Mr. Daniel. Is that man familiar?"

I slap my palm on the arm of my chair. "Elliot. I can't believe it. I actually felt sorry for him. And on the day I got fired, I thought about asking if he'd like to have lunch together sometime."

"I believe they have filed charges against him."

There isn't much left to do besides signing the agreement. So playing matchmaker, I excuse myself to go to the ladies room to give my mom and Jim a chance to speak alone. I pace back and forth in front of the sinks and call Jen to tell her about the settlement.

I have to hold my phone away from my ear as she screams. We make plans to see a movie and I hang up, not wanting to appear to have been in the bathroom an awkwardly long time. My mom is blushing and Jim looks pleased when I get back to his office. He escorts us to the waiting room politely saying goodbye to me and telling my mother he'll see her Friday night.

I wait until we're on the stairs to say anything. "So, what's happening Friday night?"

"Oh, nothing. Jim had an extra ticket to a play and asked if I'd like to accompany him."

My dad has been gone for five years. This is a big deal, but I know she's trying to play it off.

"Fun. What play?"

"My Fair Lady."

"Isn't that the one with Audrey Hepburn?" I ask.

"It is. I might have a copy on VHS at the house if you'd like to watch it."

I put my arm around her, proud of her for taking this step. "We can watch it when we get home."

We're halfway home when my mom asks what I'm going to do with the settlement money.

"I'm still trying to wrap my brain around it."

Jim had explained I would receive a lump sum payment, which is subject to income taxes, so I should set aside almost half of it for that. I don't think I'll do anything right away.

As I pull onto our street, my heart starts pounding when I see Mike's car in our driveway. "Damn it."

My mom looks from me to him and back to me. "Do you want me to tell him to leave?"

I shake my head. I'm old enough that I shouldn't continue to hide behind her. She squeezes my arm and gets out after I park by the curb, not wanting to block him in. He stands from where he sat on our front steps.

He moves out of the way, so my mom can get by. She gives me a sympathetic smile before closing the door. I know part of her wants me to consider reconciling with Mike. I know she doesn't condone what he did but is only thinking of how long we were together.

I stay by my car. I want him to come to me. I don't want there to be any possibility of him thinking this conversation will happen anywhere but outside. That way it will be much easier for him to leave.

He walks toward me. "Mike."

His hands are jammed in his pockets. "I know I messed up, Court. I'm sorry."

My arms are crossed over my chest. "What do you want?"

His shoulders sag. "I want you to come home."

I look past him to stare at the back bumper of his BMW. "I can't."

He takes another step toward me and I flinch moving back to keep the distance between us. "I still love you."

I drop my hands, fisting them. "You wouldn't have done what you did if that were true."

"I'll do anything. Please." A desperate plea.

I look at him; really look at him for the first time since it happened. My love-shaded vision finally is seeing clearly. Am I even attracted to him anymore? Did I hold on for so long out of a fear of being alone? "We weren't happy. If we were, we would have gotten married years ago. It's better this way. I'm trying to move on. You should too."

"How is this so easy for you?"

I gulp, rapidly blinking back tears he doesn't deserve to witness. "You fucked someone else, Mike. I'm sorry if I'm not showing enough emotion for you. Does it make you feel better knowing that just looking at you makes me sick? That I had to go get tested for STD's because I have no idea how long you have been cheating on me; or even better, if she was the first?"

Slipping his hand out of his pocket, he reaches out for me. "It was a mistake."

I cringe, stepping back again. "Do not fucking think about touching me ever again."

His hand drops.

"You need to leave. Don't try to contact me again." I walk past him and into my house.

He ignores me. "I need you in my life Courtney. Don't you still love me enough to give me another chance?"

"I can never trust you again. Do you get that? Do you understand there is nothing you could ever do that could fix this?"

"I don't believe that."

Shaking my head I walk away. "Please go and leave me alone."

Whatever he says is lost to me as the door closes behind me. My mom is waiting with open arms. I collapse into her, a rush of liberated tears streaming down my face. I think I hate him. I'm too sad to know for sure. I eventually make it to my room. Kicking my shoes off, but still fully dressed, I crawl into bed pulling the covers over my head. I doze off and on, but never actually sleep for the rest of the afternoon.

By dinnertime, my mom comes to check on me, worried. For her more than myself, I eat a protein bar. After that, I take a bath, only wanting to soak the day away.

Eight years. I can't get that time back. The only thing I can do is move forward. Finding out what Mike did hurt me in ways that had me questioning if I would ever get over him. The funny thing is each day that passes, I'm more certain it has saved me in the long run.

I'm not sure what direction my path in life will take, but the possibilities excite me more than anything else has in the last eight years.

I've had my bath; and suddenly, I wonder where my phone is. I head downstairs in my robe to find my purse sitting on the coffee table. My mom must have put it there at some point.

I scroll through my notifications and see a text and a missed call from Clay wanting to see how the meeting with the lawyer went. I return his call as I head back upstairs.

I smile when he answers on the first ring. "Hey."

I close my door and sink down onto my bed. "Hey."

"How'd everything go today?"

"I signed the settlement papers. I'm having a hard time processing the amount they offered."

"I hope in a good way."

"It's way more than I was expecting," I admit.

"That's great news."

"I know."

There's a pause. "Then why do you sound down?"

I pluck a tissue from its holder on my bedside table, tears prickling my eyes. "Mike was at my house waiting for me when I got home."

"Ex fiancé Mike?"

"Yes."

"What did he want?"

I press the tissue to my cheek stopping the progression of a tear. "He wants me back."

"What are you going to do?"

I stand, tightening the belt of my robe. "What do you mean? You can't think I'd consider taking him back."

"I'm happy to hear you say that."

""Yeah?"

"I'd hate to have to steal you away from him. Besides, I'd like you to come willingly."

My eyes flick to my closed door. "You would?"

"Courtney, I want you any way I can get you."

A spark of desire blooms inside my gut. "I want you, too."

He takes a deep breath. "Tell me what you want, Courtney."

I shift, pressing my legs together. "That day, in your condo."

"Yeah."

"I didn't want you to stop." I don't even recognize my own voice.

"I didn't want to stop."

I flick off the light. "What would you have done if you didn't stop?"

"Where are you?"

"In my room."

"Are you in bed?"

I wet my lips. "Yes."

"What are you wearing?"

"A robe."

He groans. "Are you wearing anything under that robe?"

I gulp. "No."

I hear the rush of air leaving his lungs. "Will you touch yourself if I tell you?"

I hurry across my room and lock my door. "Do you want me to?"

"God, yes."

Suddenly shy, I giggle.

"You think I'm funny?"

I cover my face even though he can't see me. "I've never done this before."

"Does the thought of me touching you turn you on?"

I let out a ragged breath. "Yes."

"Just imagine your hands are mine. Can you do that?"

"I can."

"Remember how you were against that window?"

"I do."

"I wanted you so bad."

"Tell me."

"Imagine my hands under your sweater, that innocent looking sweater. Put your hands on your breasts. God, they felt so good. Rub your nipples."

I do as he says, imagining myself up against that window. His body is pressed up behind me, his hands caressing my breasts and teasing my nipples. I moan.

"You like that don't you? I slide one hand down your body and stroke your clit."

I whimper.

"Spread your legs, Courtney." I do as he says, my middle finger teasing my clit.

"Are you wet?"

"So wet," I gasp.

"Fuck. I slide my hand down further and dip it right into your wetness. Do you like that?"

"Oh, yes."

"I push it deep before I pull it out and rub your wetness all over your clit."

"Oh, my God."

"I'm so fucking hard."

"Are you touching yourself?" I ask.

"I am. You like that?"

"Uh hun."

"What do you want me to do with my cock, Courtney?"

"I want you to put it in me."

"Fuck. All right, I hitch up that sexy-ass skirt you're wearing and slide your panties down. Your ass is so fucking hot. I pull off your sweater too."

"Do I move my hands off the window?"

"What?"

"To get my sweater off?" I pant."

"No keep your hands on the window."

"How do I get it off?"

"I rip it off. It's just gone."

"Okay."

"I pull your hips back to me and press you hard against the window so your breasts are pressing on the glass. I slide my cock between your legs."

"When did you take off your clothes?"

"They melted off. Fuck. I don't know."

I bite back a laugh.

"Am I losing you here?" he asks.

"No, no, keep going. Your cock is between my legs."

"Fuck. Say that again."

His tone makes me shiver. "Your," I draw out each word. "Cock is between my legs."

"God, that is sexy. All right. So, I rub it back and forth across your pussy. I'm still rubbing your clit with one hand."

"I want you in me."

"I slide my cock into your tight, wet pussy."

My finger circles my clit furiously, as I imagine him filling me.

"You like my cock, Courtney?"

"I do."

"Pinch your nipples."

I do and feel my orgasm build. "I'm so close."

"I grab your hips and bury my cock inside you."

I feel it crest. "Oh, God. Oh, God. Oh, God."

"Let me hear you come, baby."

"Yes. Oh, God. Yes."

"Fuck."

I pant, trying to catch my breath.

"That was so fucking hot."

"Did you?"

"All over my fucking hand."

I don't think I've ever been so nervous to see someone in my life as I am on my drive in to work. A blush creeps over my face as I think about our phone conversation last night. I won't even be able to look Clay in the eye ever again. My hands shake as I park next to his truck. I had hoped I could beat him here.

To torture myself even further, I wore the same pencil skirt I had worn that one day to his condo, only this time with a button up blouse. Be confident, Courtney. Own this. I step out of my car and straighten my skirt. I'm halfway across the parking lot before I see him. He's wearing a pair of well-worn jeans and a black t-shirt. He's midway opening the middle bay and stands there, arms stretched up as he pushes the metal door up into place.

The heat from his stare melts my self-doubt and I turn, changing direction to go to him. Knowing I'm coming for him, Clay pops the door into place and meets me halfway. With one hand gripping the back of my neck, the other my ass, he lifts me, crushing my mouth with his.

I coil my arms around his neck and kiss him until we need to either stop or find a room. I'm so lost in Clay I don't realize we aren't alone until I hear a throat clear behind us. Clay slowly lowers me and I turn, expecting to see his dad.

"Grant?"

Grant Offenheim stands stiffly, glancing between Clay and me before speaking. "I have a meeting with Pete Bradshaw."

"I'm over here," Clay's dad calls out from the open door of the office, winking at me.

Grant nods in my direction before continuing on to the office.

"Oh, my God." I bury my face into his chest once Grant is out of sight. "I didn't know your dad was already here."

He brushes his hand over my hair before pulling back and lowering his lips gently to mine. "I gave him a ride in."

"Do you think he saw us kissing?"

"Who? Grant or my dad?" he teases.

"Your dad," I groan.

He drops his lips to mine, speaking against them. "Pretty sure he saw."

"You're awful."

He slips his tongue in my mouth. "And you're trying to kill me wearing this skirt."

I blush.

"But this." He peers down my blouse to the small expanse of flesh visible. "Is a very different shirt."

"You like?"

He rests his forehead on mine. "There are a lot of words other than like I can use to describe what I think about your shirt."

"I like the things you say."

He closes his eyes. "We'll have to revisit that later."

I pout. "Want to walk me to work?"

"Of course. Don't want you to be late."

He gives me an extra kiss once I'm behind the counter before slipping back to the bays. I spend the next hour trying not to watch him as he works.

"I was disappointed when you broke our date."

I jump and spin around on my stool, my legs bumping into Grant. "You scared me."

His hand touches my knee and I turn to the side.

His dimples seem less charming today. "Didn't mean to startle you."

I stand and move further down the counter, straightening stacks of paper. "No worries."

He follows me and I glance into the bays to see if Clay can see us. "If you ever change your mind about going out—"

"I'm good, thanks."

He stands right behind me. "I'm sure you are."

I ease past him and around to the other side of the counter, opening the door for him. "Have a nice day."

He keeps his eyes on me as he pulls a pair of designer sunglasses from his pocket and slips them on. "I hope to see you around."

I let the door close with a whoosh behind him. How he could even try to hit on me after seeing me with Clay confuses me. Men. I walk back around the counter and knocked on the office door.

"Doing okay, Pete?"

He looks up from a stack of papers, worry-lines creasing his forehead. "Thanks for asking, Courtney. I could use Clay's help with something if you could grab him for me."

I chuckle internally at Clay's dad telling me to grab him. He is flushing out a radiator when I open the door to the bay.

Knowing he won't hear me from the door, I step into the bay and take the long route around the car so he'll see me coming.

When he sees me, he stops what he's doing and smiles. "Come here often?"

"Flirt. I came to tell you your dad needs you."

He wipes his hands on a piece of cloth and follows me back toward the office. I'm halfway up the step when I notice he's standing there watching me.

"What are you doing?"

He acts like I surprised him. "Enjoying the view."

I shake my head and he follows me in, kissing my cheek before heading back to the office. When he comes back out, he asks me if I'd like to go to lunch with him.

"Everything okay?" I ask once we're on the road.

"Yeah." He reaches out and grabs my hand.

"You seem stressed."

He nods. "That Grant guy made an offer to buy the shop."

"I thought you wanted your dad to sell the place."

We park at the diner, but neither of us gets out right away. "I think we need to find a lawyer to look everything over."

"I don't know if he does real estate stuff, but my lawyer is a good guy. I forgot to tell you, he and my mom are going out on a date."

"Speaking of dates." He leans over the console to nuzzle the spot right below my ear. "I want to take you out again."

I lean into him. "And not to your place?"

His lips nip their way down my jaw. "I want you all over my place."

My throat feels thick. "Why not take me there."

"You aren't ready."

I lean back, out of his reach. "Excuse me?"

He rests his elbow on top of the console, setting his chin on his hand. "Why rush?"

"I don't like being told what to do."

"Come here."

I give him a look.

"Please, come here."

Smirking, I inch closer to him; when I'm within reach, he grips the back of my neck and kisses me, hard.

Too soon, he lifts his lips from mine. "You liked being told what to do last night."

CHAPTER 16

CLAY

I'm trying to figure out what that Grant guy is up to. It's bad enough I know he wants in Courtney's pants, but now he wants my dad's shop, too. Is this a ploy to get to Courtney? I know the guy is loaded and could easily buy any place she worked, but he seemed surprised when he saw her here the day he dropped his card off.

Or was that what he wanted us to think? After this morning, he can't have any doubt of our being together. I chuckle picturing the look on his face when Courtney plastered herself to me and kissed me.

Once we're at the diner, I walk around to her side and open her door. "Did Grant say anything when he left?"

She takes a deep breath. "He said he was still interested in taking me out."

Fucker. I frown. "I don't like that guy."

Her hands cup my face and she leans down to kiss me. I grip her by the waist and lower her to the ground, not breaking our kiss.

She pulls back keeping her eyes on mine. "I'm with you."

"Wish he would get the memo," I grumble, tucking her into my side and closing the door behind her.

"Maybe you should take out a full page ad in the paper," she teases.

I hold the door open for her. "I'd do it if I thought it would work."

"Trust me, you have nothing to worry about."

"How about a 'property of Clay' tattoo?" I joke as we sit in our regular booth.

"I'll get right on that," she deadpans as our server walks up.

We both get burgers and a basket of fries to share. I don't tease her about her vanilla milkshakes anymore. I love the way she tastes afterward.

After we order, she goes back to Grant. "You're not really bothered by him are you?"

"I don't trust him. He seems like the kind of guy who assumes he can get whatever he wants."

She reaches out across the table and grabs my hand. "He can't get me."

Lifting her hand to my lips, I relax. "I'm sorry if I'm acting tense. I guess I need to get used to not being the only guy around who's crazy about you."

She blushes. "That's not true."

"Please," I argue. "I know of at least two guys other than me who want you."

"Well, it's a fluke, so I wouldn't worry about it," she argues.

I squeeze her hand. "It's no fluke, babe. You're a catch."

She looks away and I squeeze her hand again so she'll look back at me. "Don't worry, I got running shoes."

She laughs at my lame joke; I choose to focus on her, and not Grant. There's plenty of time to figure out what his deal is.

She quietly sips her milkshake and catches my eye. "Yes?"

She pops the straw from her mouth, and then her tongue slides out to catch a drip on her bottom lip. I've never been so jealous of another person's tongue in my life.

"I want to spend the night at your condo."

I almost choke on my fry. "What?"

She grins. "You heard me."

Gulping, I take a sip of my soda to aid my last bite down my throat. "Why?"

She smirks. "Why do you think?"

I look around us, and lean in closer to her. "I want to make sure we're thinking of the same thing."

Her mouth drops. "You, seriously, want me to say it out loud?"

I nod, already half hard guessing what she's about to say.

She wets her lips again and leans in as well, her eyes locked on mine. "I want to spend the night with you."

I push my food to the side and reach for her hand, there's only one thing in the restaurant I'm currently hungry for. "What would you like to do if you spend the night?"

Her hand grips mine tightly. "Clay."

I can take that to mean either she's annoyed at me for making her spell it out, or she wants to do me. I'm thrilled if it's the second; and I'm going to keep pushing her to make dead sure it isn't the first.

"Come on, babe. Tell me."

She groans, quietly, and I swear my balls tense at the sound. "You know I want you."

"Fuck, babe. Let's go, right now." I lift my other hand to get the check.

"Clay," she giggles, her eyes shining and reaches to pull my hand down. "We have to go back to the shop."

"It'll still be there tomorrow," I argue.

She shakes her head. "I was thinking, maybe, this Friday or Saturday. So we can sleep in."

Damn, I like the sound of that. "Are you sure?"

She nods, squeezing my hand again. I've been using the weekends to catch up on work; but if I focus the next couple of nights, she can have all my attention, all weekend long.

"That sounds like a date."

She shivers across the table from me; and I can't help myself, I slide out of my side of the booth and into hers, pulling her into my lap. She manages to get half a squeal out before my lips silence her. I don't care if the whole diner sees us.

I didn't want to rush her. I didn't want her to be like any other girl to me. So I waited, as patiently as I could, for her to let me know she's ready.

"Oh, the things I'm going to do to you," I groan against her lips.

CHAPTER 17

Courtney

"Change of plans."

I switch my phone to my other ear. "What do you mean?"

Tonight was going to be the night; at least, I had hoped it would be the night. Jen even took me lingerie shopping.

"You've always wanted to see The City Boys haven't you?"

"The who?"

"I'm not sure if you remember, but Maggie's friend invited her to see some concert. The friend's mother was supposed to be the one taking them."

"Somehow I have a feeling that changed?"

"Apparently, Amber's mother's sister or aunt or I'm really not sure who was injured and she needs to go to Texas to help out. Amber's father can't take the girls because he will be watching their five younger children."

"Five?"

"Yes, and Amber has two older brothers as well. Eight children total."

"They should get a reality show. So, you got volunteered?"

"I did. I'm so sorry. I had big plans for you tonight."

I pout. "You are such a good uncle."

"So you'll go with me?"

I pull my new undies out of my shopping bag and give them a longing look. "I'd love to see The County Boys with you."

"City."

"Huh?"

"Never mind. I have a big favor to ask too."

"Uh huh."

"Want to keep me company while I chaperone them at the hotel?"

I remembered Maggie saying something about Amber's mom booking a hotel room. "Ahhhh."

"Please. I need back up."

"I'm sad our first overnight won't be alone. I had plans for you, too," I tease.

His voice lowers in a way that has me crossing my legs. "I'd love to hear more about these plans."

I laugh. "I think I'll have to surprise you with them another time."

"They have to sleep sometime. Maybe we'll still have time."

"Ten year old girls sleep? Not a chance."

"And drugging them would be frowned upon, right?"

I laugh. "Pretty sure, yeah."

"Damn it. Pick you up in thirty?"

After I agree, we hang up. I turn, frowning in the mirror. The dress I had put on for a romantic dinner and possible sleepover with my boyfriend would not work for a teenybopper concert. I change into a maxi skirt, a long tank top, and some comfortable cowboy boots. I pack a cute t-shirt and shorts pajama set and something simple to wear tomorrow.

"That's what you're wearing?" Mom asks, as I hit the bottom step.

"We're taking his niece and her friend into the city for a concert and staying the night at a hotel." I kiss her head. "So don't wait up."

"I thought you were going out to dinner just the two of you."

"That was the original plan, but Clay was asked last minute to fill in on concert detail." I peek out the window hoping to see his truck.

"What band are you seeing?"

I shrug. "Some teenage boy band."

She sits up. "The City Boys?" she asks with a bit too much enthusiasm.

"Oh, my God, Mom. Do you like them?"

She tries to act nonchalant, leaning back in her chair as though she doesn't care. "They're all right."

"Liar," I tease as I go to open the door when I hear Clay's truck pull in.

"Take pictures," she calls out after me.

Clay is out of the truck and walking toward me. "Hey, baby."

I drop my bag before he wraps his arms around me, lifting me. The last two weeks have been full of kisses, some stolen, the majority given, heavy petting sessions, and steamy phone sex. Feeling his body against mine makes me mourn the loss of the evening I had hoped for.

While he can be forward as hell on the phone, he has had this misguided idea I need time to grieve the end of my engagement with Mike. I appreciate his letting me take my time but, by my clock, I was ready two weeks ago. Part of me has wondered if it wasn't my past but his own that has been making him hesitate.

He has told me himself what we have going is the most serious, relationship-wise, that he has ever gotten with anyone. After the falling out he had with his friend, he stopped his random hookups. He didn't go too far into it, but I know that was also around the same time something happened with his younger sister.

He never directly talks about her and I know he isn't happy about Maggie living with her. While things slipped here and there about Maggie's mom, there has never been one word uttered about her father. I don't think Clay even knows who he is.

He kisses me, moving his lips across my cheek to my ear before whispering, "You look beautiful."

I tighten my grip around his neck and inhale my new favorite scent, Clay.

He sets me down and reaches to grab my bag with one hand and my hand with his other. "Want to hear something funny?"

We walk toward his truck. "Always."

"I think my mom is in love with the band we're seeing tonight."

He drops my hand, opening my door and hands my bag to Maggie who sets it by her feet. I wave at them feeling a little embarrassed. I had not known we had an audience for our kiss.

Clay pops his head in the truck first. "Amber, this is my girlfriend, Courtney."

Hearing him call me that makes my heart pound.

"Hi, Maggie. Hi, Amber." They both smile and wave back at me.

He offers me his hand as I climb into the cab. "I heard one of them is into cougars. Maybe we can set him up with your mom."

"What's a cougar?" Amber asks from the backseat.

I cover my mouth and look at Clay as he tries to come up with something to say.

After a minute, he replies, "For me to know and you to find out."

"Real mature," I laugh as he shuts my door.

"I can Google it," Amber says, pulling out a smartphone.

"Don't." Clay lifts his hand. "It's an expression for a younger guy dating an older woman."

"What about an older guy dating a younger girl?" Maggie asks.

Clay and I both look at each other. "Maybe, George Clooney?"

He laughs as he backs out and onto my street.

"Who's George Clooney?" Amber asks.

My mouth drops, how can they not know who Clooney is?

Clay keeps his eyes on the road. "You can Google him."

We check into the hotel to drop off our bags and so Clay can leave his truck in their underground lot. The girls have fun exploring the suite. They're having so much fun we consider ordering room service for dinner; however, the girls change their minds at the last minute wanting to go out before the show.

The arena is within walking distance of the hotel. It's the main reason Amber's mom had booked a room here. We walk around until we find a gourmet sandwich shop. There aren't any tables with four chairs available but there are two tables for two fairly close to each other, which we take. The girls feel grown up having their own table, and Clay and I get a chance to speak privately.

Clay rubs his face with his hand after we order. I reach out to touch his arm. "Are you doing okay?"

He gives me a half smile. "I think I'm getting a headache."

I glance over at Maggie and her friend. "I can't imagine why."

He follows my eyes. "Exactly. By herself, Maggie is a cool kid. The two of them together though."

There had been plenty of high-pitched squealing. I put my hand on top of his.

"Think of how many ten year olds will be at the concert."

I try not to laugh as he drops his head to the table groaning. Somehow, his irritation with the girls further endears him to me. In no way has he given them a hint they have been annoying him. For them, he would suffer in silence. I move my foot between his legs and draw a circle on his calf with the toe of my boot.

He lifts his head. "Are you trying to play footsie?"

"Who me?"

He looks around before leaning in, his hand half covering his mouth. "If it isn't you, somebody around here is getting fresh with me."

I tap my finger on my puckered lips as I pretend to size up potential suspects.

My eyes lock on to his. "Who do you think it could be?"

"There's only one lady I want rubbing up on me and I'm looking at her."

Our café style table is small enough for me to lean forward and quickly kiss him.

"What'd I do to deserve that?"

I lean back as our server arrives with our sandwiches. "You're a good guy and an awesome uncle."

He glances over at Maggie as she daintily eats her sandwich, his gaze softening.

He picks up his sandwich and looks up at me. "She's a good kid."

After dinner, we walk to the arena. Our seats are amazing. We are only a few rows back on the left side of the stage. The girls are disappointed we missed the first couple of songs from the opening act. We heard them, only we were trying to make our way into our section at the time.

The singer is a teenage girl. Maggie and Amber are clearly in awe of her and sing along with most of her songs. I don't recognize her, but her songs seem cute and age appropriate given her fan base.

Neither Clay nor I are ready for the change when The City Boys came out. With screaming, nonstop for the next hour and a half, it's pointless trying to talk to him. Instead, we speak in hand gestures and facial expressions. I laugh as he dances with Maggie. Then, during a slow song, he stands behind me, his arms around me.

I put my hands over his arms, holding him holding me. His lips tease my neck as our bodies gently rock back and forth to the love song. When it ends, he turns me in his arms and kisses me as if we are the only two people left on earth. Surrounded by thousands of people, I only see him. When we break our kiss, Maggie and Amber are watching us with rapt expressions that have previously, only been reserved for a City Boy.

The band plays two encores, one of them a cover to one of my favorite songs, "Can't Take My Eyes Off of You." I cling to Clay, burying my face in his neck. I have only known him two months and, right in this moment, I know I'm in love with him.

On the way out of the arena, I pick up a t-shirt for my mom and get one for each of the girls. Clay tries to pay but I won't let him. When we get back to the hotel, we all change into our pajamas and order ice cream sundaes from room service.

Clay teases Maggie and me for getting vanilla, until I give him a hot vanilla flavored kiss when the girls aren't looking. The girls aren't tired so Clay orders a movie through the hotel pay per view. It's a newer dystopian based on a popular book.

The girls are hooked but I can only concentrate on the man sitting next to me. I'm scared by my feelings for him and not knowing if he feels the same way. I know he likes me; he is beyond vocal about that.

What also scares me is the knowledge that, now more than ever, how much of loving someone is out of your control. I had trusted my heart to Mike and he was careless with it. It's scary falling in love now I know what having my heart broken feels like.

Clay has used the excuse of my sleep shorts to touch my bare legs whenever he can. He seems to get a thrill out of the goose bumps his touch causes. Each time he gets this smug look, as he looks too sexy for his own good in a pair of loose sweats and an old t-shirt. Who knew sweats could be sexy?

When both girls yawn at the same time, our eyes meet. Are we thinking the same thing? I know we aren't going to do anything crazy, not with the girls here. We don't have to do anything, but I'd love to fall asleep in his arms tonight. The sofa folds out and a queen bed is in another room.

The girls give us little argument as we get them up to fold out the bed. They take turns brushing their teeth while Clay and I work together getting it ready. They crawl into bed as soon as it's ready, and seeing their droopy eyes, I turn off the TV.

Clay glances at his watch before rubbing one eye. "I'm wiped."

We leave the door to our room open in case either of the girls wakes up in the middle of the night. Watching each other from either side of the bed, we both seem to be waiting for the other to make the first move. Clay moves first, pulling back the covers and sliding onto his side, reaching his hand out to me. He pulls me to him, lining my body up against his.

Our legs tangle as though we have always done this.

"You are so amazing," Clay whispers against my neck, his lips kissing and nipping my skin.

I press into him; I somehow want to erase where I stop and where he begins. If we could have been alone, this night would be so different. Our passion for each other stays within a safe boundary neither of us breaches. I don't know who drifts first, him or me; one minute we're kissing, and the next I'm dreaming.

The arena is now empty except for Clay. He's sitting front row center while I have the stage all to myself. I don't know what I should do. Should I sing or should I dance? I wring my hands looking around wildly for a possible escape route. He stands and I wait. Will he leave? Will he stay?

I wake before I know the answer. Stretching, I reach out for Clay, finding the bed empty. I glance toward the open door before getting up to look for him. I pause in the doorway, leaning against it. The folding bed has been put away, the coffee table back in its rightful place. Clay is sitting on the sofa while the girls sit across from him on the other side of the table.

I cover my mouth to stifle a laugh threatening to erupt. They are painting his fingernails.

Maggie sees me first and lifts his hand for me to see. "Look, Courtney."

Clay turns his head to look at me. I cross the room and sit next to him, leaning my head on his shoulder. He kisses the side of my head while patiently waiting for the girls to finish.

I hold my hands up. "Me next?"

Clay showers while I have my nails done. He gets dressed in the bathroom as well. When he walks back into the room my mouth waters at the way his shirt clings to his damp chest, and my fingers itch to run through his damp hair. Considering our audience, I excuse myself to get ready instead. The girls and I head to the hotel restaurant to get a table while Clay goes to check us out.

After breakfast, we drop off Amber first, and then take Maggie to his parents' house. We follow her in knowing his folks will give him crap about it, if we don't at least say hello. I give Pete a hug before going into the kitchen to have a cup of tea with Judy. She is sweet, but not very subtle in her curiosity as to where things with Clay and me are going.

Clay collects me not long after. He seems distracted as we drive back to my house.

"Is everything okay?"

He squeezes my hand. "Sorry, just thinking."

"Want to talk about it?"

He's quiet, fingers tapping a beat on my hand. "While you were with my mom, Dad and I talked."

When he stops, I say, "And?"

"He heard back from the real estate lawyer your mom's friend recommended."

This doesn't sound good. "Was the offer low?"

He shakes his head. "That's the thing. It's high, too high. Almost twice what the property is worth."

"That makes no sense. Why would they offer more than it's worth?"

"We're trying to figure that out."

"Could Grant know something you don't?"

Before he answers, I get a call from my mom. Clay waits quietly for me to finish.

"Is everything okay?" he asks, once I hang up.

I shake my head, not as an answer but more out of confusion over what my mom told me. "Mr. Fulson, my old boss, called my mom. He told her he wasn't allowed to contact me before the settlement was all over with, but he wants to meet me and apologize face to face for everything that happened."

He reaches out to rub my shoulder. "That's a good thing, right?"

"I guess; part of me wants never to think about that place again. I'm not sure I've ever been more embarrassed, and knowing they thought I was capable of stealing from them. I don't know what he could say that would make that better."

CHAPTER 18

CLAY

I pop my head into the front office, letting the door to the bays rest on my back. "Let's get out of here."

Courtney thinks about it for a minute before grabbing her purse. "Where to, boss man?"

I laugh, walking in the rest of the way. "Brad and Jenna went out of town, so I'm dog sitting the next couple of days. Want to hang out with Colt and me?"

She reaches down to grab her purse. "Sure. Should I follow you in my car?"

As she straightens back up, I circle my arms around her waist. "Why don't we drive past your mom's place first and drop your car off."

She shuffles closer to me and I tighten my arms around her. "Isn't it out of the way?"

Kissing the top of her head, I reply, "I don't like the idea of you driving at night."

She smirks up at me. "Are you trying to say I'm a bad driver?"

I kiss her forehead. "Nope, but I like taking care of you and the dirt road to their place sucks at night. I'd feel better if I took you home."

She gently kisses my neck. "I like you taking care of me, too."

I grab her chin and tilt her plump lips up to meet mine. "Good. I don't plan on stopping. Let me lock up the bays."

It's hard to let her go, but it makes it easier knowing I'll have her all to myself for the rest of the afternoon. Because it was slow, my dad took off after lunch. As it is, we're only closing thirty minutes early and the extra time will be eaten up dropping her car off. We could leave straight from here, but I like the idea of making sure she gets safely to her front door.

Once I've got everything locked up in the bays, I meet her back in the office. She's shut down the computer and forwarded the phones. I surprise her, scooping her up in my arms and carry her out the front door.

"I can walk you know," she teases, wrapping her arms around my neck.

I shrug and dip her once we're through the door, so she can lock it. After it's locked, her arms coil around my neck again. I love the way she feels in my arms. I'd carry her everywhere if she'd let me.

When we get to her car, I let her legs fall to the ground and lean her against the door. Her lips meet mine hungrily. My hand drags up her leg, pulling her skirt up with it. I love the way her skin feels under my fingertips. The fact we're in a public place in broad daylight is the only thing keeping me from following the path my fingertips created with my tongue.

I'm still trying not to rush things. Part of the reason I feel safe taking her to Brad and Jenna's is because I'm not going to have our first time together happen in someone else's house. Besides, Colt will make a good chaperone.

Both of us are catching our breath when I pull away. Something about her makes me want to skip the shallow end of the pool and go right for the high dive. I'd drown happily in her arms.

She fixes her skirt as I open her door for her. "I'll follow you."

She lifts her lips; and as far as I'm concerned, there's no halfway when it comes to kissing her. Once she's thoroughly kissed and in her car, I head to my truck. I can't even deny the extra strut in my walk isn't one hundred percent because I know her eyes are tracking me in her rear view mirror.

It takes over an hour to drop off her car and get to the farm. Brad and Jenna have an electric dog fence and Colt has a doggie door he can use during the day. Other than feeding him and keeping an eye on the place, I'm only here to hang out with him.

Colt knows my truck and starts barking and jumping all over their front porch as I come down the main drive. I jump out first so he can get all his excitement out on me. I'm not sure Courtney wants him jumping all over her again. I don't expect her to be right behind me. She laughs when her hand on my waist startles me.

"You think that's funny?" I tease, putting my arm around her.

She leans into me, holding her hand out for Colt to sniff. "Uh huh."

Because it's nice out, I give her a tour of their farm. They grow Christmas trees to sell, and fruits and vegetables for their own use. Jenna also works as a human resource consultant. She does a lot of traveling and on the trips Brad takes with her, I house sit.

"This place is beautiful." Courtney sighs, leaning against me.

"Brad inherited it from his grandparents."

"It went to him, and not his parents?" Courtney wonders aloud.

"Yep, his parents are more condo people. They live in Florida."

"Do you always want to live in your condo?"

I shrug. "It's fine for now."

Someday I'd like to start a family. Have my kids grow up in a house like I did, with a big backyard to play in.

We head back to the house and grill up a couple hamburgers. All too soon, I have to take her home. I bring Colt along for the ride, letting him sit in the backseat. He's a good passenger until I go to kiss Courtney goodnight.

He leans over the console from the back, trying to push his nose between us. I give up and end up getting my goodbye kiss when I walk her to the door.

"Want to have dinner tomorrow?" I ask, not ready to let her go.

She shakes her head. "I already told you I'm meeting up with -"

"Jen," I finish for her, giving her a cute pout.

"Stop," she laughs, pushing at my chest. "You know this is important to me."

I nod, kissing her again.

Courtney's big thing is we don't lose ourselves, our individual selves, in us as a couple. I guess that happened with her ex and she's scared of history repeating itself. So, I agree to have a guys' night with Luke while she's out with Jen.

Luke and I meet up at a bar close to my place so I don't even drive, just walk there. I'm on my second beer when fingers slowly drag down my back, seductive like. The move is so familiar I assume it's Courtney and expect to see her face as a happy surprise when I turn around. It's not; there is a complete stranger, and may I add an extremely attractive brunette, standing behind me.

Aggressive girls have never annoyed me; I like their no bullshit, go after what you want approach. However, this time I can better read the desperation in her move. It isn't as attractive now as I might have thought at one time.

Courtney would have never pulled a move like that; she has too much class.

"Hi," she almost purrs, holding out her hand.

I step back, increasing the space between us. "Do I know you?"

I have to ask; she doesn't look familiar, but she is sure acting as if she knows me.

"I'm Gina. I saw you and wanted to introduce myself."

Yep, don't know her. "I have a girlfriend."

She smirks. "Oh, and you're not allowed to talk to other women?"

I ignore her question and pull Luke over. "This is my single friend, Luke."

I should be hurt by how quickly she turns all of her attention to him. Instead I watch, more curious than anything else, to see how her come –ons go over on Luke.

the other side of
SOMEDAY

For once, I'm relieved I don't have to make random chit chat with some stranger in a bar hoping it will lead to more.

I have an amazing girl. I can't help but admit I wish I were going home with her tonight.

CHAPTER
19

Courtney

"It's really your last day?" I pout.

He rubs the tip of his nose around mine and I tighten my arms around his neck. "I've been thinking about expanding. I might need to hire someone to handle the phones."

I narrow my eyes at him. "You don't need anyone and you know it."

He presses his hips to mine. "I could think of some ways to keep you busy."

"I'm sure you could."

His dad's rehab has been going well and Clay needs to get back to his own clients. He has the flexibility of being his own boss, but he has been putting in long hours nightly and on the weekends trying to keep up. This will mean we can actually see each other outside of work.

His dad has hired a young guy to help around the shop, someone he can apprentice.

"Have you talked to the lawyer again?"

"The deal seems legit, but my dad is still set against selling."

I don't know if Pete will ever give up his hope for Clay to take over the business.

"Clay." His dad is standing in the doorway of the office with the phone in hand.

Something is wrong. His arms fall from my waist as he races over to his dad. I'm a step behind him and hear his dad say something about Maggie.

"What's wrong?"

Clay grabs his keys and is already walking across the parking lot. I don't wait for an invitation; I follow him and climb into the passenger side.

"Courtney."

I cut him off. "Where ever you're going, I'm coming."

"It's not a good idea, my sister, she's…" His voice trails off.

"Your dad said something about Maggie."

He starts the truck and punches it into reverse. "My sister isn't the best mom. My parents have been trying to convince her to let Maggie live with them full-time for years but she refuses."

My stomach flips. "Is Maggie okay?"

He flips the shifter into drive and pulls out onto the main road. "My sister has a drug problem."

I shake my head. "I had no idea."

"Maggie is a great kid. With her going to school year round and spending the weekends at my parents' house, my sister manages to keep it together for the most part when Maggie is home."

"What happened today?"

He presses his lips together, dragging his hand through his hair. "I guess Nicole owes her dealer some money. He came by their house and Maggie got scared."

"That's awful."

He nods. "Nicole refuses to go to rehab; and my parents don't want to have her arrested, so there isn't a way to force her into letting them watch Maggie. Then, my dad broke his hip. They want to take care of her, but they aren't getting any younger."

We pull into a dated apartment complex. The moment Clay parks, Maggie opens the door and runs to his truck in tears. He's out of the truck and lifting her into his arms before I've unbuckled my seatbelt. He walks slowly back to the truck. Maggie's head is buried in Clay's neck as he holds her tightly. Clay turns, and still holding her, opens the back driver's side door.

As she buckles her belt, I ask if she'd like me to sit in the back with her. Her watery nod breaks my heart and sends me scrambling over the seat to put my arms around her. She folds into me, her body shaking with silent sobs. I meet Clay's eyes in the rearview mirror. He mouths 'thank you' before pulling away.

We go to his parents' house. Pete closed the shop early and is waiting for us with Judy. With Clay on one side and Judy on the other, Maggie tells us what happened. Nicole, her mom, had been there when she went to sleep the night before but must have left at some point overnight because she wasn't there when Maggie woke up.

Maggie was about to call Clay or Judy to see if one of them could take her to school, but then her mom showed up. Problem was, she wasn't alone. A man followed her into their apartment, shouting and demanding money.

He knocked pictures off the walls and pushed her mom. Maggie watched this from the doorway of her room before hiding in her closet and calling the shop. By the time Clay and I got to the apartment, both her mom and the man were gone.

"This has to stop," Clay mutters, tucking her into his side.

"I don't ever want to go back there," Maggie pleaded softly.

"Over my dead body are you going back there," Judy fumed.

Pete calls her school to let them know she isn't feeling well and would be staying home sick today. Clay carries Maggie to the room she uses here. The events from this morning have exhausted her. I watch from the doorway.

"She hasn't even had breakfast and it's almost lunchtime." Judy tsked as Clay tucked her in.

"She'll eat when she wakes up but, for now, let her sleep." Clay ushered his mom out of the room kissing my forehead before closing the door behind him.

"I'm going back over there to get Maggie's things. She'll need her stuff for school tomorrow."

"No honey. What if that man comes back?" Judy pleads.

He pauses, looking at her. "I hope he does."

"I'm coming with you."

He comes over to kiss me. "Courtney, I don't think that's a good idea."

I nod. "You're not going over there alone."

"Babe," he pleads.

"Sorry. The sooner we go; the sooner we'll be back."

Seeing I'm not taking no for an answer, he kisses me again before grabbing my hand.

Once we're outside, he pins me against the door of his truck. "You are so fucking amazing."

I offer him my lips, parting them. His lingering, limb-tingling assault on them ends too soon. He's quiet on the drive over, his hand tightly clasping mine.

When we park, he tries to convince me again to wait for him in the truck; but I refuse, needing to be with him. So many times during my relationship with Mike, I let him make my decisions for me. I know I'm being stubborn; and as stupid as it seems, I need to protect him.

"You have a key?" I ask when we get to the door.

He knocks first, pausing before saying. "Nicole? Are you home?"

When there is no response, he opens the door and I follow him in. Despite the sparse furnishings, the room feels unlived in. There is an outdated flowered loveseat facing a small TV on a plastic table.

"Her room is back here."

We pass a bare kitchen before entering the first lived-in feeling room of the apartment. A clouded comforter cloaks the twin bed on the far wall. Clay lifts her book bag from the floor and fills it with stuffed animals from her bed.

"What can I do?"

He opens her closet, pulling a small rolling bag from it. "Pack whatever you can into it."

There aren't many clothes hanging in the closet. I fit those and move to a small dresser by the door.

Clay looks under her bed before glancing around the room again. "This is good. Let's go."

"You can't take her."

Our heads turn to the figure leaning on the wall outside the door. I know instantly, this must be Nicole. The family resemblance is unmistakable, only time clearly, has not been kind to her. Heavy makeup and too tight clothes are her mask. She is thin to the point of being scary and her blue eyes seem dead.

"Watch me," Clay growls.

A panicked look flashes across her features before she attempts to play it off with false bravado. "I can call the cops."

Clay advances on her, his tall frame towering over her. "I dare you to."

She grabs his arms in desperation. "Please, don't take my baby."

He shrugs off her hold, gesturing me to walk ahead of him.

Her eyes widen when she notices me. "Who'd you bring into my house, Clay?"

He ignores her and follows me into the 'unliving' room.

"I swear, I'll kill myself," she screeches behind us.

I turn, my eyes snapping to his face. He holds Maggie's book bag in one hand, rubbing his other hand over his face.

He turns to face her. "Don't say that, Nicole."

She hugs herself, shaking. "I will. I will."

"Stop it." His words are forceful, his tone gentle.

She turns, knocking her head into the wall three times before he pulls her into his arms. "Try to think about Maggie."

Whatever she says dissolves into incoherent sobs.

Clay looks back at me. "I'm going to try to calm her down. Can you make sure the door is locked, and call my mom? I don't want her to worry."

I flip the deadbolt and sit on the loveseat to call Judy. After I've assured her we are fine, I hang up and wait for Clay. My head turns at a buzzing sound. When it doesn't stop, I begin to search for its source. A cellphone is on the kitchen counter; I don't remember seeing it the first time we walked past.

It continues to buzz and curiosity gets the better of me when I glance at the screen. A new text flashes.

I can't do this anymore it reads from a Grant O.

I pick up the phone. I tell myself not to pry but can't stop from opening her contact list to look up Grant O. I compare the number to the one on my own phone for Grant Offenheim. They are the same. I'm still leaning against the counter when Clay walks back toward the living room.

I reach for him as he passes the open doorway. "Clay."

I hand him both of our phones. "I shouldn't have looked, but the phone wouldn't stop buzzing. That was wrong. I'm sorry. But, look who is texting her."

His mouth drops as realization hits him. He starts to scroll through the messages before slamming the phone down.

Even though he's shaking, I'm not afraid. I touch his cheek, moving his face until he faces me.

His eyes are pinched shut; he blinks them open, his blue eyes intense. "She calls him Maggie's dad in these texts."

"Oh, my God."

"He's been giving her money."

My eyes flick toward the hallway he led her down. "Is she asleep?"

He nods.

"We should go."

"My dad is going to flip out."

I tug him toward the door. He rambles in half sentences. "Why is he trying to buy…does Maggie…I just don't…"

For the first time in a long time, he doesn't hold my hand as he drives. He nervously strangles the steering wheel instead. Once we're in the driveway of his parents' house, he cuts the engine but makes no move to get out of the car.

"I don't know what to do."

"Hey." I reach for him and he leans across the console toward me.

I catch his face in my hands and hold him up. "Everything is going to be okay."

I lean in to meet him, my lips a reassurance against his. "It will."

"Should I tell them?"

"Your dad should know. It might have something to do with the sale."

My hands move up and down as he bobs his head in agreement.

His hands cover mine, holding me, holding him.

"I think I love you," I blurt.

I hadn't meant to tell him. I hide, ducking my face into the crook of my elbow; my embarrassment brings tears to my eyes.

His grip tightens on my hands. "I love you."

Not too. Not because I said it first. He said it as though nothing else mattered.

I lift my watery eyes. "You do?"

He doesn't answer me; he kisses me gently, sweetly, his hands now on my face, catching my tears. He loves me. Our moment ends, reality reminding us there are things his parents need to know.

"The same Grant?" Pete asks, shell-shocked.

Judy places her hand on Pete's knee, leaning forward. "Do you think the offer for the shop has something to do with Maggie?"

Clay's eyes flick to the hall, which leads toward her room. "Why else would he offer twice what it's worth? Something isn't right here. I think we need to ask Grant what he hopes to gain in purchasing the shop."

Pete calls Grant's office and, through his assistant, sets up a lunch meeting for next Monday. There has been no sign of Nicole since we saw her at her apartment. Clay starts to take me back to the garage to get my car but I stop him. After everything that happened today and everything that was said, I don't want to be away from him yet.

I fish my phone out of my purse and notice an email from Mike asking me to call him. Sorry, but delete. I call my mom to let her know I'm spending the night at Clay's place so she won't worry. When he hears me say that, he flashes me a heated look, his grip tightening on my hand. A pulse beats within me, a low beat of a drum that gets stronger the nearer we get to his place.

The air in the elevator as it climbs seven endless floors is thick. His hand fumbles as he unlocks his door, evidence of the nerves we both seem to be experiencing. The door is closed, the deadbolt is flipped, and there is nothing to interrupt us. We both want this.

The windowed wall does not end; it continues down the hall and turns the corner into his room. His bed faces the city, the view the only visible artwork in his room. He leads me to the foot of his bed, turning me, and easing me down until I sit in front of him.

He kneels and lifts my feet, gently slipping off one, and then the other of my shoes. His shoes and socks come off next; and on his knees, he moves between my legs. We kiss, his hand wrapped around my waist, my head dipped down to his. When he stands, he takes me with him and moves us further onto his bed.

A pillow meets the back of my head as he lowers me, lowering himself to me. The press of his weight against me is not enough; I want more. I need our skin to touch at every possible point. The need to have him fill me is like taking a breath after holding it. We shift to our sides and face each other. I hold his face to mine, my fingers threading through his silky brown hair.

Strong hands are fastened to the curve of my hips, his thick cock hard against me. Desire pools between my legs as, without command, my body shifts to move against him, to feel the delicious contradiction of my soft to his hard. A clever hand releases each button of my blouse one by one. After the last is freed, he moves his lips from mine, down my neck to the soft globes still bound by my bra.

The tip of his nose tickles, making me shiver against him.

He lifts his head. "Are you cold?"

I shake my head and tug at his shirt. A lazy smile precedes the pull of fabric over his head. Shortly, my blouse joins his shirt somewhere off the side of the bed.

I stretch onto my back; he hovers seemingly undecided on where to touch me first. His fingers glide up my stomach to cup me through my bra. It isn't enough. We work in harmony; as I arch my back to undo its clasp his fingers drag the straps down my skin.

I clutch him to me after he lowers his lips to pull one nipple between them. Fingers calloused from work tease, pinch, and pluck at my other nipple.

"You are so beautiful," he whispers against my skin.

It had never felt like this with Mike. I don't want Clay to stop but I want more. I need to touch, kiss, and learn every nuance of him. Hands firm, I push him; and like putty, he moves under me.

"Clay," I gasp.

I've never seen him without a shirt before. My fingers leading him he rolls to his side, his back to me. I knew he had a couple tattoos. He told me of their existence that day we had lunch in the back of his truck. I haven't thought of them since. The artwork covering his back is unreal.

"How long did it take to get this?" My fingers trace the monster on his skin.

He shifts further, onto his stomach. He keeps moving until his head is in my lap, his arms circling my waist.

His lips brush across the skin above the top of my slacks. "A long time."

He'll have to tell me later I think, stretching my legs out under him. Another button freed, his fingers easing the zipper down as our eyes stay locked on each other. I fall back, my head hitting his pillows, as I lift my hips so he can undress me.

Simple cotton underwear is now the only thing covering me.

I reach for the waistband of his pants, sitting up to kiss the contours of his abs as I unfasten his belt. His hands move to help but I push them away wanting to do this myself. His fingers weave through my hair. He gathers it in one hand, holding my hair back so he can look down at me as I undress him.

Limbs move to assist me and before long his pants land on the floor. He's on his back, looking down at me. With fingertip caresses, and my lips lingering as I taste his skin I crawl up his body. His eyes widen, holding my gaze, as I brush my cheek up his hard length.

"Fuck," he hisses.

In an instant, I'm pinned beneath him, his hard length pressed between my legs.

He kisses me hard, pushing against me. I open my legs wider, grinding into him, my fingers fisting his hair.

His eyes are hooded when he breaks our kiss and stares down at me. "I'm going to tear you apart."

"Do it," I pant.

He kisses his way down my body, freeing me of my panties until I am bared to him. The afternoon sun through his wall of windows exposes me fully. Fingertips part me and dip just inside my core. I try to shift wanting them deeper, but a hand locks me in place.

I watch, fascinated as he lifts his fingertips to his mouth, his lips closing around them as he sucks me from them. I only have time to gulp before his mouth is on me. His tongue, his fingers, his teeth all focused fully on torturing me. I start to pull back; it's too much. Mike didn't like pleasuring me with his mouth.

His arms circle and lock around my thighs, spreading me wider, his tongue circling my clit.

"Oh shit," I pant, my body surrendering control to him as my hips move shamelessly to grind his face.

His eyes stay on my face. I try in vain to keep my eyes on his; but as each sensation hits me, I thrash, throw my head back, and arch my back. He is relentless, not stopping until I'm quivering and pulsing against his lips. My hand covering my face, I try to catch my breath.

My closed eyes flutter open when I feel the bed shift. He grins down at me, licking his lips. I would blush, but I'm not embarrassed. I think no further than knowing I want this man. Hands on his shoulders, I push him onto his back and kiss him. Tasting myself, I reach down to stroke him through his boxers.

His moan against my lips makes me feel powerful. As I push the elastic down, he lifts his hips to help me pull them off him. I pump him up and down, his skin hot in my hand. Pulling back, I shift lower, his lips parting when I lick his cock. I move until I'm between his legs. He opens them making room for me, and then he pushes my hair from my eyes so he can watch me.

With one of my hands firmly wrapped around the base of his cock, his hips twitch as my lips wrap around its swollen, thick head.

"Christ." His fingers tighten in my hair.

I keep my eyes on his as I take as much of him as I can, sliding my hand up until my mouth touches it. I find a rhythm, my mouth and hand pulling back before meeting again. Clay groans, closing his eyes when my fingertips brush across his balls.

After a few feather light caresses, he grabs me around the waist, pulling me to him and crushing me against his chest.

"You are so fucking hot," he growls against my lips.

"I want you inside me," I beg.

He reaches into his nightstand and pulls out a condom. I take it from him and roll it down his length before lying down.

Gently, he dips his face to kiss me. "I love you."

I gulp, my hands cupping his face. "I love you."

He eases into me, stretching me, filling me, a moment of love, and nothing else. It builds into a tension we need to quench.

He grinds his hips against mine, his hand sliding up to hold the back of my neck. "You ready?"

I tug his lower lip between my teeth, teasing it with my tongue before releasing it. "Give it to me."

A determined glint flashes in his eyes as he slowly pulls out until just the tip of his cock is inside me. I mourn the loss of him, pitching my hips up trying to refill myself with him. He swivels his hips in a torturous tease before slamming back into me. The force pushes the breath out of me.

I wrap my legs around him, reaching around, digging my nails into his ass pulling him back into me, over and over again. He seems to possess inhuman strength; his body's splitting mine apart in a way I never thought possible. His teeth sink into the top of my shoulder and I lose myself entirely.

When I try to smother my own moans with my hand, he grabs my wrist pulling it away. "I want to hear you."

I let go, fully, loudly as I convulse around him, his face tilted up and eyes pinched shut as he comes.

Dropping his forehead to mine, he grins down at me before peppering my face with kisses, and then he reaches my mouth and kisses me hard, fully. Shifting me in his arms, we are on our sides with my body cradled against his.

His lips move to my neck. "I should probably feed you now."

I walk my arms up his arm. "Putting out before dinner, whatever will you think of me?"

He pushes my hair away from my face, smoothing it back and dropping his lips to mine. "I think I'll never let you go."

"Is that a Titanic reference?"

CHAPTER 20

CLAY

I don't know what I was expecting, what I had imagined our first time together would be like. Even my wildest fantasies couldn't hold a candle to what happened between the two of us. I knew Courtney was sexy as fuck, but she took sexy to a completely new level.

Sexy? That word doesn't seem to do her justice. I throw on a pair of sweats and head toward the kitchen. Pulling on one of my shirts, she follows me. I don't have an appetite for anything other than her right now. I tug her against me and kiss her.

"You sure you want to eat?" I joke against her lips.

"Mmm hmmm. Need energy for round two," she mumbles, her tongue peeking out to tease my lips as she speaks.

"Want to order takeout?" I ask, picking her up and setting her on a stool.

She spreads her legs and I stand between them. "That sounds good. What do you feel like eating?"

My hands drift up her legs. "I know what I want to eat."

She blushes. "Clay!"

I capture her lips again. "You'll be my dessert."

I pull back, grinning as I see the lust in her eyes. "Is Chinese good?"

She nods and tightens her arms around me. I'm in no rush to leave her embrace; even for the short time it takes to grab my phone. I angle my head so I have access to that delectable neck of hers. Whatever I'm doing she likes, tilting her head back so more of her neck is free for me to suck, nibble, and kiss.

The thin cotton of my shirt she pulled on does nothing to disguise the way her nipples have hardened. God, I can't get enough of her. My only dilemma is what to do first. I want it all, to taste her, to touch her, to drive my cock inside of her.

"Clay."

My name, almost a plea from her lips, somehow makes my already engorged cock harden even more. I need her. Moving my lips lower, I suck her nipple into my mouth through the shirt and drop my hand from her hair to tease her cunt.

My eyes snap up to hers. "Christ, you're wet."

She lifts her head, her eyes slowly opening to meet my gaze. "You're touching me."

"I'm about to do more than that."

Leaving her panting I go and grab a condom. I'm back to her in no time. I push my sweats down enough to free my cock, sliding the condom on. Then her hands grab me, guiding me into her.

"Fuck," I groan, sinking into her.

Whimpering she grinds against me, her hands reaching around to grab my ass.

"Put your arms around my neck and hold on."

She wastes no time doing what I ask; and I lift her, slipping each of my arms under her knees. Her eyes widen as gravity pulls her deeper on to my eager cock. Stepping back from the stool and into the middle of my kitchen, I let go. Her head tips back, a groan bursting from her lips as her body slams fully against mine.

Her legs wrap around me, my hand's vice grips on her incredible ass as I pump in and out of her. One of her hands moves up to fist her fingers in my hair. The tug, the pull of it, is fucking amazing as she yanks my head back until our eyes lock.

We stay that way, our lips a breath apart, mouths slack, staring into each other's eyes as her body explodes around mine. The grip and pulse of her around my cock is too much. With my eyes still locked on hers, I clench my teeth and come hard.

My arms shake as I ease her gently back onto her stool. Her hands still grip my shoulders tightly as we catch our breath.

"That was -," she starts.

"I know," I finish.

Absolutely fucking amazing. I'm part super human when she's in my arms.

"I'm just going to clean up." She blushes, slipping off the stool and into the bathroom. While she's gone I chuck the condom into the kitchen trash.

As I hang up the phone, she returns and begins lightly kissing the tattoo on my back.

I wasn't in the best place when I got that tattoo. It served as a reminder of the ugliness that lived inside me; a part of me, which I only allow to live as artwork on my skin. The man I was, egotistical, angry, and careless of the feelings of those around me, I buried a long time ago.

He would never have been worthy of a girl like Courtney. As painful as the lessons I went through were, they have made me the man I am today.

I turn, circling my arms around her waist and pulling her tightly against me. "Thank you."

She lifts her arms up and drapes them around my neck, pulling her shirt up with it. "For?"

My hands drop to her ass, now uncovered by my shirt but covered with a pair of cotton boy shorts.

Distracted, I ask, "Why'd you put these on?"

She smirks, looking up at me.

I slip my thumbs under the thin cotton. "You think these will keep my hands off of you?"

Her smirk falls as her mouth goes slack; damn, I meant to kiss that smirk off her face first.

I dip my head to hers and take her mouth before picking her up and carrying her to the couch. Slowly, I lower her to the cushions before stepping away from her.

"You stay right there," I order her. "We are going to eat before anything else happens."

She blushes, covering her face with her hands. "I'm not doing anything."

Christ, she's right and I still want to attack her.

"Here." I pull a throw blanket off the back of the sofa and toss it to her. "Cover up all that hotness, please."

She pulls the blanket over herself; and suddenly, I'm jealous of it. Shaking my head, I step back into the kitchen to get both of us some water. I pass a glass to her, careful to stay away.

"You're being so silly," she teases, taking a sip.

I shake my head and start to argue, but the phone rings, letting me know our food has arrived. I grab some cash from my wallet.

"Don't move," I remind her, before heading downstairs to get our food.

I probably should have put on a shirt to do it. There're three girls in their twenties who ride the elevator back up with me. I can't tell if they're drooling because of my chest, or how good my food smells.

"Feel like sharing?" one asks, stepping close to me.

"No, thanks. My girlfriend is already waiting for me," I answer, stepping back.

She pouts. I suppress a laugh, *not interested, sweetheart.*

Courtney is right where I left her.

CHAPTER 21

Who needs an alarm clock in a room with a wall of windows? My attempts to bury my face into Clay's neck to delay waking backfire. He smells too good. I nuzzle into him as his arms squeeze around me.

"Good morning." His husky whisper tickles my ear.

I stretch, loving the way he feels against my skin. "I'm sore."

Last night was insane. We made love, ate, made love some more, ate again. We finally fell asleep sometime after twelve.

"So I can't have my way with you this morning?" He teases.

Desire pools in my belly. It seems I'm insatiable. "I never said that."

Like magic, he hardens against me, but he argues, "I don't want to hurt you."

"You won't." I inch impossibly closer to him.

He chuckles, my body shaking with his. "What about a hot bath?"

I pop my head up, nodding. A bath sounds like heaven. I had drooled over his bathroom last night. It is almost the size of my bedroom. The wall behind the double sinks is the lightest of blues, almost gray. The other walls and floors are tiled with white subway tiles. There is a jetted, soaking tub and separate shower with a rainfall showerhead and a built-in bench.

He slips from under me and after pulling his boxers on goes to start the water. I steal his t-shirt from yesterday and follow him.

"You like tea, right?"

I hug the doorway, enjoying the view as he leans over the tub to test the water. "Tea would be amazing."

He moves past me, pausing to kiss my head. "I think that can be arranged."

While he's in the kitchen, I quickly relieve myself before stepping back into the hallway. "Hey, do you have an extra toothbrush?"

He finds one for me and we brush our teeth together. It's amazing how easy it is to be with him. I can be silly as we fight over the sink; I can be sexy when I want to turn him on; I can be confused as I learn how to change my own oil; I can be every single part of me, and he loves them all.

The whistle of the kettle calls him back to the kitchen. He uses a French press and makes coffee while my tea steeps. We carry our mugs with us back to the bathroom and rest them on the edge of the tub. Losing his shorts, he gets in first. I follow, easing myself into the hot water and my back against his chest.

"God, this feels good," I moan, relaxing further against him.

His hands reach around to cup me. "I can think of a way to make it feel even better."

After a long and pleasurable soak, we end up back in his bed. I finally get my chance to look at his tattoos. He has a skull on his calf. He's embarrassed by it. He was only eighteen when he got it and an old friend did it. His friend wasn't a professional, but it doesn't look that bad.

His back piece, though, is equally terrifying and beautiful. It's all teeth and horns; a monster, part dinosaur, part alien.

He twitches as my fingertips graze the outside edges. "Why a monster?"

"There are worse things in life to fear."

He flips over, my exploration clearly finished, and pulls me to his chest. "Do you want me to run you home?"

My heart cracks. "Oh, right. You probably have stuff to do. I didn't mean to -"

"Courtney, shut up. Do you want to stop by your house to pack a bag so you have clothes to wear to lunch tomorrow?"

I try to hide my face, embarrassed; but he doesn't let me. Grabbing my wrists, he straddles me. I close my eyes.

He scatters kisses across my face. "So, will you go to lunch with Maggie and me tomorrow?"

He laughs when I only open one eye and nod. "Maybe, you could even pack a few extra things to keep over here."

My other eye pops open at that. "What are you saying?"

He rolls next to me and props his head up on his hand. "Starting Monday, we're not going to see each other every day at the shop. I figured you could come over here." Rolling onto his back, he pulls me on top of him. "And spend the night."

"But -"

He lifts his head to silence me with a kiss. "I don't know how this works. This isn't anything I've ever done before."

I lower my lips to his, relaxing. "I don't want there to be any pressure."

He cocks his head to the side. "Do you feel pressured?"

I cover my face. "I'm scared. Everything is so good."

Pulling my hands down he sits up, pulling me with him until his back rests against the headboard. "I don't want to frighten or upset you; but at the same time, just know falling in love with you has been scary as hell."

"Why are you scared?

His hands cup my face. "I've never been great at trusting people. I've been burned so many times by Nicole, and she's my own blood, but I still have let you in."

"I won't hurt you." I drape my arms over his shoulders, resting my hands on top of the headboard.

His hands drop to the hem of the shirt I'm wearing, dragging it over my head. "We can pick up your stuff later."

"Don't you think you two are rushing this?"

While Clay is waiting for me downstairs, my mom has come up to help me pack. "How long did you know Daddy before you got married?"

"Touché." She starts folding the clothes I've put out.

"Why don't you go hang out with Clay while I finish up? Get to know him," I suggest.

She agrees, leaving the room to go make small talk with him. I use the opportunity to sneak my sexy lingerie into my bag. It'll be a fun surprise for Clay tonight. I throw a couple more things and a book in before closing up the tote. I doubt I'll have any time to read; but I don't want to be completely dependent on my boyfriend to entertain me.

One mistake I made in my relationship with Mike was losing myself along the way. I need to make an effort not to do that. While the thought is fresh in my mind, I text Jen to see if she wants to see a movie sometime next week, go out to dinner, or something. I don't expect a response so fast. She has met someone through that dating website, and she wants to introduce him to me.

I text her back to see if it'd be cool if Clay tags along; if he's free and wants to. Her instant yes makes me grin. Mike and Jen never really got along. She has an amazing bullshit radar, so her opinion about Clay will mean a lot to me.

My mom and Clay are in the kitchen when I come downstairs. "Hey, guys."

She passes Clay a packet of something and he tries discreetly to put it in his pocket. "What's going on?"

He produces the packet from his back pocket. "I asked what kind of tea is your favorite so I could pick some up for you."

I meet my mom's eyes and she's glowing. "Aww. That is so thoughtful."

I lean over to give him a kiss. "Thank you."

He waves bye to my mom. "It was nice seeing you, Mrs. Grayson."

"Please call me, Melissa."

As we drive back to his condo, Clay asks if he can take me out to dinner.

"Sure. Where do you want to go?"

"There's a great place we could walk to; they serve a bit of everything."

"Sounds great." I glance at the clock. "Is it cool if I shower first?"

"Only if you don't mind company."

The thing about taking a shower with someone who has an insane body is you forget to do anything other than rub soap all over them. Luckily, Clay has no issues soaping me up. The thing that surprises me the most is his offer to wash my hair. His fingers massaging my scalp, as he works the shampoo and conditioner into my hair, is so unexpectedly sweet.

Because of our height difference, I have him sit on the bench so I can do the same for him. It's impossible to concentrate when he won't stop touching me. I threaten to make him sit on his hands but he ignores me. Rinsed and halfway dried, we end up making love again before we get dressed.

Afterward, I make Clay leave the room while I get dressed so I can surprise him later.

"You're killing me," he grumbles through the door.

"No peeking, Bradshaw," I tease.

I wear a tight purple corset with black ribbons, a matching thong, and lace-topped black stockings attached to a garter belt. I glance in the mirror. On the outside, all anyone will see is a simple black dress. It gives me a thrill knowing what's underneath it all.

Clay looks edible in charcoal slacks and a crisp white dress shirt. I start to think about what's hiding under his clothes as well, his monster. The restaurant he takes me to isn't well marked from the street but busy inside.

"Hey, Clay." One of the waiters greets as we walk in.

"Hi, Luke, this is my girlfriend, Courtney."

I smile and wave. I wasn't expecting introductions.

"It's nice to meet you, Courtney." He turns to Clay. "How'd you land such a hottie, Clay?"

He shrugs. "Still trying to figure out what she sees in me, Luke."

I blush.

"Is anyone joining you two?"

Clay shakes his head. "Just the two of us."

We follow Luke further into the restaurant and he seats us in a booth. As I look at my menu, I ask Clay about going out with Jen and her date later on this week.

"Can I talk you into staying over after?"

Our table is in the back corner. I slip my foot out of my shoe and rub his calf with it. "I think that can be arranged."

He leans forward wetting his lips. "Don't look now; but I think that person who started rubbing up on my leg that night of the concert is back."

I giggle. "Who do you think it could be?"

He glances around, naming possible suspects. We're laughing by the time Luke comes back to take our orders.

He starts to walk away but stops, and looking at Clay, says, "It's real nice to see you looking so happy, man."

Clay reaches across the table for my hand and squeezes it, thanking him.

"I can't picture you unhappy."

"Shit with Nicole got bad there for awhile. I hope she hasn't tried to pull anything with my parents today."

"Wouldn't they call you if she did anything?"

He nods. "I'll probably call them when we get back to the condo to check on them."

"Of course, we could swing by there too, if you want."

"Nah. We'll see them tomorrow when we pick up Maggie for lunch."

"You are such a good uncle; I have to tell you that is a big turn-on."

He raises a brow. "Really? Is that what attracted you to me?"

"It's a part of it. You not being hard to look at doesn't hurt either."

His mouth drops. "Not hard to look at? I feel like I should be offended."

Leaning in, I whisper, "You know you are fucking hot as hell so there."

That seems to placate him. "I don't have anything on you, babe."

My cheeks redden. "Stop."

He lifts my hand to his lips. "Courtney, you're going to have to get used to me telling you how gorgeous you are because I don't plan on stopping."

Luke saves me from replying when he arrives with our drinks. Clay ordered a draft of a microbrew unique to the restaurant. I played it safe with a Riesling.

"Do you ever want kids?" Clay asks suddenly.

I start coughing when my drink goes down the wrong way. He starts to get up and I can picture everyone watching as he thumps my back. I wave my hand for him to stay where he is as I catch my breath.

"Kids?" I manage, finally.

"I wasn't trying to kill you, I swear. It's just that you said my being good with Maggie was one of the things you liked about me. Made me wonder how you feel about kids."

"That makes sense. I wasn't expecting the question right then. Honestly, I thought I'd have kids by now. I'd like to someday, you know, get married, start a family." I hesitate. "What about you?"

"I've never really thought about it. I've always been careful because I never wanted to get a girl pregnant. Maybe I was extra sensitive because of Nicole having Maggie."

"Just so you know; I'm on the pill," I offer, hoping it will relax him.

"So we could maybe do it without a condom?"

"It doesn't protect against STDs. I was tested after I found out Mike cheated on me, so I know I'm clean. Have you ever been tested?"

"That's straight forward." I start to say something, but he continues, "I have. It's also been a while for me since I was with anyone."

"Why?"

He waits when he sees Luke heading toward us with our food.

After we're served, he keeps going, "After things got crazy with Owen, I reevaluated my life. Started spending more time with Maggie and focused on my job."

"But that was five years ago. You aren't saying you haven't been with anyone in that long, are you?"

"You have a good memory. No, it hasn't been that long, but the changes I made in my life started around then."

"Oh."

Clay pauses before asking, "Do you want to, without?"

Our shared shower and bath would have been very different. "I do."

If it's possible, Clay blushes when he replies, "Wow."

He looks extremely uncomfortable so I stutter, "If you don't want to, we don't have to."

He shakes his head and says, "That wasn't what I meant. I've never done that."

"Do you want to?"

The look on his face is answer enough. A switch has been flipped, ratcheting the intensity of our meal up a notch. I already have figured we are going to have sex after dinner, but somehow now knowing that he won't be wearing a condom has made it suddenly extremely hot in here. He is turned on. I am turned on. There is something powerfully erotic in knowing I will be his first.

We skip dessert. There is a pull between running back to his place and taking our time walking there. The anticipation builds. We both encourage it. In the elevator, we retreat to opposite walls and stare hungrily at each other. When we get into the condo, he advances on me.

When he puts his hands on my waist, I pull back. "Weren't you going to call your mom?"

He groans, dropping his forehead to rest on mine. "They're probably fine."

"Clay."

He smirks but pulls out his phone to make what may be the fastest check-in call on record before his lips find my neck.

I wrap my arms around his neck. "What'd she say?"

"Huh?"

"Your mom? What'd she say? How's Maggie?"

"Everyone is fine. No sign of my sister."

"Hey, Clay?"

He lifts his head. "Yeah."

"I love you," I sigh before dropping my lips to his.

He lifts me, my legs moving to wrap around him, and he carries me over to the couch. "I love you."

I kiss him again before pushing up and off him. "I got you something."

With surprise apparent in his features, he reaches for me. "You didn't have to."

I evade his grasp, stepping closer to the window. "Can you help me with my zipper?"

He jumps up and comes to me. I turn, offering him my back. He pushes my hair over to one side, kissing the back of my neck as he eases the zipper down. I reach back, gripping his thighs. Once the zipper reaches the end, I turn, face him, and let my dress fall. It pools softly around my feet.

Clay's eyes widen, his fingertips reaching up to trace the top edge of the corset. "You were wearing this the whole time?"

I nod and turn slightly, so he can see the back.

"Fuck."

"You like?"

He crouches in front of me, smoothing his hands up my stockings to tease the exposed skin along the top of my thighs. His lips follow, my fingers threading in his hair, as he kneels in front of me. He shifts my legs apart and I lean back, the cool glass of the window pressed to my shoulder blades. His eyes trail up my body, latching on my mine as he peels back the scrap of fabric covering my sex.

He watches my face as his hands grip my ass and he sucks my clit into his mouth. In no time, he has my knees buckling, his hands the only thing keeping me upright. He stands, making sure I don't fall and kisses me hard before turning me so I'm facing the window.

"You want me to fuck you against this window?"

"God, yes." I've fantasied about it ever since that day.

I hear his belt hit the floor, followed by what must be his shirt. With my hands pressed to the cool glass, I look back at him. His slacks hang on his hips. I can see the bulge of his hardened cock from where I stand. He holds my gaze, reaching down to slip off one of his shoes, and then the other. With one downward pull, he removes his slacks and boxers, now naked.

He pumps his cock in his hand as he advances on me. I drop my head forward when I feel the press of him against me. He reaches around to tease my nipples from their cups.

"You are so fucking hot," he groans.

"I want you."

My hands slide down the glass as he pulls my hips back and pushes my back down. He starts to push my thong to the side.

"There are ties, on the sides."

Nimble fingers at my hips free the fabric from my body. He shifts his cock between my legs, teasing my entrance. I swivel my hips trying to encourage him inside me. His hands clench on my hips as he slams into me with one powerful stroke.

"Yes," I pant.

He bucks wildly against me. "God, you feel so good. Shit."

"Give it to me," I beg, "harder."

He listens, pounding into me as my hands stay pressed against the window. He leans over me, tilting my head back to find my lips as he continues to slam into me. As he comes, his whole body tenses and he groans against my lips. Still inside me, he walks us backward as I watch my handprints disappear from the glass.

I'm turned, lifted, and carried to his bed. He slips my heels off, unclips, and then rolls my stockings down and off. He buries his face in the offering of breasts my corset serves him.

"This." He slides his hands up my sides. "Is fucking hot, but I want you naked."

I giggle as I'm turned and he begins to unhook me. The corset is tight so I revel in the sweetness of expanding my chest. Once I'm freed, I turn back into him and we tangle up in each other. Is it possible to be addicted to a person? The first step is admitting you have a problem.

As I awake, I realize this morning is a repeat of yesterday. When I try to burrow under the covers, I feel the rumble of Clay's chest as my avoidance of the sun amuses him.

"Should I invest in some curtains?"

"No," I mumble into his neck. "I love the windows. It's the sun I'm not crazy about right now."

"It makes a good alarm clock." He kisses the top of my head and I snuggle closer to him.

Tonight, I'll be back at my mom's missing this. I stay blissed out in him until I can't put off nature's call. I didn't wash my face last night so I freshen up and brush my teeth before diving back under the covers.

"Do you want some tea?" Clay starts to get up but I pull him back, wanting to cuddle a bit longer.

He doesn't seem to mind and coils his arms around me. It's ridiculous, but I already miss him. When we do finally get up and eat breakfast, neither of us addresses the elephant in the room. We will be driving right past the shop and my car on the way to lunch. The logical thing would be for Clay to drop me off there after lunch so I can pick up my car and head home. I don't want to go home.

Interrupting my gloom is a call from Jen. I know it can't be good when she asks if I'm sitting down.

I catch Clay's eye. "No, I'm not sitting. What's up?"

"Honey, I really think you need to sit down."

I move over to his bed and sink onto the edge of it. "You're scaring me, Jen."

"Courtney, Mike may have tried to kill himself."

The wetness flooding my eyes is too much for the rapid blinking of my lids. Tears flow over and down my face as Clay rushes over to me.

"No, please, no. That's not true."

I have been so angry with him, but I have never wished anything like this.

"I'm so sorry, honey."

Clay is beside me, pulling me into his arms.

CHAPTER 22

CLAY

Watching Courtney break down after learning what Mike tried to do to himself is awful. She blames herself, or a bare minimum thinks there is something she could have done to prevent his attempted suicide. He had his own demons, made his own choices. Trying to convince her of that seems impossible.

Not caving in to him had been out of character for her. At least that's how she tries to explain it to me.

"This isn't your fault," I repeat.

She doesn't argue in words; but she folds into herself, almost trying to shrink the space she occupies to leave more room for her guilt to grow.

I pull her into my lap. At first, she sits stiffly, fighting the relief my arms offer her. When she finally gives in and sags against me, I relax as well. Bad stuff happens to good people. How you react to the things outside of your control defines your inner strength. The last few months have been a roller coaster for her.

This is a bigger drop then she can handle. Tightening my arms around her, I'm strangely relieved when her silent tears wet my shirt. If she's crying, she's dealing with it. Her bottling her emotions up would scare me more. What Mike tried to do has gotten to her; the idea that the person she had planned to spend the rest of her life with might have suddenly been gone.

"I got you," I breathe against her hair, giving her the only thing I have to comfort her, me.

"I just don't understand why," she whimpers into my chest.

He didn't leave a note; and as far as we know, he hasn't been able to speak to anyone about it yet. He took a bunch of pills, and his condition was touch and go there for a while.

Multiple phone calls have come in. Mike's parents contacted Courtney's mom directly since they didn't know her new number. We've learned of some financial troubles he had that Courtney hadn't known about. The more we learn though, the more accidental it appears. There was no one around him in the days leading up to it, who noticed anything different.

His money issues have something to do with taxes, exactly what we weren't told. Selfishly, for her, I'm relieved she left him when she did, so he wasn't able to drag her down with him. Given their break-up, we might not ever know to what extent his secret troubles have been.

Cheating on her and hiding financial issues from Courtney makes me wonder if this is the tip of the iceberg as sad as the outcome could have been, maybe this will get him moving in a better direction. With Courtney in my arms, it's clear to me how lucky I am to have her.

"Maybe he'll be up for talking soon." I tip her chin up and brush a tear from her cheek.

Her chin wobbles. She feels responsible.

She tucks her head back into my chest and slowly breathes in and out. I don't need to be anywhere else. If it helps her heal, I'll hold her forever.

"Want to lie down?"

She nods and I carry her to my room.

"Thank you," she whispers against my chest.

"Like there is any other place I'd rather be." I drop my lips to the top of her head.

"You're too good to me," she argues.

"You deserve so much more."

"More than you?" She scoffs.

Grinning, I run my fingers up and down her back. "Yep."

"You are crazy." She wiggles closer to me.

"Crazy for you," I counter.

She giggles and it's music to my ears. This whole mess with Mike has exhausted her emotionally. It's nice to hear her laugh again. I stay with her, curling my body around hers until she falls asleep. I could get up; I have a ton of stuff I probably should be doing right now, but I stay with her instead. Even in sleep, I don't want her to feel alone.

She takes on too much; I know, I'm wired the same way. She might not know it, but her mere presence in my life has done more to relax me than anything else before her ever has. I want to be the same for her. She's still holding back, not letting herself go when it comes to us.

She has this Mike-planted fear she'll lose herself in me, and there will be nothing left if anything happens to us, relationship-wise. All I want to do is prove to her that no matter what, I'm not Mike. I'm not going to make the same mistakes he did; and at this point, I don't see my life without her in it.

Maybe instead of losing herself in me, I can give her the support to find herself instead. We've been open and honest about all of our shit since day one. I can't think of a firmer foundation than ours. Life has a way of testing us. This is another one of those tests for her.

She'll probably want to talk to Mike once he's up to it. I'm not thrilled about that, but I'll be there for her every step of the way. He doesn't deserve the power he has in her guilt right now. She deserves the opportunity to have closure when it comes to him.

She turns her face into my neck and I relax against her. My arms briefly tighten around her before slacking as I fall asleep.

"Clay."

I blink. "Huh?"

"Clay, babe, we should probably get up."

My arms react on their own, pulling Courtney back down to me. She doesn't fight it, melting against me. My lips move to her neck, my hips rocking against hers.

Her legs open and I roll her onto her back. I'm wide awake now and trying to be thoughtful of her emotional state.

"Are you sure?" I nip at her collarbone.

"I need you," she whimpers.

I tug her shirt over her head and pull her nipple into my mouth through her bra. Her back arches up off the bed as her fingers fist my hair. My hand slides down her body and into her pants. I lift my head to capture her lips as I sink two fingers inside her.

"Please," she pleads, tugging at my shirt.

I'd have to move my fingers to get it over my head, so I ignore her as she continues to buck against me.

"Please," she begs again.

I hook my fingers inside her and rub her clit with my thumb. "Please what?"

"I need you inside me," she gasps.

I move my lips to where her ear meets her neck. "You want me to stop what I'm doing?"

One of her hand moves down to grip the wrist of the hand I'm finger fucking her with. "No," she moans, pressing my hand harder against herself, grinding against it.

Thought so. I suck her lobe between my teeth.

"You gonna come all over my hand, babe?" I whisper wickedly in her ear.

Her eyes roll back and her grip on my wrist tightens.

"What are you gonna do after you come?" I ask.

"What...ever...you...want," she pants.

"I want you to ride my cock. Does that sound good, babe?"

"Yes...yes...Oh, God...yes," she moans.

Fuck, I might come only listening to her.

"You are so fucking sexy."

My words and my hand push her over the edge. The rest of her body stills, as her pussy pulses around me.

It takes her a moment to open her eyes. When she does, I slowly drag my fingers from her and bring them to my mouth. She watches, wide-eyed as I suck her juices from them.

As soon as my fingers are out of my mouth, she crashes her lips to mine, pushing me until my back is on the bed.

CHAPTER 23

Courtney

No one blames me directly. I blame myself. I was so angry with him the last time I saw him. The email I deleted haunts me. All I think now is how I almost didn't have an opportunity to say goodbye. We were together eight years.

Clay has been with me as much as he could be. The day I got the call, he drove me straight to my house; and later that day, he drove Jen to the shop to bring back my car. I felt bad for missing lunch with Maggie, but everyone understood. Pete told Clay to tell me not to come in until I felt up to it.

I have tried to convince Clay my grief has not been regret for refusing to take Mike back, but only shock because he tried to end his life. Part of me feels like I never knew him. He had always been so confident, so sure of himself. When I found out he was cheating on me, I assumed the fault was with me, not him.

It has been hard accepting his action might not have had anything to do with me at all. I emailed him. I'm not sure if I can handle seeing him face to face; but I gave him my new number and told him once he's feeling better, it'd be okay for him to call. Clay isn't thrilled but he knows I would never take Mike back after what he did. I want to forgive him. If he hadn't cheated, I might not be with Clay.

Clay's family has been dealing with the fallout that comes with taking Maggie away from Nicole. As for Nicole, no one has seen or heard from her since that day. Pete met with Grant and confirmed Grant was, in fact, Maggie's father.

They met eleven years ago when Nicole happened to talk her way into a party at Grant's house. As he explained it, to say he was a bit of a partier would be putting it mildly. He panicked when she told him she was pregnant.

His family was extremely conservative; and he and Nicole both knew there wasn't a future for the two of them together. He had promised to help support Nicole and Maggie; but recently, he had stopped giving her money when it became clear it was going toward coke and not Maggie.

The offer on the shop had been his attempt to filter additional funds to Maggie when it became clear Pete and Judy were actually supporting her. He wants, if the Bradshaws are willing, to become a bigger part of Maggie's life. Clay still doesn't like Grant because he thinks Grant is still attracted to me. They are going to have a paternity test done before anything else happens.

"Why is Grant comfortable with people knowing he has a daughter now?"

Two weeks have passed since I found out about Mike. I'm at Clay's condo. We haven't had sex either because, somehow, it feels disrespectful. He's careful with me, tender and sweet. He holds me and never asks for anything in return.

"When Nicole gave birth to Maggie, Grant's grandfather was still living. Apparently, that guy was a complete asshole. He passed away a couple years back, so Grant has been thinking about going public ever since."

"He should've been a better dad right from the start," I argue.

"He should have," Clay agrees. "I can't knock him for trying to make things right now though." He stretches out, putting his head in my lap. "He's okay as long as he doesn't try asking you out again."

I brush his hair back before stroking his cheek. "I'm such a mess right now and you've been so amazing. What did I ever do to deserve you?"

He pulls my hand to his lips, his blue eyes piercing mine. "I'm the lucky one."

I scoff and his sits up only to drag me down so I'm lying with him.

His hands cup my face. "I love you, Courtney. I didn't even think that was possible. I want to be here for you. It's killing me that you're hurting."

I melt against him. "I feel guilty for being here. I feel like I broke a promise to him."

His arms tighten around me. "He broke a promise first. You can't beat yourself up for leaving him."

"I know. You're right; I know it. It's so strange."

"I don't want to push you. I feel like I am."

I reach up to pull his lips down to mine. "You have been amazing. Thank you."

"Are you still up for going tonight?"

I nod. "When do we have to leave? I'm comfy."

He lifts his hand to check his watch. "Not for another couple hours."

"Mmm." I snuggle closer to him. "Do we need to bring anything?"

"Nope, but I'm still bringing a pony keg of Luke's microbrew. We're picking up Jen and her date on the way, right?"

"His name is Justin. Jen and I MapQuested it. His house is less out of the way, so we'll get them from there if that's okay with you."

"Sounds good."

He gently plays with my hair, twisting little chunks of it, and then finger combing it. I doze in his arms as he watches TV.

His hand shakes my shoulder. "Hey, sleepyhead."

I blink up at him. "What time is it?"

He pushes my hair from my eyes. "We need to leave in twenty minutes."

When I don't immediately get up, he asks if I still want to go.

I bob my head, stretching my arm back. "Just groggy."

"You're cute when you're groggy."

I kiss his chest. "You're cute all the time."

His arms give me a delicious squeeze. Other than checking my hair to make sure it doesn't look crazy from his naptime styling, I'm ready to go.

"Did you sleep?" I ask from the bathroom.

He leans against the door jam. "Nope, watched the game."

"Do I look okay?" I glance back at my reflection.

He comes up behind me, coils his arms around my waist, and kisses the side of my neck. "You look beautiful. Come on, let's go."

He still loves to open my door and help me into his truck. I tease him, telling him it's because he likes to cop a feel.

"Can you blame me?" He grins as he buckles his belt.

Our hands find each other and I give him directions to Justin's house. He lives in a townhouse community with small, hard-to-see house numbers. We drive around trying to find his unit until I give up and call Jen. Using the landmarks she gives us, we finally find it.

"Sorry about that," Justin says, as he and Jen climb in. "No one can ever find it."

We're all heading to Brad and Jenna's for another movie night on the side of the barn. Brad and Jenna are Clay's closest friends, and Jen is mine. So we thought it'd be fun to get everyone together. I warn Jen about Colt on the way over. She's more of a cat person; dogs jumping on her always freak her out.

"He's super sweet though, so don't worry about it."

Clay's glance my way paired with the impish grin on his face makes me wonder if he's thinking about how Colt scared me the night of our first date. I don't ask, it would contradict what I told Jen. Once we turn onto the dirt road, I learn something new about Jen. Apparently, dirt roads weird her out; who knew?

Lucky for us, it isn't the longest of dirt roads and we pull up at Brad and Jenna's house. Colt is already outside and runs over to the truck to greet us. My eyes pass over their front porch, half expecting them to be walking down the steps like last time. Then, I notice them out of the corner of my eye getting set up over by the barn.

Jen only mildly freaks out when Colt jumps on her. Brad manages to distract him with a Frisbee while we make our way to the barn. As introductions are being made, Jen and Jenna bond over possible spellings and pronunciations of their names.

Tonight, three loveseats are set up on the lawn, making me wonder how many they own and where they store them. The grill is going so we can have burgers, hot dogs, and corn on the cob during the movie. Brad hugs Clay when he produces the microbrewed pony keg.

"This will go great with the burgers."

"What movie are we watching?" I ask Jenna.

She tilts her head and smirks at Brad.

With a bold flourish, he gestures toward the white side of the barn. "If you build it, they will come."

"Field of Dreams?" I ask.

He snaps his finger and points at me with a nod for placing the movie quote so quickly.

"I haven't seen that movie in forever." Justin puts his arm around Jen's shoulder. "Have you seen it?"

She shrugs. "It's the one about baseball, right, with Kevin Costner?"

When Justin nods, she goes on. "I think I've seen pieces of it, but not the whole thing."

Brad moves some burgers to a plate. "It's a great movie and we're celebrating."

Brad's eyes flick to Jenna, who smiles and rests her hand on her stomach. "We're pregnant."

"Congratulations!" Clay booms, hugging her first, and then Brad.

He had mentioned to me a while back they had been trying.

He points at Jenna. "No microbrew for you."

Brad drapes his arm around her shoulders. "She's already getting weird cravings and everything."

Clay puts his hands up. "No one wants to hear about your sex lives."

Jenna snorts and Brad shoves Clay. "Wiseass."

Clay and I get the center loveseat because we're the common denominator, Brad and Jenna the one closest to the grill and their house. The good thing about a movie night when meeting new people is there isn't any forced conversation.

I snuggle up to Clay and feel completely relaxed for the first time in days. The initial shock is starting to subside and watching a movie on the side of this barn makes me happy. It hasn't even been two months since our first date and I'm already reminiscing.

When Jenna gets up to grab something from the house, I excuse myself to go with her. I have needed to use the bathroom but haven't wanted to walk into their house all by myself.

"That's the thing about guys. They just go pee in the tree line. They have it so good." Jenna grumbles as we walk together.

"I know," I agree. "The whole being able to pee standing up without worrying about peeing on yourself."

"And periods." Jenna adds.

"Eh, I don't really get them anymore, but I still have PMS. What is that about?"

"It's not fair."

"It really isn't."

"And the whole aging thing. Why do guys get to look distinguished when they get older?"

I snort and tell her about Clay telling Maggie and Amber to Google Clooney.

"How is Maggie doing? Any word from Nicole?"

I shake my head. "What sucks is that's good and bad news."

She nods, putting her hand on my arm. "I don't want to overstep myself or anything, but I need you to know we have never seen Clay this happy. We heard about what happened with your ex. If there is anything you need, please let me know. Clay is like a brother to Brad; and we're so happy things are going good with the two of you."

We end up hugging right before she points out the bathroom to me. My thoughts wander to Mike, and I end up comparing him again to Clay. I wish he had given himself enough time to see that opportunities outside of us existed. On what was possibly the worst day of my life, I didn't give up, but it feels like he did.

My pity dissolves the lingering anger I have toward him. Now I'm just sad he felt like he needed pills to cope. I hope now he knows no matter how angry I was with him, I always have wished him well.

I help Jenna carry a tray of éclairs out to the gang. I laugh when I see Clay eyeing them. He has to know he won't be getting a repeat of my last dessert performance; maybe I'll have Jenna wrap one up for us to take home.

I've seen the movie before, so I watch Jen and Justin, and Jenna and Brad instead. Jenna and Brad have been married for years. It's sweet to watch her steal bites from his plate while his hand rests on her stomach. With Jen and Justin, their relationship is even newer than Clay's and mine. They sit close but they haven't relaxed into their 'them-ness' yet.

I sneak a glance up at Clay, loving the way he keeps me tucked into his side; feeling my gaze, he looks down at me, and smiles with crinkly eyes. I tilt my chin up, offering my lips, which he takes with no hesitation.

"Doing good?" he whispers in my ear.

I nod, holding him as he holds me. When the end credits start rolling, we notice Jenna has fallen asleep. Clay goes with Brad to hold the door open for them as Brad carries her sleeping form inside. I leave Jen and Justin in the light of the torches as I unplug the projector and put it away the way Clay had the last time we were here.

I jump when he finds me. "Hey, I could have done this."

He tugs me to him. "I wanted to help."

"Brad said to leave everything else. He'll take care of it in the morning."

We walk back to where Brad is standing with Jen and Justin.

"Sorry, Jenna passed out. We read it's normal during the first trimester."

"I'm so excited for you guys. You're going to make great parents," Clay says, punching his shoulder.

Brad nods, looking suspiciously choked up as he quickly looks away. On the drive back to Justin's, Jen asks if we'd like to have dinner over there soon. I agree for us. I'm just so happy to see her happy. She hasn't had the best track record with some of the guys she's dated, and Justin seems like a genuinely nice guy.

When we get back to Clay's condo, we quietly undress and tumble into bed together. "Move in with me."

"What?" He squints at me when I switch the light back on.

"I'm serious. I want us to live together."

I don't think; I just jump. "Yes."

He sits up. "Yes?"

I crawl into his lap and kiss him. "Yes."

He hasn't pushed me in anyway since I found out about Mike. He's supported me and been everything I never knew I needed. Our kiss deepens. It's time. I won't say I'm healed, but I'll never know what we can be unless I try. He peels from me the t-shirt I had changed into to sleep in. I need him.

"Please," I plead.

He shifts to slip off his boxers, somehow managing to keep me in his lap. When he sets us back down, I reach for him and position myself over him. His lips find mine as I slowly impale myself on him. His hands grip my hips to lift me up and down.

We break our kiss, fighting to breathe. Our noses almost touching, our eyes holding, as he fills me in more ways than physically.

My eyes flutter as I feel the pressure start to build deep inside.

"Let go, babe," he urges me.

My head falls back breaking our eye contact as I begin to convulse around him. He isn't far behind me, his groan shaky as he releases.

We cling to each other, and then his hands cup my face. "Really? You will?"

I kiss him, smiling against his lips. "Yes."

After the best night of sleep I've had since I learned of Mike's suicide attempt, I find myself again trying to hide from the rising sun.

"Today we're buying curtains," Clay mumbles against me.

"You don't have to," I argue.

He kisses my head before slipping out of bed. "Anything for you, sleepyhead. I don't mind. If we mount the rod high enough, it'll be like they aren't even there when they're open."

I squint at him. "You said we. I don't know how to install curtains."

"I'm a great teacher." He winks and walks out of the room.

I follow him, pit stopping in the bathroom on the way out to the kitchen. He has the kettle going and starts making toast.

"Nutella or jam?"

"Mmm, both please."

He slices a grapefruit in half and passes me one. I don't think I'll ever get bored of watching him in the kitchen, especially when he isn't wearing a shirt.

"Should I get a tattoo?" I wonder aloud.

"Only if you want to, it's hard to change your mind after the fact."

"That's what's always held me back from getting one. When I was eighteen, I came this close." I hold up my thumb and index finger with a small gap between them. "To getting my zodiac sign on my ankle."

"I don't even know when your birthday is." He passes my toast to me.

"You have time. It's not until June. When is yours?"

"January fifteenth. You never said what day yours was."

I coat my toast with hazelnut spread. "The seventh."

He unplugs his phone and programs it. I smile at him as I eat.

"What?" He laughs.

"You're cute."

He steals a bite of my toast. "You're gorgeous. So, what kind of tattoo would you get?"

"I was thinking about getting something for my dad. One of his favorite things to do was garden. He loved the idea of taking something from a seed and nurturing it into a plant or a flower. Those lilies, in the front yard of my mom's house, my dad and I planted those together."

"So maybe a lily?"

I nod, lifting my mug to my lips.

"Where would you get it?"

I set my mug down and turn in my stool, sliding the strap of my tank top down. "I was thinking my shoulder blade."

His lips grace the spot I bare. "I know a guy if you want to do it."

I spin back around, pulling my strap back up. "Does it hurt?"

"It's not like a flu shot. It feels like rough rubbing." He points to a part of his that touches his side. "It hurt like a bitch right here."

"Do you think my shoulder will hurt?"

He dips his head down to kiss me. "Maybe a little."

"I'll think about it."

He moves to sit on the stool next to mine, pulling me into his lap. "After lunch do you want to start moving your stuff?"

My mouth drops. "You want me to move in today?"

He steals another bite of my toast and nods.

I bring my lips to his ear. "You jump, I'll jump."

CHAPTER
24

CLAY

Her face splits into a smile guilty of stealing my heart. I indulge in a Nutella flavored kiss so heated, we impatiently fumble out of enough clothes to make clumsy love right there in the kitchen. We enjoy a shared shower after since her elbow somehow ended up covered in Nutella.

Because I won't take no for an answer, we head to a local furniture store to get her a dresser to match mine. I want to argue when she goes to pay for it but know better. As we drive back, she gets quieter than normal.

"Not second guessing moving in with me are you?"

"I want to split the mortgage," she blurts out as we pull into the garage.

"No can do," I reply, parking.

She starts to argue but I'm already out of the truck. She jumps out to join me around back.

"I want to contribute."

I grab her hand, pulling it to my lips and kiss it. "You being here is all I need."

She stops, digging her heels in as I try to keep walking. "Clay Bradshaw. You will let me pay my way. What's half of the mortgage?"

I crouch down in front of her and pull her over my shoulder, and then keep walking. "Zero. Your half of the mortgage is zero."

I set her down in front of the storage cage. "You are being stubborn. Why won't you let me help out? It's only fair if I'm living here, too."

I unlock the gate and pull a dolly out before relocking the gate. She follows me arguing all the way back to my truck.

I pull the tailgate down and tug of war style pull the blanket the dresser rests on toward the edge of the gate. I carefully lower the dresser onto the ground, balling up the blanket and tucking it into the top drawer.

"Clay," she groans.

I turn to her grabbing both of her hands and bringing them to my lips, looking directly into her eyes. "I don't have a mortgage. That's why you can't pay half."

She tilts her head. "Why didn't you just say that in the first place?"

I shrug, shifting the dresser onto the dolly before flipping my tailgate back up. "You're cute when you're annoyed."

She smirks. "So, what can I pay?"

We make our way to the elevator. "If you must, we can split the condo fee. It covers the heat, air conditioning, trash, and maintenance stuff."

"Deal, and how do you not have a mortgage?"

I push the button for our floor. "It's a one-bedroom condo so it wasn't that expensive to begin with. I got a fifteen-year mortgage but threw extra money at it when I had it. I don't spend a lot and I make decent money."

"I feel like asking how much you make; but I can't think of a way to do it without it sounding tacky and that I care about money."

I pass her the keys and follow her with the dresser. "It can vary from year to year depending on how many jobs I take on, but I average out at just under a hundred grand a year."

Her mouth drops. "That's a lot of money. That's way more than what I make."

I smirk; plucking the keys from her hands, I unlock the door. "I know how much you make."

She holds the door for me as I navigate through it with the dresser. "I don't want to be deadweight."

I stop, lowering the dolly. "You're being silly."

She closes the door as an excuse to turn away from me, her shoulders sagging.

"Hey." I turn her, lifting her chin up until our eyes meet. "Don't make this into something it isn't."

"Are you too good for me?"

"Babe, you are so out of my league, it isn't funny." I kiss her sweetly. "I'm lucky you're slumming with me."

She throws her arms around my neck. "I love you."

"All good?" She nods, so I kiss her. "I love you."

Her new dresser isn't an exact match to mine but they work together. Once we have it situated, we leave for lunch, me pulling the dolly behind us. When we get to my parents' house, we find Maggie sulking.

"What's with the sad face?" I ask, sitting next to her on the couch.

She glances around before answering. "Did my mom die?"

"Why would you ask that?" I inquire.

"She hasn't come to take me back."

Courtney's eyes find mine over the top of Maggie's head. I blink rapidly, my heart breaking for her.

Taking both of her little hands and holding them in mine. "Your mom loves you so much, sweetheart; she just has some problems to work out."

"Did she go to the place where you stop taking drugs?"

I drop my head to rest my forehead on our joined hands. No ten year old should have to wonder if their mom is in rehab or not.

Lifting my head, I take a shaky breath. "Maggie, I'm not going to lie to you. I'm not sure where your mom went, but if you ask me to, I'll go find her. Do you want me to?"

Courtney moves around the sofa to sit next to me, putting her hand on my back. Maggie has pinched her eyes shut.

"Maggie?" I ask gently.

"Am I a bad person, if I say no?"

I gather her up in my arms, rocking her. "Don't ever think that, not for one moment."

My mom pauses in the doorway, looking at us, her hands pressed to her chest.

"Promise?" Maggie whispers.

"Cross my heart," I reply. "Did you want to stay here and order a pizza?"

She lifts her head, shaking it. "Can we still go out to lunch?"

I stand, taking her with me. "Course we can. Besides." I glance back at Courtney. "We have something to celebrate."

She follows my eyes to Courtney, gasping excitedly. "Did you ask Courtney to marry you?"

Marry Courtney? Why the hell not?

Given all the bullshit I've had to deal with recently, she has been the one thing that has kept me sane. I love her; I can't imagine my life without her. Last thing I want to do is rush her. Moving in together is a big step on its own. When the time is right, I'll ask her.

CHAPTER 25

My eyes widen.

He frowns. "I did not."

"Oh." Her expression falls.

"But," he continues, "I did ask her to move in with me and she said yes."

A smile blooms across her cheek. "You did?"

He nods. "I sure did."

After he sets her down, she pauses and looks at me with a serious expression. "Did your mom say you could?"

I blink and glance at Clay. "I haven't asked her yet."

Her shoulders sag. "What if she says no?"

I lean over to rub her arm. "She won't, sweetie."

She looks between us. "Are you pregnant?"

Clay chokes. "What? No, no, Courtney is not pregnant."

I stand. "Anyone hungry?"

Clay and Maggie are on my heels as Judy pulls me in for a hug on our way out the door. "We are so happy you two found each other."

Clay leans down to kiss her cheek before taking my hand and we follow Maggie out to the truck. We keep the conversation light over lunch. Maggie admits she's bored living with Pete and Judy, something about not having Wi-Fi or a TV station she likes.

We invite her over for a sleepover next Saturday night. Then we can drop her back off after Sunday lunch. After lunch, instead of just dropping Maggie off, we stay and hang out at Clay's parents' house for a bit. Maggie shows Clay stuff she's working on for school while I excuse myself to call my mom.

I don't want us coming over to pick up my stuff to blindside her. When I tell her, she surprises me by telling me Clay had talked to her about it last week. That sneaky boy, I had no idea. She isn't surprised I have said yes, but she does take a few minutes to caution me about moving too fast.

I can't explain why everything with Clay seems so right. I only know it doesn't feel like we're rushing at all. I don't tell her this because she would only argue it. Instead, I agree to take it slow even though I'm still moving in with him.

I call Jen next. She is even less enthusiastic. She and Justin had a fight; so instead of us talking about my good news, the call turns into twenty minutes of me listening to her grumble about him. Clay comes over to sit by me after fifteen minutes and I lean into him. It makes listening to her easier somehow.

When I hang up, Clay tilts his face toward mine. "Ready to move in with me?"

I throw myself into his kiss. "Yes."

We break apart at the sound of a cleared throat behind us. It's Clay's mom. I almost mounted her son on her couch. I hazard a glance in her direction; and even though I'm still embarrassed, it's a relief to see she doesn't look annoyed.

We say our goodbyes and head to my house. My mom has pulled out some boxes since I spoke to her. Once I fill a box, Clay carries it down to his truck. I have more now than the last time I unpacked, but not by much. When he puts the last box is in his truck, my mom walks out with us.

"Are you sure you know what you're doing?"

I shake my head; I know there are no guarantees. "The only thing I know for sure is I love him."

My car is still at his...our...condo. I give her another hug before climbing in. Our hands find each other somewhere in the middle. We don't let go. He has me wait by the truck as he uses the dolly to move my boxes up. I give him a kiss with each reload, the intensity ratcheting up after each trip.

When the last box is stacked and his truck is locked, we go together. Groaning, I grind against him as he pins me to the wall in the elevator. Who knew moving could be such a turn-on? Once we're inside, the boxes are forgotten as he lifts me and carries me to the couch. We struggle out of our clothes franticly; my need to have him inside me is intense.

There's no foreplay. My need for him to fill me seems only equaled by his desire to do so. Our impatience is quenched once we are joined. Whatever need to rush, which pushed us at first, dissipates. We slow our movements. My hands drift to hold his face as a gentle pace takes over.

We're almost nose-to-nose. I get lost in the ocean of his eyes as, like waves lapping my shore, he pushes into and then retreats from me. I felt so lost and fractured when I met him, but somehow this beautiful man has solved the puzzle I didn't know I was.

For so long, I told myself I was happy. I told myself things were good enough. After Mike and I split up, I thought my future happiness was something almost unattainable, a maybe someday kind of thing. My maybe some days will never live up to the real thing Clay and I have.

I loved Mike. I even mourn his absence from my life; but what we had was a shell of something real. I know with the same certainty that the sun will rise each day that Clay loves me. As pressure builds up within me, a tingling wave peaks, and then crashes pulling Clay's release from him as well.

Before long, we untangle so I can start unpacking and Clay can start dinner. He isn't making anything fancy, just a baked chicken and rice dish. Once it's in the oven, he comes to hang out with me in our room. The boxes we moved today are mainly clothes. He sprawls out across the bed as I fill the new dresser.

I make a pile on the bed of things needing to be hung. He figures it out and starts hanging them up for me. There isn't enough storage space for everything, so I keep one box out for the summer stuff we can store somewhere else. The food is done before I am. Clay turns on the TV and we sit on the sofa to eat, our plates on the coffee table.

"Should we get a kitchen table?" Clay asks.

"Do you feel like you need to step up your game now that I'm here?" I tease.

He swipes my fork and sets it on my plate before pinning me beneath him. "You want me to step up my game?"

I pull his face down to mine. "You got all the game I can handle, babe."

He kisses me soundly before pulling back. "I don't know how to live with someone, and I want to do it right."

I melt and tug him back to me; between kisses, I ask, "Why do you think we need a new table?"

He leans back, holding himself up with one elbow and reaches to trace my lips with his fingertip. "I think I'd rather watch you eat than watch TV."

Eating is the last thing I'm thinking about right now. "I'd rather watch you than TV any day, too."

He stands, pulling me up with him and walks us over to the windows. "What about a small table right here?"

I press both of my hands to the window and look over at him. "Right here?"

He ducks under my arm so his back is to the glass and pulls me tightly into his arms. "You're right. We definitely need this space free." He tilts his head to the left. "Maybe over there."

"I like the way you think."

Later that evening, comfortably tucked into Clay's side as we watch TV, my mind wanders to Mike. As if he can sense the shift in my mood Clay asks if I'm okay.

"Well," I cringe. "I want to call Mike; however, I won't if it would bother you."

"Why do you want to talk to him?"

I take a deep breath. "I wonder if what he did was an attempt to get my attention. Yes, if it was, it worked. I want, no I need, some closure."

He reaches for my hand. "I respect whatever you want to do, babe. Do you want me here when you call him?"

Comforted by his support, I nod. "Please. I'd like to do it now, if that's okay."

"Of course."

After so long together, I'm still able to remember his number off the top of my head. He answers right away.

"Mike."

He's surprised to hear my voice, his own voice wobbling as he says my name.

"I heard about what happened, Mike; and I wanted to hear from you how you're doing."

He assures me that he is alright, that he's recovering. The desperation in his tone makes it hard for me to believe him. It's as if he's trying to sell me something. When he changes the subject to tell me how much he misses me I have to stop him.

"I only wanted to call and let you know I'm not holding any grudges. I want you to get help if you need it so you can be happy someday. I'm not implying I think we'll ever be friends; but I want the last conversation I have with you to be a good one and not one where things are said out of anger," I explain.

During our relationship, I was never this confident, this clear; and when he stutters that it was an accident, that he's getting his life back together and his hope, that maybe we could get back together I have to interrupt him again.

"Mike, I've moved on. I'm extremely happy in my new relationship; and I hope someday you find your happiness as well."

He repeats apologies and what he did to me was a mistake. I didn't have it in my heart to cut him off again, so I quietly wait for him to finish while Clay holds my hand.

When he finishes speaking, I say, "We can't undo what happened. We can only move forward."

He starts crying and telling me, he still loves me. Knowing what I do about love, it's clear to me he loved the idea of us more than he ever truly loved me.

"I have to go, Mike. Please, try to move on with your life. Goodbye."

I wait for him to say goodbye back, which thankfully he does.

"Are you okay?" Clay asks, pulling me into his lap.

"I feel drained."

"Let's call it an early night," he says, lifting me and carrying me to our room.

I bury my face into his neck. "We forgot curtains."

His chest shakes as he tries not to laugh. "Want to pick some up after work today?"

"I think we'll have to special order them," I mumble against his skin.

"Maybe my mom can make them. She likes doing stuff like that."

Not thinking, I pop my head up, only to quickly tuck my face into his neck when the sun shines in my eyes. "Really?"

He drops a kiss to the top of my head. "She'll probably make them today if I tell her they're for you."

"What? No way," I argue.

"You think I'm joking? Want me to call her right now?"

I shake my head. "It's early, you might wake her."

His body beneath me shifts slightly as he reaches for his phone. "Nah, she's probably on her second cup of coffee."

I eavesdrop on their conversation as an excuse not to get up. He holds the phone away from his ear and turns up the volume. Just as he said, the moment he tells her the lack of curtains in the bedroom annoys me she offers to make some. She even asks him if she should call me to find out what kind of curtains I would like.

"She's right here, Mom. Do you want me to ask her?"

I put my hand out and he sets his phone in it. "Hey, Judy."

"Hi, darling. How are you?"

I lift my eyes to Clay's, his arm holding me snuggly to his side. "Never better. How are you?"

She updates me on Maggie, the pain in her voice clear through the phone as she admits there still has been no contact from Nicole. Clay and Pete are going to drop by her apartment today. They are also trying to figure out what to say to Maggie about Grant.

She is smart enough to know something's is up when they try to swab her cheek. They are going to see if they can do it one night while she sleeps. The only fear is she might wake up during it.

"Hopefully, she won't wake up. She and Amber both slept hard the night of the concert."

This seems to relax her and she goes on to ask about the curtains. One thing I love about Clay's place is how simple everything is. When she asks what color I'd want, I cover the mouth of the phone and ask him if the same color of the walls would be good.

Whatever you want, he mouths, smoothing my hair back.

After I tell her, she asks how tall the windows are and I pass the phone back to Clay since I don't know. He promises to measure them for her and says goodbye for me before hanging up.

"See?" he asks, setting his phone on the bedside table. "The second she knew they were for you, she was all over it."

"Your mom rocks." I kiss his neck lightly before getting up.

I envy his ability to work from home. He doesn't even have to get dressed. Working with Pete is fun though, much more relaxed than my last job. Only bummer is now that Pete is back and spending more time in the office and not the bays, I know they don't really need me. I plan to start a new job search between customers today. Now that I know there will only be positive stuff from Mr. Fulson's office, applying for positions seems less stressful.

Lingering in bed has me running late. I take my toast to go and hurry out the door after a quick kiss at the door. I wasn't able to find a visitor spot and parked on the street, a block up. Being stuck behind every driver who is driving under the speed limit in North Carolina doesn't help either.

I'm fifteen minutes late when I dash into the office. "I'm so sorry," I mumble, tossing my purse behind the counter.

Pete lifts his hands, smiling. "Judy called and said you might be running late and it's her fault for talking your ear off."

My mouth drops; guess she does like me. We get right to work. My favorite pickup truck pulls in just shy of lunchtime. I prop my chin in my palm and watch Clay strut across the parking lot. He catches my eye half way and grins.

"This is a nice surprise." I lean forward as he walks in so he can kiss me over the counter.

After a thorough hello kiss, he leans back. "I thought I'd surprise you for lunch."

I grab my purse and slip off my stool before walking back to see if we can get something for his dad while we're out. I know something is wrong the moment I peek my head in the door. Pete is bent over his desk, his breathing labored.

"Clay, call 911!" I shout, rushing over to Pete's side.

He isn't able to speak but remains conscious the five minutes it takes for the ambulance to arrive. Clay tells Victor, the apprentice Pete hired to head home early today. I call Judy while Clay quickly locks up before we follow the ambulance to the hospital.

Since their house is closer to the hospital than we are, Judy beats us there. She is pacing when we arrive. There is no news from the ambulance yet other than confirmation Pete is now being seen by an ER doctor. Clay and I get Judy to sit and flank her.

I shift in my chair trying to find a more comfortable position. We don't wait long before someone comes back for Judy. Pete is still being evaluated, but he has not lost consciousness.

"Why don't you go back with your mom?" I offer.

He glances back and forth between us before giving me a hug. "Are you sure?"

"Absolutely, I can hang out here. Just text me and keep me posted."

He nods. "Before I go back there I'm going to call Amber's Mom and see if Maggie can ride home from school and stay the night with them."

"I could go pick her up instead if you want," I offer.

"Thank you, but I'm not sure how long we'll be here and I don't want to worry her. Are you sure you'll be okay out here?"

After I nod his lips find mine and with a quick press of a kiss, he's gone. I move to a quiet corner of the waiting room. I'm torn between surfing the web on my phone to pass the time and being afraid to run down the battery in case Clay needs me. Luckily, there's a TV. It's set to a hospital channel, which highlights the different services they offer in the community.

I don't realize I've dozed off until someone sits next to me. I jump, already inching away before I realize it's Clay.

He drapes his arm across my shoulders and tucks me into his side.

"Hey. How's your dad?"

My heart starts racing when he doesn't immediately reply; but instead, presses his lips to the side of my head.

I pull back, tipping my face up to his. "Is he all right?"

Inhaling through his nose, he nods before squeezing his eyes shut and pinching the bridge of his nose. It dawns on me how dark it is and how long we must have been here. I put my arms around his neck and pull him to me. He buries his face in my neck and clings to me.

I just hold him, this man I love. I know his dad is okay; but whatever happened behind those doors, shook Clay. I will hold him for as long as he needs to process what it was.

"It's okay. Everything is okay. I'm here. I've got you," I murmur on a loop until the tension slowly ebbs from his shoulders and he slightly sags into me before pulling back.

He rubs his face and blinks a few times, as he clears his throat. "He had a mild heart attack."

I reach for his hand. "But he's okay, right?"

He nods again and stands pulling me with him. "They set up a recliner in his room for my mom. I'm exhausted. Let's head home."

"Do you want me to drive?"

He contemplates his response before digging into his pocket and passing me his keys. I drive a small sedan and have never driven something as big as his truck before. Nervous as I am, I want to take care of him and I know he's too wiped to drive.

"Should we call Victor?" I ask, pulling out.

"I don't even know his number."

"I have it, grab my phone."

I glance over at him when he doesn't move. "What?"

"Already got the new guy's number programed in your phone?" He jokes.

I laugh. "I guess I have a thing for mechanics."

He adjusts his seat to more of an incline, relaxing as he lays his head back so he's facing me. "Is it because we're good with our hands?"

"You got it. Now, please call him. I'm sure he's worried about your dad."

He peeks into my purse, and grabs my phone. "Do you think we should open up tomorrow?"

I chew on my lip as I try to recall our appointment schedule by memory. "I think there are a couple customers scheduled for pickup. We should at least take care of them." I turn my head toward him. "What do you think?"

He sits up and leaning over the console, surprises me with a kiss on the cheek. "I think you're amazing."

I smack my lips at him as he dials Victor and updates him on Pete's condition and the game plan for tomorrow. He surprises me by telling him he'll be coming in as well.

"Will that be okay with your projects?" I ask after he hangs up.

He drops my phone back in my purse. "Should be fine."

He's quiet as we pull into the garage and in the elevator up to the condo.

"Doing okay?" I slip my hand into his.

He looks down at his feet before shrugging. "Still trying to process it."

CHAPTER
26

CLAY

This is it, the final straw. He needs to sell the place and retire. Maybe after today my mom will finally put her foot down and make him stop working. It kills me how stubborn he is. Can't he see how not caring about his health is affecting all of us?

Maggie needs stability and security, not losing her grandpa to a heart attack.

"Babe?"

Shit, I completely missed what Courtney said.

Dragging my hand across my face, I shake my head. "I'm sorry; I didn't hear what you said."

She drops her purse by the door and puts both of her hands on my chest, leaning into me as she lifts up her lips up to gently kiss me.

"Are you hungry? Or do you want to crash?"

My arms circle her waist. "Crashing sounds perfect."

Neither of us moves though. We just stand there, holding each other until my knees feel like they're going to buckle under me from exhaustion. Stepping back she takes my hand and leads me toward my, scratch that, our room. I'm half-dead as she undresses me.

It's enlightening, being so taken care of by someone who loves you. I need to figure out a way to thank her for everything. Every day she is becoming my rock, my safe place.

I try not to think about Mike and the once over he did to her self-worth. Courtney is a woman to be cherished. I hate he didn't; but if he had, there's no guarantee she'd be in my life right now. My life, hasn't been easy with my dad being ill and the whole mess with Nicole.

I need to make sure she isn't putting herself last while she's busy taking care of me. I need to take care of her too.

I don't move to lie down until she ready to as well. It's all I can do to stay awake for her.

"Come here." I motion as she starts for her side of the bed.

She crawls into my lap and I take her with me as I stretch out onto our bed.

I bury my face in her hair. "Thank you. I love you so much. You kept me from losing it today."

"Shh," she murmurs, nuzzling into my chest.

"I mean it. Thank you."

"Want something to eat, drink?" she asks still taking care of me.

"I'm not sure my stomach could handle anything right now," I answer truthfully.

Seeing my dad like that isn't an image that will go away any time soon. I thought he was going to die.

"You should try to get something down. How about some tea?"

I nod, more for her than me. If it'll make her feel better to take care of me, I'll let her. I don't know what I would have done without her today. I'm sure she is the only reason I haven't lost it.

She slips away and I mourn the loss of her touch, but she's back quickly with a cup of tea for each of us.

"I added a splash of milk so it won't be too hot," she says, passing me my mug.

I hazard a sip, relieved when it stays down. The warmth flows down my chest and into my gut. She's right. I needed this. My lips are dry against the ceramic rim as I drink more. The tension that had coiled itself deep into my muscles slowly ebbs. It isn't gone but it no longer hurts to breathe.

"Come here." I motion to my lap and she crawls over to me.

"Are you okay?" she asks, settling herself against me.

"Better now." I set my mug on the table next to the bed and run my nose up and down the side of her neck.

"That was pretty scary." She reaches for her mug and takes a drink.

I nod, my chin touching the top of her shoulder with each downward motion.

"He'll be just fine," she says, reassuring me.

"I know."

The doctors are adamant he is out of danger, but I'm still waiting for my brain to process that. Right now it's still stuck on not knowing what I'd do if I lost my dad. We don't always see eye to eye but he is still larger than life to me. I lean back and take another sip of my tea.

"Feeling hungry yet?" Courtney asks.

I shake my head. "This is about all I can manage right now. Are you hungry?"

"No, I'm not. Just worrying about you."

"All I want to do is pass out."

She slips off my lap and starts undressing me. I go to stop her but she pushes my hands away. My shoes come off first, then my socks. She unbuttons my jeans and slides the zipper down next. If I weren't so bone tired, this would be turning me on. I'll have to remember to tell her that later.

I shift, lifting my hips as she eases my jeans off me. Then I lean forward for her to pull my shirt off over my head. Once I'm down to my boxers, she tucks me in and undresses herself. I watch with heavy lids as she pulls on one of my old shirts and climbs into bed with me. I pull her tightly against me and try to hide my yawn from her.

"Shh," she coos, dragging her fingertips slowly up and down my back until I pass out.

CHAPTER 27

Pete is home from the hospital. Judy has had her hands full taking care of him, so Maggie has been spending Friday and Saturday nights with us. Clay and I let her stay up real late one Friday night and swabbed her cheek once she passed out. We are all anxiously waiting for the results of the paternity test.

There has been no sign of Nicole. It kills me how well Maggie is taking the fact her mother just took off. That's the hope, that she left, verses something bad happening to her. Clay's family hasn't filed a missing person report with the police. They want to confirm if Grant is her father before pursuing any legal custody claim on Maggie.

Clay can't admit out loud what we all know; unless she comes back clean and ready to stay that way, it's probably best for Maggie that Nicole stays gone. During Pete's stay in the hospital, Clay was coming into the shop everyday but is now down to Tuesdays and Thursdays.

My eyes find him through the window into the bays. His back is to me while he leans over the engine of Mrs. Baker's Camaro. I don't think I'll ever tire of the way his t-shirt stretches across the wide expanse of his shoulders. I was only joking when I told him I was into mechanics. The funny thing is how truly turned on I get watching him work on cars.

It doesn't take much for me to imagine those calloused fingertips on my skin. I blush when he suddenly looks up, catching my obvious stare. He laughs, making Victor look over at him confused by his sudden outburst. He shakes his head, slowly walks over to the sink in the shop, and holding my gaze, leisurely, methodically washes his hands before heading my way.

My mouth drops, he has plans for those fingers. Desire pools in my belly as I turn my back to him. I try, and fail, at pretending to be busy. I glance over my shoulder at him as he walks into the office. "See something you like?"

"Huh?" I act as if I have no idea what he's talking about.

Undeterred, he advances on me, tipping my chin up to look at him. When he claims my lips, I can't hold back my lusty moan in response. There is no place I've ever been more comfortable than in his arms.

"Office?" he asks, already lifting me.

Not breaking our kiss, my legs wrapping tightly around his waist is answer enough. Once we're in the back office, the door locked behind us, my legs slide to the floor. Clay's hands ease their journey southward, still supporting my weight.

"I love this fucking skirt." Clay growls against my lips, his hands drifting up under it now that my feet are on the ground.

"Babe," I plead, needing him.

He captures my bottom lip between his teeth briefly before lifting his mouth from mine. My busy hands have freed his cock as he pulls my panties to the side and pushes two fingers into me. I ride his one hand as his other pulls the front of my shirt down to expose my bra. My grip on his cock tightens as I stroke him. He dips his head, latching on to my nipple through the mesh of my bra.

Clutching his head to my chest, I come hard. My body is still pulsing as he pulls his fingers from me, spinning me so my back is to his chest, and bending me over the desk. I have no time to mourn the loss of his fingers because now I'm deliciously full of his cock.

Stretching my arms across the desk, I grip the edge as he pounds me, lifting onto my tiptoes so he can go even deeper. His nails bite into the flesh of my hips as he powers into me. His pace is frantic, turning me on even more. Barely coming down from my last orgasm, I find myself barreling toward another.

"God, Clay," I pant, pushing back against him each time his body presses into mine.

Fast and rough, slow and teasing, every way Clay touches me makes me want him even more. He groans, his hips bucking wildly, as he comes. Neither of us moves for a moment while we catch our breath. He recovers before I do and, pushing my hair aside, leans over to kiss the back of my neck.

"You are so fucking sexy," he whispers against my skin.

I reach back and tangle my fingers in his hair, shifting my hips against him.

"You keep that up and we'll never get back to work," he warns.

"Promise?" I tease.

He didn't shave this morning so his stubble tickles my neck as he nuzzles it. I pout when his weight leaves me and he slips from me. Grabbing a couple tissues from the desk, he crouches behind me and cleans me, stroking one hand up and down my leg as he kisses it.

When I start to stand, he squeezes my legs. "I want these wrapped around my head tonight."

My mouth drops, it takes me a moment to recover. "And you say I'm bad. How am I going to get any work done now?"

He fixes my skirt while I check my top. Once I'm properly dressed again, I turn to tuck him back into his pants, my hand lingering on his cock while Clay leans down to kiss me. When he starts to deepen the kiss, I smack his arm pulling back.

Trying, and failing to be stern, I say, "Back to work, boss man."

He pouts, making me laugh as we nonchalantly exit the back office. I peek through the window to the bays and relax when I see Victor still preoccupied with the transmission tune-up he was working on. Clay gives my ass a squeeze as he moves past me to head back into the bays. He pauses in the doorway, catching my gaze, and slowly lifts his fingers to his nose. Sporting a naughty grin, he inhales deeply and winks at me.

My mouth drops as the door swings closed behind him, blocking him from my view. Not wanting to embarrass myself in front of Victor is the only thing keeping me from following Clay and mounting him on the hood of Mrs. Baker's Camaro.

My phone distracts me from my inappropriate thoughts.

Thankful she didn't call fifteen minutes ago, I blush when I see it's Clay's mom.

"Hey, Judy."

"The results came."

Hurrying toward the bay, I knock on the window to get Clay's attention. "Have you opened it yet?"

"We have, I was hoping you could put Clay on the phone. I tried to call his a minute ago and it went straight to voicemail."

When he turns, I motion for him to come to me. "He's in the bays. Give me a minute to get him."

Clay's at the door in no time, a frown on his face when he notices the phone at my ear.

"It's your mom. They got the paternity results," I explain, handing him my phone.

He doesn't waste time with pleasantries. "Is Grant the father?"

I clutch at his arm and he looks down at me, shaking his head. My relief is bittersweet. As complicated as Grant being Maggie's father would have been, at least we would know.

Clay holds me close as he finishes talking to his mom. When he hangs up, he leans down to press his lips to the top of my head.

"Are you okay?" I ask.

His breath rushes out, pushing past my ear. "I'm pissed off at my sister. I hope she at least thought Grant was the father. If not..." His voice trails off.

My mind completes the sentence; she trapped an innocent man with her lies.

"Did your mom know if Grant has heard yet?"

He pulls back from me, leaning his hip on the counter. "He probably got the same letter."

I shake my head. "I wonder what it would feel like to go from thinking you're a father to knowing you're not from a letter."

Clay's eyes soften and he tugs me into his arms, resting his head on mine. "Maybe he's relieved."

I don't argue; but part of me is certain Grant wouldn't have begun to fight for her, if he hadn't wanted to. "Still no sign of Nicole?"

His silence, my answer. With Nicole gone what will happen to Maggie?

Clay kisses me once more before returning to the bays. There's work to be done. I'm distracted. I close and open the same customer record three times before remembering to call Mr. Stone to let him know his Jetta is ready. After I finish the call, I look out into the bays, wondering if Clay is as distracted as I am.

To anyone else he would seem unaffected, but to me, his movements are hesitant. He's pensive, pausing more often than he normally would as he works. A simple oil change and transmission flush take him twice as long as it normally would. His movements appear frustrated and jerky. Watching him is driving me nuts, so I give up and go out to the bays. Victor sees me coming and steps outside for a smoke break.

"Babe," I murmur, before putting my hands on his shoulders so I don't startle him.

His head dips forward, his hands bracing his weight against the car. Wrapping my arms around him, I mold my front to his back and hold him. I kiss his shoulder before turning my cheek to rest my face against him.

"I'm so angry at her," he finally admits.

Saying nothing, I hug him tighter and give him the air to say aloud the things that have been weighing on him. It's like a bottle of water, fallen over, words like a stream, rushing out.

"How could she do this to Maggie? She's never been gone this long. I don't know what to do, Courtney."

Making sympathetic sounds, I continue to hold him.

"My parents can't handle the stress of raising Maggie. Hell, my dad needs to sell this place and retire. There's no way he'll do that if he has to worry about paying for college. That leaves me, Courtney."

I stiffen and feel his body tense.

"I'm scared taking on the responsibility of Maggie will mess up what we've got going. I love you and I don't want to lose you."

Feeling as though I've been silent long enough, I pull back, pushing at him until he turns to face me. My hands reach up to cup his face, his lips turning briefly to kiss the palm on one before gazing down at me.

"I'm not going anywhere. If you want to do this, I'm with you."

His eyes widen briefly, tension easing from his stance before he lowers his lips to mine. My hands move from his face to wrap around his neck as his arms band around my waist, lifting me.

The click of the side door opening, and then clicking again as it's quickly pulled shut, lets us know Victor has finished his cigarette. He's probably waiting outside right now for us to finish up. I start laughing first against his lips, his body shakes as he still holds me once his laughs join mine.

Walking me back to the office, further proof chivalry isn't dead; he kisses me quickly on the forehead before hurrying back into the bays. He works quickly, no longer burdened with the worries from before. He's only here helping his dad but I'll never tire of watching him work on cars. Now, because he's in a better mood, it's hard not to watch.

Victor cranked up the radio after Clay popped his head out the side door to let him know I was back in the office. I think we embarrassed poor Victor. The music gives him an excuse to avoid small talk after seeing Clay's tongue down my throat. The rest of the day goes by quickly.

We're in Clay's truck and on the way to his parents' house. He wants to run the idea of Maggie coming to stay with us full-time by them. I'm not worried about his dad; his mom, I think, will pose the true opposition to the idea.

"What do you think they'll say?"

His fingers drum the steering wheel. "We just moved in together. Moving Maggie again will unsettle her. We only have a one bedroom. We aren't married..."

He stops at my sudden intake of breath. He said marriage. I love him. He knows me; but after everything that happened with Mike, the whole concept of a lifelong commitment scares me. I'm happy living together. Will that be good enough for Clay?

He deflects smoothly. "Maybe you can hang out with my dad and Maggie while I talk to her alone."

I nod. "Sounds good."

After he parks, I lean over to give him a quick kiss on the cheek for encouragement. Once we're inside, we head straight for the den. Maggie jumps up to give me a hug. The idea of having kids always seemed so far away when Mike and I were together. There was a plan, marriage, and then kids. When the marriage planning never started, I didn't let myself think about stuff that should come after.

I let Maggie lead me to the sofa so I can hear all about everything I have missed over the last couple of days. Clay uses this time as an opportunity to catch his mom's attention and motion for her to meet him in the kitchen.

Maggie didn't notice, still excited to share her stories, but Pete didn't miss a thing though. His eyes follow her out of the room before turning back to meet mine.

"Courtney?"

I blink, looking back at Maggie. "Sorry, sweetie. I missed that last part."

Now, because she's certain she has my full attention, she continues, "There's this movie coming out I really want to see."

"Cool, what's it called?" I ask.

She looks down and starts making a circle with her toe in the plush of the carpet. "Well, the thing is, it's rated PG-13 and I was wondering if maybe…"

I stop her before she goes any further. "We should check with Clay first."

She frowns. "But, all the kids at my school are going."

Pete pats the arm of his recliner until she looks over at him. "You heard Courtney, don't argue."

Crossing her arms across her chest, she leans further back into the sofa. "Yes, Grandpa."

I reach over to squeeze her knee and she gives me a small smile. If this is the worst, a ten year old asking to go to a PG-13 movie, maybe I can handle it. It's a snap generalization. Her battles won't always be this easy, but Maggie is a little girl who deserves someone fighting for her.

CHAPTER 28

CLAY

I talked to my mom about Maggie moving in with us. She didn't flat out say no but she didn't say yes either. I'm giving her some time to let the idea settle before I bring it up again.

"Are you sure about this?"

Courtney reaches across the table to grasp my hand, nodding.

Most couples follow a certain pattern, dating, moving in together, getting engaged, marriage, and then children. Not for Courtney and me. We are going straight from moving in together to, hopefully, having a ten year old.

I never would have considered taking Maggie full-time, if I wasn't with Courtney. Well, maybe I would have considered it, but it would have scared the fuck out of me.

What do I know about raising a girl? Nothing, I know nothing. Somehow, with Courtney by my side makes taking care of Maggie less scary. She could handle all of the girl stuff and I could handle scaring off any guys interested in dating her. It seems like a fair compromise.

"I'm still not sure if my mom will go for it."

Courtney releases my hand and picks up her burger, pausing before taking a bite to say, "We'll just have to convince her."

I fiddle with a fry, dipping it in ketchup, but not moving to eat it. "What if Maggie doesn't want to live with us full-time?"

She holds a hand up over her mouth as she chews, her eyes doing all the talking.

"Fine," I concede. "I know she'll want to live with us for the Wi-Fi alone."

Courtney laughs behind her hand.

"Do you think we should have a plan of attack when it comes to talking to my mom?"

She shakes her head, swallowing. "Nothing crazy. We should think about what her arguments will be, so we're ready to squash them."

I grin. "Squash them?"

She nods. "Like a bug."

That's my girl.

We head straight from the diner to my parents' house. Maggie's at a birthday party, so we won't have to worry about her listening in.

My mom's sitting at the kitchen table, tea laid out. She stands and comes to kiss Courtney on the cheek when we walk in. Me, I get a wary stare in greeting.

"Hey, Mom." I ignore her stare and kiss the top of her head.

She lifts one head up to squeeze my side.

"So, what did you kids want to talk about?"

The use of kids was intentional. I glance over at Courtney to see if she picked up on it as well. She's cool as a cucumber.

"Can I pour you a cup, Judy?" she asks, reaching for the teapot.

My mom nods and looks up at me when I clear my throat.

"Have you thought about Maggie, maybe, moving in with us?"

Her shoulders droop. "I don't know if that's a good idea."

After Courtney passes the cup of tea to her, she reaches out to hold her hand. Courtney briefly hesitates before placing her hand in my mom's.

"You have made my son so happy." My mom reaches her other hand out for mine. "I worry this is too much for you both to take on so early in your relationship. You both need time for yourselves."

I squeeze her hand. "We know, Mom. Maybe we could work something out to where Maggie spends a few nights a month here."

My mom frowns as she considers it. "But, where would she sleep. ? You live in a one-bedroom condo, in the city."

Courtney and I had talked about this over lunch. "We talked about it. We can sell the condo and move to a place where she could have her own room."

"You want to buy a house together?" She arches a brow looking back and forth at us.

I put my arm around Courtney, and kiss the top of her shoulder. "Yes, Mom, we want to buy a house together."

"But you aren't even engaged," she argues.

Courtney blushes. "We're aware of that."

She frowns. "Courtney, you know I adore you. I worry you two are rushing into this. Taking care of Maggie would be a big change to your relationship. You two should be free to enjoy your time together and not have to worry about a ten year old."

I start to talk, but Courtney squeezes my leg and looks at me. "Judy, I adore you too, and Maggie. We want this, we really do. Clay and I have thought long and hard about what taking care of Maggie would mean. We already take her some weekends; and yes, we do understand that having her full-time would be a big change, but it's what we want to do."

I tighten my arm around her. "Please think about it, Mom. Dad has been so stressed out recently. You could focus on taking care of him without having to worry about anything else. If we really needed a break for a date night here and there, we could always call you or have her spend the night at a friend's house. We want her."

She doesn't say a word for the longest time before taking a deep breath. "Let me talk to your father about it and see what he thinks."

Courtney sags against me. My dad's a piece of cake. If my mom is open to the idea, he'll be no problem.

"So are you two going to get married?"

"Mom," I snap, as Courtney tenses right back up next to me.

"Well?" She lifts her hands up.

"That is something we need to discuss; but we won't be doing it to fall in line with any timeline other than our own."

When the house phone rings, my mom excuses herself to go get it.

I turn to Courtney. "Was what I said okay, about the marriage part?"

She laughs, blushing. "People are going to ask; maybe we should have talked about it, so we'll know what to say when they do."

I gulp. "Do you see us married someday?"

Her eyes widen. "Do you?"

I dip my lips to hers. "Way to dodge; but yes, I want that."

She exhales, putting her arms around my neck. "Thank God, because that's what I want too."

"You got a timeline?"

She shakes her head. "We got plenty of time, babe."

CHAPTER 29

Judy had some concerns before she would seriously discuss Maggie living with us full-time. Her biggest concern, the fact we lived in a one-bedroom condo.

"Well?"

I cup Clay's face. "Well what?"

He leans in to ghost the tip of his nose up, then down mine. "Are you okay with selling the condo?"

My hands fall, his lips so close to mine distract me. I ignore his thoughtful question and kiss him instead.

"Courtney." He groans against my mouth.

He's clearly distracted too.

I lean back. "It's your condo. I'm comfortable with whatever you want to do."

His blue eyes soften as he lifts my hand from my lap to kiss my knuckles. "This is your home. The decision is as much yours as it is mine."

"Good thing your mom never got to those curtains," I joke.

His face splits into a grin. His favorite part of every morning, or so he claims, is my attempts to burrow into his chest to avoid the rising sun.

"I'll make sure the master bedroom of the next place we get also faces east."

I glance past him to look at the full floor to ceiling windows. "I will miss the window."

His arms snake out to wrap around my waist before pulling me into his lap. "We haven't moved yet."

Our condo won't be the only property on the market. Clay finally has convinced Pete to sell the garage. A realtor has already been meeting with him to set the asking price.

Like magnets, the pull of his lips is irresistible to mine.

He kisses his way to my neck. "Where do you want to live?"

"Ahh," I moan, my fingers in his hair. "Close to Maggie's school is fine."

He lifts his head, his baby blues dazzling me. "I love that you're all in."

I lean back until I'm stretched out on our sofa, his body following mine. "I want this, all of it, with you."

"You won't regret it, babe," he says, before his lips take mine again.

The conversation effectively is over for the moment.

"I'm not sure how I feel about a first floor master," Clay mumbles.

"It only seems logical to give Maggie her own space." I raise the blinds in the kitchen window to peer into the backyard.

"Will you be okay being that far away from them if we have kids?"

I turn to face him, my mouth falling open. "Kids?"

His hands find my hips as his lips press to my cheek. "Yes, Ma'am. That is if you want to have my babies someday."

I'm prepared to start making Clay's babies on this countertop with our realtor as witness.

I coil my arms around his neck. "No first floor master then."

I'm lucky I'm holding onto him because the smile he gives me would have knocked me on my ass otherwise. He presses a hard, fast kiss to my lips before pulling me toward the living room where our realtor, Darcy, is waiting.

"We'd like to eliminate any properties with a first floor master."

She glances between us, and smiles. "I have another property not far from here with all the bedrooms on the second level."

We follow Darcy back out of the house and to her car. Even though he could use the extra legroom, Clay refuses to ride up front. He is the master of the multiple small gestures, which show me he cares. He opens my doors, he holds my umbrella, he draws a bath for me if I mention any sort of ache or pain, and he never makes me ride in the back seat if he can help it.

He's the personification of my southern gentleman come to life, except for in the bedroom. There, he's all things and some of them not very gentlemanly, and I love it.

It's a short ride over to the next house. As the relator pulls into the neighborhood, we both recognize it since one of Maggie's friends lives here, but on a different street.

"This is a good neighborhood," Clay remarks.

When we pull up to the house, we both cringe at the paint on the shutters, a vibrant orange. Otherwise, it's a simple two story colonial with off-white siding. The house is set back from the street with a wide green lawn. There is a stone path leading from the sidewalk right to the front door, joining with another path from the end of the driveway.

"Be a good place for a basketball hoop." Clay points to the garage at the end of the driveway.

"Let's see the inside first," I tease, slipping my hand in his.

Darcy gets the key from the lockbox hanging on the doorknob and opens the door.

Inside the smell of fresh paint lingers.

I turn back to her. "How long has this house been on the market?"

She shuffles through the files she has in her giant, posh purse. Clay starts exploring as she looks.

"Only a week."

"Was it vacant before going on the market?"

She shrugs, slipping her purse off her shoulder and setting it on the floor next to the front door. I'm not surprised. I've seen carry-on luggage smaller, her purse must weigh a ton.

She pulls out her phone, finger at the ready. "Want me to ask the selling agent?"

I shrug. Finding out how long the house has been vacant isn't a big deal. I'm just curious.

"Let's see what Clay thinks of the place first," I reply, turning around to go find him.

He's in the kitchen, looking at the appliances.

"Do these come with the house?" he asks as we walk into the room.

Darcy nods. "The washer and dryer also convey."

Clay holds out his hand and mine easily slips into it. "What do you think?"

Sure, we haven't seen the whole thing; but compared to the other houses we've looked at so far, it's one of the better ones. Being in a familiar neighborhood is also something going for it. The layout is appealing; front foyer with a living room and dining room on each side of it. The kitchen is past the dining room, and a family room next to it, off the living room.

"I'm guessing this is the home office." Clay leads me into a small room off the family room.

"It's on the small side." I glance around.

"It's big enough for a desk, and these built-in-shelves are perfect for all your books."

Turning, I let him paint the picture for me.

"We could put a comfy chair for you right here."

"I wouldn't want to bother you while you're working."

"Hush, woman." He grins down at me. "It'd be a cool space for both of us."

I caught a glimpse of Darcy heading back toward the kitchen. She's smart. Clay's selling this place good enough all by himself.

"Let's check out the second floor."

There are three average sized bedrooms and a decent sized master. Sadly, not a floor to ceiling window in sight; the recently redone walk-in shower in the master bath might make a good substitution.

One glance to Clay and I can tell he's thinking the same thing. I blush and pull him out of the bathroom before he tries to bend me over the sink.

"What do you think?" he asks, as we head back down to the first floor.

Not ready to commit, I hedge, "Let's look at the backyard first."

"Did you guys see the screened-in porch?" Darcy asks from the kitchen.

Excuse me? Screened-in porch?

Sight unseen, I look back at Clay. "I love it."

He whoops, lifting me up while I gasp. "I knew I wanted it when Darcy pulled into the driveway."

Darcy laughs at the two of us. "So, I'm guessing you'd like to make an offer."

He sets me back on my feet and we nod, grinning.

"Need anything from the store?" I ask Clay, picking up my purse.

He pushes back from his desk and stands, stretching his arms up over his head. His shirt pulls up, revealing a mouthwatering stretch of his waist above his jeans.

"Want company?" he asks, pulling my attention from his stomach to his face.

"Always," I grin.

He crosses the room to me and offers me his hand. It doesn't matter what we're doing, even something as simple as running to the grocery store is made better by being together. When I compare what I have now to what I had with Mike, it's a comfort impossible to deny. Subconsciously, I never relaxed with Mike.

I forced myself to bend to what made him happy versus what comes natural with Clay. I'm not twisted up like a pretzel trying to guess the right things to say or do.

As we're walking out to Clay's truck his phone rings. After a hello and a moment of talking on the other side, he presses the phone to his chest. "It's my mom. She wants to know if we'd like to have dinner with them tonight."

"What's she cooking?" I tease.

Clay laughs, still holding the phone to his chest. "I'll tell her you said that. Knowing her, she's probably going to order some Chinese or pizza."

"That sounds good. I still need to stop by the store though." I laugh, knowing Judy doesn't like to cook.

"We can stop there on the way."

After I nod, he lifts the phone back to his ear to let his mom know we'll come. Since we don't have to worry about making dinner now, I only need to pick up body wash and conditioner.

Once we get to the store, Clay remembers we're out of paper towels so we split up to divide and conquer. I'm grabbing body wash when I hear someone say my name.

I turn, my eyes widening when I see Grant. "Hi."

"I thought that was you." He looks away almost embarrassed he spoke.

"How are you?" I hazard.

He hesitates. "Fine, I suppose, considering I've learned I haven't been a father for the last ten years."

I cringe, the anger in his tone almost a physical blow. "I'm so sorry."

He rolls his eyes. "What do you have to apologize for? You did nothing. It's honestly poetic. I was ashamed for so long; and the moment I was willing to step up and do what I should have from the beginning, it all blows up in my face."

"There is no excuse for Nicole to deceive you for so long."

"You reap what you sow, right? I was the one who screwed her life up. Here I thought being a father could somehow save me."

I have no idea what he means by that. "Grant." I reach out to touch his arm.

"What's going on?" Clay's growl behind stops me.

"Grant was just saying hello," I explain.

"He can just as easily say goodbye." He waves before draping his arm across my shoulders. "Goodbye, Grant."

Grant smirks; drops his eyes to Clay's feet, and then slowly drags his gaze up to his eyes.

"Clay, be polite." I elbow him.

He looks up at the ceiling as though I'm causing him pain before looking back at Grant. "I'm sorry my sister lied to you. Just so you know; she's been doing that to all of us for a long time."

Grant nods. "It's nice to know I wasn't the only one." He glances at me. "It was nice seeing you, Courtney."

Then he turns and leaves as we stare after him.

"Whoa," I mumble once he's out of eyesight.

CHAPTER 30

CLAY

"It's Darcy," I say, muting the TV before answering

Courtney turns, faces me, pulls her knees up to her chest, and rests her chin on them. I hold her eyes as Darcy talks.

Once she's done, I ask her to hold on.

I cover the speaker of the phone. "We got an offer on the condo."

Courtney's face breaks out in a wide grin. "Is it a good one?"

I nod. "Full price."

We set the price for the condo under the current going rate for the area hoping for a quick sale. Considering it went on the market less than a week ago, it seems to have worked.

"When do they want to close?"

"Thirty days."

She reaches out to put her hand on my knee. "Are there any conditions?"

"Just an inspection."

She launches herself at me and I set the phone on the coffee table while she peppers my face with kisses.

"So you're saying I should accept it right?" I joke, hugging her tight.

"Yes," she breathes against my neck.

I quickly grab my phone and tell Darcy it's a go as fast as I can because it turns out real estate transactions make Courtney horny.

"Where were we?" I ask, lifting her shirt over her head.

The last month has been full of all things real estate. We made an offer on the house with the screen porch after bringing Maggie to see if she liked it. My mom also came along, but it wasn't her opinion I was worried about. Luckily, they both loved the place as much as Courtney and I did.

Dad accepted an offer to the sell the garage. Victor and a couple of his cousins were approved for the loan and bought the place. It's been helping my dad let go, knowing the garage is going to someone who he knows. He's finally let go of the fantasy that I'll take over.

Once we move into the new place, I'll buy a beater heap of a car, Maggie, him and I can work on together. He'll love it.

After selling this place, we'll barely have a mortgage. If Courtney had her way, we'd use all her money from the settlement and have no mortgage. Since we've gotten serious, she's stayed true to her need to keep some things separate.

I respect her for it. She keeps me on my toes. There will never be a time when I take her for granted. So, every other week Courtney has a girls' night with Jen or Darcy, now that they're tight. It gives me a chance to work out with Luke, or hangout one on one with Maggie.

I want her to hold onto her money because I never want her to feel dependent on me for anything other than my love. She has all of that. So, we both put equal amounts toward the house and we'll have a mortgage for the next few years. Since the condo sold, I won't have to pull my chunk from my retirement account.

"I want you," she groans, clearing thoughts of real estate from my brain and slipping her hand into my pants.

I tug at her yoga pants as she fumbles with my fly. We're both still half-dressed when I enter her. Her frantic pace slows as we lock eyes. Gently, I lift her up then lower her back down as she reaches up to cup my face. Nothing before her ever was like this. She fits me, like an ingredient I never knew I was missing. Together we're delicious, and apart we were just that, apart.

"I'm gonna miss this place," she sighs.

I tighten my grip on her hips. "I'll fuck you up against the window every night until we move."

She moans and the sound goes right to my balls. I'm already inside her and she's still turning me on.

"You like that?" I pant.

She nods, dropping down to my chest to kiss me. My hands move from her hips to grip the back of her head, holding her there while I take my time kissing her back. Her lips are my ultimate weakness. We're half on, half falling off the couch but don't stop.

She swivels her hips, grinding down on me. She starts to tense up so I know she's close. I slide one hand down her back to hold her ass. She gasps against my lips when I squeeze it, hard. Close turns into gone as she shatters above me.

There is nothing fucking hotter on this planet than my girl coming on my cock. I get a couple more thrusts in before I go, spilling into her. She goes all liquidy on me like she has no bones. I chuckle and, somehow, manage to set us upright, her in my lap, still on my cock.

If my shoes weren't still on, and my pants weren't around my ankles I'd carry her to the bathroom to clean up.

"I would sell this place every day for that kind of reaction."

She blushes. "I still can't believe that beautiful house is going to be ours."

"Believe it, babe."

"I have to call my mom." She grabs her clothes and leaves me.

It's dumb to miss our connection but I do. I kick my shoes off under the coffee table and pull my pants back on.

I've never known someone I could be in the same room with but still miss. She comes back a couple minutes later, dressed and with her phone.

"Is it cool if I call her now?" she asks, tilting her head at the movie that's been on mute since Darcy called.

"Of course."

Her smile is infectious, I'm happy about the house; but I'm fucking thrilled she's loves it. Once the phone is ringing, she switches hands and threads her fingers through mine. I lazily drag my thumb across the back of her hand while she talks to her mom.

It's comforting to know they have such a good relationship. Mrs. Grayson has been nothing but supportive of our moving in together and buying the new place. The only thing she worries about now is where Courtney will work because the garage has been sold.

While ownership transfers over, she's still going to stop by and sit with Victor's younger sister so she can learn how to run the office. My dad had a mass mailing sent out to all his existing customers to let them know he was retiring and the shop was now under new management. She will be busy with all of that stuff for the next week; but after that, who knows.

"So, how's your mom?" I ask, once she hangs up.

She pulls her hair down from the loose bun on the top of her head only to twist it back up again. "She's good. She said to congratulate you on the sale and wants to know if there's anything she can do to help with the move."

Glancing around, I shrug. "We don't have a ton of stuff. I figure we'll rent a truck and get Luke and Brad to help move the big stuff. We can pay them with pizza and beer."

She raises a brow. She's met Luke and heard me gripe about his green smoothies.

"Fine, pizza for Brad and we'll pick up some sprouts for Luke."

I stand, reaching out my hand to help her up. "Let's run by Darcy's and sign off on the offer."

"How much does this thing weigh?" Brad groans from one side of the sofa.

"I told you it was a sleeper," I huff from the other.

His mouth drops when Luke walks past us carrying a stool. "Not fair, man."

I'd laugh but this shit is heavy. I catch my breath once we load it into the truck. Courtney and our moms are already at the new house setting up Maggie's room. We want to surprise her with it when she gets out of school. She thinks we aren't moving for another couple of days.

"What else is left?" Brad asks, reaching his hand out for a bottle of water.

"A couple of dressers." I watch his face fall and add. "They're empty and we can use the dolly. The mattress and box springs are gonna suck."

"Man, these are light," Luke calls out, a box spring under each arm as he walks up to the truck.

"Looks like you got it covered. We'll hang out while you get the rest of the stuff," I joke, grabbing one box spring from him.

"I felt bad not helping with the sleeper. That looked heavy."

Brad flops back onto it. "It was."

"Leave him," I laugh. "Let's go grab the mattress."

As we ride up the elevator, Luke hesitates then holds out his hand for me to shake. I squint at him but he motions for me to shake it. Okay. I shake his hand.

He clears his throat once I drop his hand. "I'm happy for you, Clay. You got a great girl and your new place is awesome. I'm proud of you, man."

I pop him on the shoulder. "Where's this coming from?"

He shrugs. "We've known each other a long time. I've never seen you this happy, especially after everything went down with Owen. You've been just going through the motions, not really living. Since you met Courtney, it's like you're a new man."

"I don't know what to say. You're right though; from the moment I met her, my world changed. I'm lucky to have her."

CHAPTER 31

"It's perfect."

I straighten the purple shag rug and stand. "You think she'll like it?"

Judy puts her arm around my shoulders. "Maggie is going to love it."

The new furniture for her room was delivered this morning. After Clay and Luke set it up, they went to the condo to get the rest of our furniture. While they were gone, Judy and I went to Target to get new linens and fun accessories for her room. We've spent the afternoon putting it all together.

"The bedding should be dry. I'll go grab it."

"Thanks, Judy."

I use one of the store bags to collect the packaging and set it in the hallway to take out to the trash next time I head downstairs. We might be living out of boxes for the next couple of weeks, but Clay and I both want to surprise Maggie with her new room.

"The boys are here." Judy walks back in, her arms full with a purple sheet set and matching comforter.

"I can't wait for Clay to see all the cute stuff we got her."

"Don't spoil her too much." She passes me one side of the fitted sheet. "That's Grandma's job."

I laugh. "It's Clay you should worry about. He can't say no to her."

We move to put the flat sheet on. "He'll learn."

Once the pillows are arranged, we both step back to take in the completed look. It looks like any tween girl's dream bedroom. Everything matches and we have gotten her bigger furniture to grow into. She has a desk for homework and a bookshelf already packed with some of her favorite books. Next to it, a giant beanbag chair where she can read.

We are lucky she already likes the color on the walls so we didn't have to paint. We did get some fun prints and wall clings to jazz it up though.

"This looks amazing."

I turn to see him standing in the doorway to her bedroom. "Hey, babe."

I walk over to hug him. His arms coil around me as he holds me tightly. "Thank you so much for doing this. You're incredible and I'm one lucky bastard."

"I want to do this. Besides, I can't take all the credit. Your mom has helped so much."

"I love you."

I press a gentle kiss to his cheek. "And I love you."

Judy brought most of Maggie's things from their house so we will have almost everything set up before she gets out of school. The neighborhood we live in is close enough to the school that she gets to ride the bus now.

She hasn't done it yet. Judy is going to pick her up today, so her first ride will be tomorrow morning with her friend Lisa.

"She's going to love it." Judy beams at us from across the room.

She was hesitant at first at the idea of her grandbaby coming to live with us. It makes the most sense long term. Given Nicole's disappearance, Judy and Pete have been given temporary legal guardianship. Clay has been working with a family law attorney to begin the process of legally adopting her.

It's convoluted at best, complicated by Nicole being out of the picture. He has had to run a newspaper ad along with the formal missing persons report to attempt to locate her. It will have to run for a certain period of time, giving her the chance to come forward before her rights can be taken away.

It will all be worth it though; in the end, we all know Maggie belongs with us.

"Thanks for all your help, Mom," Clay says.

"I'm so happy you found, Courtney." She smiles and looks right at me. "You call me if he ever annoys you and I'll knock some sense into him."

"Hey." Clay blusters, his eyes widening.

She walks over to us, pats Clay on the shoulder, and leans in to kiss my cheek. "I'm going to go pick up Maggie. Want me to call you when we're on our way?"

Clay shakes his head. "You don't have to."

With that, we follow her downstairs. She waves hello to Brad and Luke before leaving. Brad and Luke sit on the sofa, each downing a bottle of water.

"Are you guys ready to bring the bedroom furniture in?" Clay asks, popping Brad on the back of his head as he walks past him.

Brad groans while Luke grins almost as if he was looking forward to it. Clay won't let me lift anything heavy but between the four of us, we quickly unloaded the truck into the living and dining room. Clay and Luke work on getting the dressers upstairs while Brad follows with the box springs.

I'm moving the last stool into the kitchen when they finish. We still need to put our bed together but that's something Clay and I can do on our own. Luke has left with Brad to return the rental truck we got for the move while I order pizza.

Clay's rearranging stuff in the family room when Judy comes back with Maggie.

"I get to sleep here tonight?" Her excited question carries from the foyer.

Clay and I both stop what we are doing to go greet her.

"Hey, Mags," Clay says, leaning against the stair rail.

"I didn't know we were moving today," she shrieks, bouncing on her heels.

"Want to go check out your room?" I grin, excited for her to see it.

"Yes!" she shouts, bounding up the stairs two at a time.

"Wait outside the door," Clay orders as we all race after her.

Impatiently, she waits for us to catch up to her and stands staring at her closed door.

"Now close your eyes." He moves in front of her, putting his hand on the doorknob.

Once he's sure she can't see, he quickly opens the door and steps to the side.

"Ready?"

"Yes," she pleads.

"Okay, open your eyes."

None of us is prepared for the tears instantly springing from her eyes as she looks at her new room.

I cringe, my heart crushed, fearing she doesn't like it.

"Are you okay, Maggie?" Clay asks, stepping toward her.

She flings herself into him, wrapping her arms around his waist. "It's the most beautiful room I've ever seen and I can't believe it's mine," she sobs.

Overwhelmed, tears of my own threaten to fall as I watch his shaking arms tightly hug her to his chest.

"It's all yours, Sweetie; it's all yours," he murmurs against the top of her head.

It only takes a moment for her to calm down and pull away, excited to investigate her new room. I move to Clay, linking my arms around him and resting my head on his chest, watching her.

Glancing at Judy, I catch her discretely brush a tear of her own from her cheek. Her eyes lift, meeting mine, and we both nod, so connected in sharing the joy putting her room together brought Maggie.

Working on the house has taken up most of our free time. Moving from a one-bedroom condo to a four-bedroom house meant we had plenty of new furniture to buy. We have put the sofa set from the old place in the family room and bought a new one for the living room.

Otherwise, that room is still empty. Because we have the family room, neither of us really knows what to do with the living room. Clay's thinking about putting his office in there, but I think he deserves a room with a door so we won't bother him if he has to work late. Currently, it's still being debated.

We picked up a farmhouse-style table and chairs for the dining room and a queen bedroom set for one of the upstairs spare bedrooms. I'm more worried about getting stuff on the walls and making everything look homey than Clay is.

We're having a house warming party this weekend. I've never met Clay's aunt and uncle, and I want everything to look perfect. Maggie has been my co-decorator. Any worries Clay and I had about her not feeling at home here are gone. She's blossoming into an even more confident young lady.

Since I'm not working, I've been volunteering at her school. I've applied for a teaching job there as well. The principal seems to like me so hopefully I won't be unemployed long. Either way I enjoy the time I spend at her school. It's given me a chance to watch her interact with her friends. With everything that has happened with her mom, it's clear they have banded together to support her. Clay and I still keep a close eye on her. It's hard for us to accept she isn't going to break down.

Maybe that's why people say kids are resilient. We've gone out of our way to make the transition easier on her. We've tried to mimic her schedule from Judy and Pete. I walk with her to the bus stop every morning then head over to her school after lunch and help in the library until school is over.

On the days when she has chorus, I stay and hang out so I can drive her home. Otherwise, she rides the bus home. The exception to this is rainy days; she hates riding the bus when it's raining. It's a chorus night tonight, so I pull my e-reader out of my purse and sink into an armchair outside of the music room.

I've been plowing through my TBR list. Reading was one of the things I lost while I was with Mike, parts of my identity that were separate from us as a couple. My loaded e-reader is a gift from Clay, the gift card to load it up with books from Judy.

One of the things I love about Clay is how he has embraced this about me, instead of reacting negatively. By buying me books and my e-reader, he is supporting things I love even if they don't have anything to do with him.

Thoughtful and sweet, the things he does make me also more conscious of ways I can support the things he loves. Maggie has helped me with one surprise for him. Since he works at home on his laptop, he tends to migrate from room to room in search of sunlight. He spends a lot of time working on the screen porch.

Our makeshift outdoor furniture wasn't comfortable and was the main reason he didn't work out there all day. Together, Maggie and I surprised him with a lounge chair and matching table. Ever since our lunch, in the back bed of his truck when we both still worked at the garage, I've known how much he loves being outside.

Now, weather permitting, on the porch is where, more often than not, he is. The cold doesn't bother him as much as it does me. I'm looking forward to a long spring where I can hang out with him while he works.

Through the door muffled melodies and sweet voices flow. It's not loud enough to distract me from my book. For whatever reason, light background noise makes it easier to read than pure silence. Before I know it, the music room door is opening and girls are streaming out.

Maggie finds me quickly and happily chatters away as we walk to my car. She wants to try out for a couple of solos. Her unabashed excitement has my eyes stinging with tears. There are still times where she is sullen, confused, and hurt by Nicole's disappearance.

My heart fills as I witness those moments occurring less and less; and moments like this, her joy unsullied by her mom, becoming more of a daily occurrence. Clay has dinner ready for us when we get home, nothing fancy, just tacos.

Maggie runs up to her room to change and put all of her school things away while I set the table.

His arms circle me from behind as he kisses the back of my neck. "Hey, babe."

I lean back against him, lifting my arms to rest over his. "Hey."

"How was your day?"

"Great. I talked a sixth grader into reading *Anne of Green Gables* last week. She loved it and came in today for the next book."

He steps back, spinning me in his arms to kiss my lips. "You make reading sexy."

I wrap my arms around his neck and inhale him. "You make everything sexy."

"I do?" He teases, sounding way too pleased with himself.

When we hear Maggie on the stairs, he quickly kisses me again before pulling away to greet her. She goes straight for a hug, squeezing him tightly as he drops a kiss to the top of her head.

"I hear you're going to try out for a solo."

She steps out of his arms, blushing as she goes to get a drink. "I probably won't get picked, but I'll never know unless I try."

Clay pulls my chair out for me, his eyes still on her. "Why would you say that?"

She shrugs bringing her milk back to the table with her. "I'm not as good as the other girls."

"As long as you're having fun and try your best, you'll be great," I say, passing her a plate with taco shells.

She takes two and doesn't argue, so I turn to Clay. "How was your day?"

"It's better now I have my girls with me."

Maggie beams.

CHAPTER 32

CLAY

"All set?" I ruffle Maggie's hair as I look out the front window.

She nods, smiling. "Courtney's going to be so surprised."

I only hope it's a good surprise. "You let me know when they pull into the driveway."

We needed her out of the house to pull off our surprise. My mom came to the rescue, inviting her over to learn a secret Bradshaw family recipe, which has been passed down through the generations. The truth is she downloaded it last week from Pinterest.

"She's here!" Maggie hollers from the front room. I glance back into the family room, double-checking the door to the office is closed.

"Remember, act natural."

She grins, rushing over to me. "I'm trying."

Courtney walks through the front door and meets us in the kitchen a moment later. "Hey, guys."

I'm pouring ice into a bucket for the house warming party. "Hey, babe."

She leans up and gives me a soft kiss, laughing when I drop the bag of ice to deepen it. She gets shy about kissing in front of Maggie, scared we're a bad example. In my opinion, it's good for Maggie to see a loving, affectionate, committed relationship.

Courtney's eyes are glazed and her breathing heavy when I pull back. If the house was empty and we didn't have people showing up in the next hour, I'd love to have my way with her. No one has ever affected me physically like her; it's easier now we live together. I don't feel as insane about needing to be around her.

Thank God, neither of us travels for work. I don't think I could sleep without her curled into my side.

I nuzzle my nose against her neck, breathing her in as she grips my shoulders. "How was cooking?"

She laughs. "I've always wanted to bake a cake from scratch, but I think your mom's distracted about something. She had to keep checking the recipe and couldn't remember how long to cook it for." She pauses, turning her face to meet my eyes. "You don't think it was me, do you?"

I have to stop myself from laughing as I picture my mother cooking this family recipe. "She's probably peeved at my dad for something. You know how much she loves you."

Her relief is instant, the stress melting away from her stance. "I'm going to go change."

"You aren't wearing this?" I ask, my hands sliding down her back and over her yoga pant-covered ass.

She playfully bites at my neck. "No, I am not wearing yoga pants and your hoodie to our house warming party."

She turns her head, slipping out of my arms to look at Maggie. "Want to help me pick something out?"

Maggie grins, sliding off her stool. She loves spending time with Courtney.

"People are coming in less than an hour," I call out after them.

I don't know what they do, but sometimes they can goof off with clothes and nail polish for hours. I finish getting the ice bucket filled and move it to the screen porch. I fill and set another one up next to it. One I fill with beer and fruity drinks, the other with sodas and sports drinks.

The counter and dining room table are all set with bowls of chips, pretzels, and cheese trays. Our friends are bringing side dishes and desserts. My dad and I are grilling the rest.

Courtney's mom is the first to arrive.

"Hi, Melissa," I greet her, giving her a quick hug. "The girls are upstairs."

She hands me a casserole dish and hurries upstairs.

"Is Jim coming?" I ask after her.

"He's stopping by later," she replies from the top of the stairs.

I start to worry about Courtney being late to our own party, but she comes back downstairs before the next guest arrives. She always looks amazing; but whatever she did up there, bumped her up to flat out stunning.

"Come here," I growl.

She holds my gaze as she slowly struts over to me. She knows she looks fine as hell, but tries to act innocent about it when she reaches me. I grab her by the neck, my fingers in her hair and plant one on her. Christ, whose idea was it to have a party? All I want to do is drag my woman upstairs and bury myself in her, caveman style.

The doorbell interrupts any hope I have of talking her into canceling this shindig. I wouldn't actually call it off; I haven't even given Courtney her surprise.

Maggie dashes down the stairs, beating us to answer the door. There's a small crowd on our doorstep and more people walking up the driveway. It gives me a chance to take it all in, this amazing moment.

Maggie's beaming as she grabs Jenna by the hand, excited to show her new room off, my dad looking more relaxed than I've seen him in years, and best of all, my girl leaning into me with my arm around her waist. Before Courtney walked into my world, I was hell-bent on shutting everyone out.

I had my circle and no desire to expand it. I probably would've died all alone in my condo, only to be found when my neighbors complained about the smell. That was the path I was on; and in some twisted way, I was cool with it because I had no idea the alternative could be this good.

Thirty minutes into the party, Courtney comes looking for me. "Hey, babe. I can't open the office door; it's locked. Do you have a key for it?"

I catch Maggie's eye. "I do have the key. Here-" I take her hand in mine. "Let me open it for you."

Maggie swings into action, quietly corralling our guests behind us, into the family room. Courtney looks around, confused when I pause by the door.

"Maggie and I planned a surprise for you today," I start, pulling the key from my pocket.

Turning to everyone, I add. "Courtney thought this room would make a great home office for me, but Maggie and I thought it would make a much better..." I trail off, opening the door so everyone can see the shelves filled with all of Courtney's books.

Her eyes widen as she slowly steps inside.

"Mom?" Courtney gasps, her fingertips slowly caressing the spines of her father's books.

Melissa steps into the room, to pull her into her arms. "Clay thought you'd like to have some of your dad's books."

Maggie joins them. "Look at the ones on this shelf."

Courtney eases one book from where Maggie pointed, hugging it to her chest. "They're some of my favorites; but I don't understand, I already have some of these."

"Open it." Maggie urges, bouncing on her heels.

Courtney's mouth drops when she does. "It's signed. Oh, my God, are all of these signed?"

I shrug while Maggie bobs her head.

"How?"

"EBay," Maggie and I both answer at the same time.

"Jinx, you owe me a Coke," I laugh, ruffling her hair.

"This is unreal," Courtney whispers, turning to take in the whole room.

Maggie and I fixed it all up while she was cooking with my mom this morning. The books have been in boxes in our garage for the last couple of weeks, and Brad picked up the settee Maggie and I got for her one morning. Jen framed a bunch of pictures, old and new, to decorate the shelves with.

This room is one hundred percent Courtney, a place for her to be surrounded by her favorite things.

"Do you like it?" I ask bending down to one knee as her back faces me.

When she turns to answer me, her eyes fill with tears when she sees me.

She covers her mouth as she nods.

I pull the small velvet box that's been burning a hole in my pocket out and reach for her hand. It's shaking as she lowers it into my hand. I slowly drop my lips to her knuckles.

"Courtney, I love you so much. I never knew I wasn't living until you showed me what being alive truly felt like. What's mine is yours, everything I have. I want to feel alive with you for the rest of my life."

She drops to her knees, tears streaming down her face as she tucks her face into my neck and says yes over and over again. I almost laugh; I haven't even shown her the ring because I'm too over the moon she said yes. I curl my arms around her, clutching her to me and angle my face in search of her lips.

When our mouths touch, I don't want to let go. One of my hands slides up to hold the back of her head as I keep our kiss going. I only pull away when my mom says, "For Christ's sake, Clayton, let her breathe."

Her eyes flutter open and lock on mine. She giggles, reaching up to wipe her eyes. I reach for her left hand, and gently ease the ring Maggie helped me pick for her onto her ring finger. Her eyes dart from the ring to me and back again.

I gulp. "Do you like it?"

Her hands cup my face. "I love it. I love you."

The spontaneous clapping of our friends and family remind us again we're not alone. I stand, helping her to her feet and wrap my arm around her waist. Maggie comes to us first, hugging us both but Courtney for a little bit longer than me.

Our moms next, they both gush over the ring and my father pats me on the back for falling in love with a good woman.

EPILOGUE
ONE MONTH LATER

Courtney

"Hello, Mr. Bradshaw."

"Hey there, Mrs. Bradshaw."

When Clay asked when I wanted to get married, I think even he was surprised I didn't want to wait. I've done a long engagement before; all I wanted was to be married to my man. We had a simple ceremony, immediate family and a justice of the peace.

We are all heading to Judy and Pete's for a reception. After that Clay, Maggie, and I are heading to the coast for a family vacation / honeymoon. Now that I'm teaching history at Maggie's school we timed our trip around one of their marking period breaks. It might seem weird to bring a ten-year-old on our honeymoon; but at least, we booked a rental with a first floor master.

When we get to their house, Maggie runs ahead of us and inside. Clay leads me to his parents' room where he helps me change out of my dress. My dress is simple, traditional, and has a million buttons up the back.

"Don't get any ideas," I tease as he makes his way through them.

"What?" he asks innocently.

"You know what."

"So, I'm taking that as you being opposed to me having my way with you on my parents' bed?"

I nod. "Yep."

"What about up against the wall?"

I pause and his eyes light up. Then I gasp.

"What's wrong?" he asks, his brows coming together.

I cringe. "Did I turn off the flat iron before we left for the ceremony?"

A grin spreads over his face. "Yep, I know for sure because I packed it in your overnight bag."

My strapless dress pools around my feet as he unfastens the last button. He takes one look at my corset and pulls me into his arms.

Best day ever.

THE END

Want more?

Sign up for my newsletter today:

www.careyheywood.com

Coming this fall get Luke's story in Book Two of the
Carolina Days series

Yesterday's Half Truths.

ACKNOWLEDGEMENTS

You.

If you are uncertain if this applies to you, please allow me to elaborate. If you are reading this, it applies to you. If you have written a book I've read or read a book I've written, for all the mint chocolate chip ice cream in the world this applies to you. If we're related, by choice or not, this most definitely applies to you. If you tell friends about the books you've read and loved, and if any of my books fall into that category, it abso-freaking-lutley applies to you. If you've reviewed a book and or emailed me or any writer after being moved by something they've written, it will forever apply to you. If you help craft an author's words into its beautifully finished product by editing, proofing, or creating a gorgeous cover to show it off to the world, it without a doubt applies to you. If you've been there for me during my moments of self doubt and offered me words of encouragement on this incredible journey, until I have no stories left to tell, it will apply to you.

Thank you.

ABOUT THE AUTHOR

New York Times and USA Today bestselling author with six books out and many more to come. She was born and raised in Alexandria, Virginia. Ever the mild-mannered citizen, Carey spends her days working in the world of finance, and at night, she retreats into the lives of her fictional characters. Supporting her all the way are her husband, three sometimes-adorable children, and their nine-pound attack Yorkie.

I'd love to hear from you!

info@careyheywood.com

www.careyheywood.com

OTHER BOOKS
AVAILABLE EVERYWHERE

Better

Her

Him

Sawyer Says

Stages of Grace

Uninvolved

A Bridge of Her Own

Made in the USA
Charleston, SC
26 July 2014